DUMPSTER DICING

Julie B Cosgrove

A Bunco Biddies Mystery
Book 1

Published by Prism Book Group
ISBN-13: 978-1533137135
ISBN-10: 1533137137
First Edition, 2016
Published in the United States of America
Contact info: contact@prismbookgroup.com
http://www.prismbookgroup.com

ENDORSEMENTS

"Julie's a genuine jewel when it comes to dishing this delightful tale of sleuthing by seniors." Mary Daheim, author of the *B&B* and *Alpine/Emma Lord* mysteries

"The Bunco Biddies are here to serve. From the moment the gals decide to help the busy local police solve a murder on their territory, Betsy Ann, Ethel, Janie, and Mildred will wiggle their way into your heart with their determination to learn "real" detective work while protecting Sunset Acres and serving the best bakery and tea." Lisa Lickel, author of the best-selling *Buried Treasure* mysteries

"What a wonderful start to a new series! Ms. Cosgrove's *Bunco Biddies* cozies will be a welcome addition to many reading lists, mine included." Sharon McGregor, author of the *Island* and *Boarding Kennel* mysteries.

"What happens when you find body parts in the dumpster? You investigate! What a delightful read! Julie Cosgrove has created a laugh out loud mystery with quirky older characters. Bring on the next book!" Cynthia Hickey, author of the *Nosy Neighbor* Mystery Series

DEDICATION

To all who are getting older, but are still sharp.
May society recognize your worth.
And to my son, James, who recognizes mine.

Sunset Acres

to Highway
Alamoville

Get 'em and Go

Front Gate

RM 1275

Hedgerow

Rainbow Road

Park
Picnic Area

Office

Sunbeam Apartments

Tennis Courts

Sunset Drive

Club
House

Library

Sunbeam Lane

Beauty
Parlor

Barber

Pools

Rec. Center
Dining Hall

Day Clinic

Sunnyside Lane

Golf Course

Post Office

Rosy Skies Trail

Skilled Nursing

Assisted Living

Rosy Skies Trail

Amber Rays Lane

Sunny Ridge

Rehab
Long-term Care

Aurora Rd

Sunburst Court

Sunbeam Lane

Sunrise Court

Sunshine Way

Sunray Terrace

Solar Boulevard

Radiant Way

West Woods

Westwood Creek

N
E
W
S

CHAPTER ONE

Betsy Ann Hunt huffed up the hill, breathing in time to the slap of her sneakers on the early morning dew-dampened pavement. The lavender, velour-covered backside of her neighbor and Bunco playing buddy, Janie Manson, wobbled ahead of her, her elbows swinging in sync with her steps, no doubt to some early Beatles song on her I-pod. Janie claimed to be one of the privileged few who squealed on the first row of the band's concert at Sam Houston Coliseum during their first British Invasion tour in April of 1965. But Janie bragged about a lot of things, such as her physical stamina—which appeared to be ebbing at the moment as a result of the sultry Texas humidity.

Betsy Ann urged her sore calves to accelerate on the incline. With every ounce of gumption mustered in her quivering ligaments, she edged alongside Janie. Exhaling a slight wheeze, she tapped her friend on the shoulder. "Can we slow down?"

"Huh?" Janie pulled out the left ear bud. She waited at the top of the lane near the entrance to the club house parking lot in their fifty-five-plus community of Sunset Acres. The rumble of the sanitation truck on its Tuesday morning rounds to empty the dumpsters drowned out Betsy Ann's breathless response.

"What did you say?" Janie jogged in place as she leaned closer.

"Have...to...stop." Betsy Ann raised a hand with fingers spread and then pressed it to her thigh as she bent over. Her ample breasts bounced with each chest heave under her fuchsia zip-up jogging jacket.

"Okay, all you had to do was say so." Janie clicked off her music. "It's only been three weeks since you slipped on your tailbone, Betsy Ann. I realize you gained six pounds lying around, but are you sure you should be power walking so soon? Dr. Pearson gave me strict orders about exercising when I chipped my hip bone two years ago."

Always knows everything. With gritted teeth to keep her from speaking her mind, Betsy Ann straightened upright in slow motion as she counted to ten. But the sincere concern on Janie's apple-cheeked face dissolved her angst. She edged up to her friend's ear and spoke louder to compensate for the trash vehicle's droning engine. "I'm fine, really. Just need a breather for a moment or two." A whiff of three-day-old, fermented garbage combined with diesel fumes left her a tad lightheaded. She waved a hand over her nose. "Whew, away from that monster."

"Oh, okay."

The two widows eased to a bench under one of the many sprawling live oak trees dotting the community. Their eyes followed the commercial dumpster as it rose in the air. The sanitation lorry's built-in forklift maneuvered the box up and over the cab.

"Amazing how they lift and dump, isn't it? The dumpster must weigh several tons."

Janie nodded. "Hydraulics, no doubt. My brother became a mechanical engineer, you know. Explained them to me one Thanksgiving, oh, back in 1972..."

Betsy Ann's eyes glazed over. Janie exhibited the epitome of a walking encyclopedia. Her mind, even though encased in seventy-two-year-old wrinkles, still resembled a sharpened pencil lead.

Her attention left her jogging mate's diatribe on modern mechanics and turned to the labored whir of the metal arms grasping the garbage container. Black plastic sacks, white ones, and various cartons tumbled into the truck's receptacle like upturned chocolate-covered mints into a wide open mouth. Then, something long and blue-jean colored caught Betsy Ann's eye. She jolted to her feet.

"Oh, my word. A leg! With an orthopedic shoe attached."

"Dear, I thought you quit taking oxycodone for pain." Janie pushed a sweat-dampened silver curl off her brow.

"I'm serious. Look."

Janie's gaze followed her friend's finger. "Oh, my heavens. It is!" She jumped up as she waved her hands over her head. "Stop. Stop."

Her words didn't reach the city worker's ears over the automatic grinds and thunks.

Betsy Ann dashed in front and proceeded to slam her hands onto the driver's door.

A middle-aged man knitted his thick black eyebrows. He jerked the lift to stop and rolled down the window. "What?"

The community's trash receptacle dangled at a precarious angle.

The senior citizens sputtered in unison. "Stop. There's a body."

The man shook his head in confusion.

Betsy Ann motioned to the back. "A body. Get it? Dead person."

The man shut down the engine. "¿Muerto?"

"Yes. Uh, sí." She bobbed her cropped, reddish-blonde hair.

The worker crawled down from his seat and walked to the back of the sanitation truck, which rumbled and spewed more putrid fumes. The dumpster titled down at a forty-five-degree angle. Suspended in time clung numerous trash bags, pizza boxes, a broken lawn chair and...an arm?

"Blessed Mary, Mother of God." The man crossed himself and dug a cell phone from his back pocket. He punched in a number and began sputtering Spanish rapid fire like a machine gun from a 1940's film noir movie.

The two spinsters edged around to peer up into the dumpster's contents, their cupped palms shading their eyes from the morning sun's rays. Janie scrunched her mouth to one side. "If I am not mistaken, it's Edwin Newman in there."

"Who?" Betsy Ann swiveled her torso towards her sprinting partner.

"You know. The old grouch who moved down the street into the Williams' old condo last Friday."

"Oh, yes. The Williams transferred to the assisted living units, didn't they? He developed advancing Alzheimer's and she's recovering from double hip replacements. Or a knee and a hip? Oh, dear, I get fuddled sometimes about all that medical stuff. So many of us are losing body parts and getting titanium joints..."

"Betsy Ann!" Janie hissed. "Body. Dumpster. Remember?"

"Yes. My, aren't we testy?" She brushed her jacket with the palm of her hand. "Why do you think those belong to... What did you say his name was?"

"Newman. Edwin Newman. He chewed out Mildred Fletcher because her Yorkie barked at him. Threw a coffee mug at the poor animal. Whack! Right on the nose. It left a raw, sore spot."

"He did?"

Janie gave her a quick nod. "Mildred must apply a special salve on him three times a day. Says it cost her $22.95."

"On Mr. Newman?"

Janie scoffed into her velour v-neck. "No, the Yorkie."

Betsy Ann's lips formed an "O."

Janie pointed to the dumpster. "Mr. Newman's in there all right."

"Are you sure?"

"Yes." Janie bent to Betsy Ann's ear. "I see his head."

CHAPTER TWO

Sirens pulsated from the highway. In minutes, the red hook and ladder truck from the Alamoville, Texas, fire department wound past the oak tree-dotted entrance like a barrel racer steering a trusting mare around the metal drums in a rodeo arena. It screeched to a halt as the wailing abruptly ceased mid-cadence. Close behind, an emergency medical services van bumped through the front gates, followed by two police cars and a Texas Department of Public Safety vehicle.

Janie and Betsy Ann sat on the bench to take in the orchestrated mayhem. Residents shuffled toward the scene, some in robes and others in street-wear. Betsy Ann clicked her teeth. "The sounds of sirens draw folks in this community the way the ice cream truck's jingle once attracted my kids "

"Yep. Everyone wants to find out who fell, croaked, or suffered a heart attack."

Ethel MacDaniels, one of the Bunco Biddies, as they fondly dubbed the twelve of them who gathered for the game each Thursday at 6:00 p.m., sauntered towards them, wrapped in her fleece housecoat. Day-old mascara smudged across her crow's feet. "What's going on?"

"Morning, Ethel." Janie grinned. "You fell asleep watching TV again didn't you?"

"How d'ya guess?"

Janie motioned to Ethel's lower eyelids.

Ethel wiped across the right, darkened half-moon and stared at her forefinger, now sporting a grayish smudge mark. "Oh." She dabbed her digit on her tongue and began to rub.

"Hardly shows, hon." Betsy Ann waved the gesture away. "No one will notice, not with all the commotion."

Ethel peered over at the row of emergency vehicles. "What happened?"

Janie stretched her legs out in front of her. "We found a body in the dumpster. Well, pieces of one, that is."

Ethel's mouth opened as wide as her eyes.

Betsy Ann became animated. "Janie thinks they belong to a mean old man who moved into the William's condo on Solar Boulevard." She turned her head back to Janie. "What did you say his name was? Edmund?"

Janie straightened her back. "Ed-win. Edwin Newman."

Ethel's head bobbed in rapid jerks. "Oh, the one who beats up dogs? Yes, I heard. Poor Poopsy. Mildred seemed quite irritated with him."

"With Poopsy?"

"No, Betsy Ann. With Mr. Newman." Janie rolled her bluish-silver eyes.

A black car with a red light pulsating on its dashboard pulled into the drive. A forty-something man in a dark suit and gray tie hopped out. His baritone voice acknowledged the caller broadcasting through the Bluetooth in his ear. "Yes, Mr. Mayor. I'm at the scene. Well, the first responders with the Alamoville Fire Department are here. So are two of my officers and a Texas state trooper. No, sir. I'm not sure why he's here. No signs of the coroner, yet." His boots crunched the asphalt gravel. "Yeah, tape's going up now." He whistled. "Hey, Officer Jenkins. Get those people back behind the barrier."

"Hi, Blake. How's my daughter and the kids?" Janie flashed the professionally dressed man a sweet smile.

Detective Blake Johnson tapped the ear device to end the call as he walked over to the bench. "Hi, Janie. They're fine..." He halted mid-sentence. "For Pete's sake. Can't they follow instructions? Excuse me for a moment, ladies." He took several purposeful steps toward the crowd, his shoulders arrow-straight.

Janie bent closer to her friends. "Melody doesn't think they're 'fine.' Last night, she sniffled to me on the phone about Blake missing yet another of Ellie's volleyball games. Plus, he had to leave before Jamie gave his recital last Friday. Got a call and skedaddled. Ever since they put his partner on medical leave two months ago..." Her thought process halted at the sound of her son-in-law's bellow.

"Jenkins. Now?" Blake jerked his thumb to the growing crowd of on-lookers, now peppered with local TV reporters.

The underling officer shrugged his shoulders and continued his efforts to corral the silvered heads and camera-toting press into a contained area as uniformed police taped off the perimeter around the dumpster.

Blake shook his head and walked back to the trio. "Sorry, ladies. Your neighbors are being a little too curious."

Betsy Ann flipped her wrist. "They always are."

"Might as well be herding cats away from a bowl of cream." Janie humphed. "Half of them are deaf, and the other half just pretend to be."

He snickered and bent to peck his mother-in-law's cheek. "Good to see you. Melody says you are coming to dinner next Friday?"

"That's the plan." She narrowed her focus. "Hope you'll be there."

"All depends." He tipped an imaginary hat rim. "Betsy Ann. Ethel. Nice to see you as well. You ladies should return to your homes now."

Janie rose to her feet. "I think you'll need us to stay here."

"Why?"

"We discovered the body." She pointed back and forth between herself and Betsy Ann. "Well, some of him anyway."

Betsy Ann shuddered.

Blake rocked back on the heels of his boots. "You're serious? Are you ladies all right?"

Both motioned that they were.

"In that case, why don't you wait here, out of the way of the mayhem? I'll call you over in a few minutes to get your statements."

Ethel gasped. "Just think. A murder." She danced on her tiptoes and clapped her hands. "Oh, I've never witnessed a real one before. Only on TV."

Janie patted her arm. "Yes, sweetie." She turned to her puzzled son-in-law with a smirk. "Ethel owns four bookcases filled with cozy mystery paperbacks. Catalogs the crimes in alpha order."

Blake pursed his lips. "Um, hmm." He back-stepped before pivoting on his boot tip. He strutted to speak to the emergency medical technician tending to one perplexed, pale-faced sanitation worker wrapped in a disposable silver blanket.

"Humph. What a wimp. None of us are falling apart." Janie jutted out her chin and sat down on the bench again.

Ethel leaned against a tree trunk. "Well, he is sort of young, so it stands to reason he hasn't witnessed that many dead people."

Betsy Ann re-crossed her legs. "Me, I have visited dozens of people in caskets. My parents, elder brother, my beloved late husband, Joe..." She made a sign of the cross over her heart with a pout. "Next came Aunt Gertrude, Uncle Ted, oh, and Shannon Perkins when she keeled from an aneurysm during a Bridge match three years ago." She stopped on the seventh finger. "And, of course, President Johnson was my first. We stood three hours in line at the Capitol to pass by him lying in state. But I was much younger then."

Janie arched a penciled-in eyebrow. "Would that be Lyndon Baines Johnson or Andrew Johnson?"

"Very funny." Betsy Ann scrunched her forehead. "Wait, shouldn't we be saying a prayer or something?"

"I guess." Janie shrugged. "Even though nobody liked him."

Ethel waggled her finger. "Don't speak ill of the dead, my dear. You're right, Betsy Ann. We should." She bowed her head.

The other two did the same. A few minutes of silence followed, despite the commotion in the background near the club house.

After a moment Betsy Ann whispered, "Amen." She crossed her chest with a reverent sigh and then reached over to pitty-pat Janie's arm. "Your daughter married well. Detective Johnson is such a nice man."

Janie sighed. "I suppose. He'll never be as good of one as my late husband Jack, but then few ever could be."

"Man or detective?"

Janie's eyes gleamed with pride. "Both."

Betsy Ann shot Ethel a smirk. Anyone who spoke with Janie for more than five minutes learned how amazing a police detective Jack Manson had been. Let her jabber for another ten, and she relayed three of his most notorious cases, four if she drank too much caffeine. Janie's Texas drawl revved to rival a New Yorker's fast-paced delivery after the third cup.

Blake turned to the three ladies' direction and wiggled his finger for them to approach. As a policeman and two firefighters rummaged through the dumpster for the rest of Edwin, a latex-gloved medic placed the leg, arm and head on a gurney and covered them with a thick, black plastic sheet. Murmurs and groans waved through the community's gawkers.

The three widows traipsed as proud as peacocks toward the crime scene, knowing all eyes of their fellow Sunset Acres neighbors, and a few reporters, rested on them.

Janie winked. "We'll be the talk of the town for at least a week."

"I know. Isn't this fun?" Ethel giggled.

"Girls, please." Betsy Ann clucked her teeth. "A man has been brutally killed."

Her friends' smiles dissipated.

However, Betsy Ann's eyes twinkled. "But, you're right." She pressed her lips to keep from grinning like a cat after catching a lizard.

Janie lifted her nose a bit higher. "Well, we're bound to gain some notoriety if we help Blake solve this mystery. Poor man is spread too thin. He needs us, whether he realizes it or not."

Ethel gasped. "Do you think we can?"

"We have every right. After all, this happened in our neighborhood. I've lived here for six years. Betsy Ann, you signed on as one of the first residents eight years ago as I recall."

"True."

"And Ethel, people trust you, so they tell you their life stories. Together, we three can glean more information in one day than the police could scrounge up in three weeks."

The other two women eyed each other. Ethel pushed her mouth to one side. "She has a point."

Betsy Ann sighed. "Very well. I for one won't sleep knowing a killer is on the loose, so the sooner they get him, the better."

Janie set her jaw. "Good. Then it's settled. Let's meet over tea and lemon poppy seed cake at my place in half an hour. What ya say?"

Ethel let out a giggle. "Oooh, I can't wait."

CHAPTER THREE

Janie hummed as she got out her grandmother's high tea set along with slices of fresh cake and a bowl of strawberries dipped in sugar. Pencils and pads of paper perched on the edge of the table. A pitcher of ice water sweated droplets onto a trivet set upon the china bureau. She placed three goblets in a triangle, and with one more eye-sweep, clasped her hands in approval as two quick raps pounded on her front door. Janie shuffled to peek through the peephole even though she recognized Betsy Ann's woodpecker-like tap. "Come in, come in."

Now in more appropriate street attire, Ethel and Betsy Ann set their purses on the sofa and made themselves at home around Janie's Queen Anne dining room table. The three widows lived within close walking distance in the condo section of Sunset Acres. Ethel lived in a three-bedroom unit at 125 Sunburst Court. Betsy Ann and Janie resided in the two bedroom models one block over at 131 and 134 Sunny Ridge Blvd.

"Oh, strawberries, too. My favorite." Betsy Ann plopped one on her mouth. "Yum."

Janie laced her hands to her chest. "Do y'all want peach or green tea?"

"Peach." Betsy Ann slid the floral napkin into her lap and reached for a piece of cake.

"And you, Ethel?"

"Did you drink up the raspberry tea I gave you for Christmas?"

"Quite a few weeks ago during that freakish cold snap when the weather lingered in the forties for days on end right after Easter. I greatly appreciated its flavor and warmth."

Ethel pressed her lips together as a rosy tint pushed into her cheekbones. "Peach, then."

Janie tipped the teapot over each cup, the not-quite boiling water swirling soft plumes of steam. "Okay. Let's get down to business. I want each of you to write down what you remember about the scene. Give at much detail as..."

Betsy Ann huffed. "Yes, Janie. I wrote a column each week for the Alamoville Weekly Gazette for almost thirty years. I know how to report."

Ethel cocked her head as her hen scratch scraped against the paper. "On flowers, vegetables, and open houses. Not on crime. I, on the other hand, can access a vast storehouse of information about murder." She tapped her temple.

Janie blew on her tea. "Yes, yes. And I was married to a detective for forty-three years. Of course he started out with a beat, but..." She took a sip and set her cup back in its saucer. "I mean to say we are all qualified to sleuth. Which is why, ladies, we can be of valuable help to my poor over-worked son-in-law. After all, as I said, this is our community. I don't cotton to murders tainting our peaceful surroundings."

Ethel inched her shoulders to her ears. "But this does get the blood flowing, doesn't it?"

Betsy Ann clunked her pencil onto the table. "Ethel!"

The woman's cheeks crimsoned deeper than before. "Sorry, bad pun." She shifted in her chair, but a glint of humor still shone in her eyes. "Besides, that mean ol' Mr. Newman would never fit in anyway. Lots of us own pets. I am surprised the association didn't screen him better."

Betsy Ann chomped on another square of lemon poppy seed cake and wiped the crumbs off the edge of her mouth with her pinkie. "Mmm hmmm."

Janie snapped her fingers. "I've got an idea. Wait here." She scampered away, her rubber soles squeaking across the linoleum floor. None of the condos were carpeted to make it easier for residents to maneuver orthopedic equipment. She returned with several pieces of copy paper and a roll of tape. She secured the edges together until the sheets almost filled the tabletop. "Okay let's draw the layout of Sunset Acres."

Within a few minutes, she'd sketched a fairly accurate bird's-eye view rendition. In the east, she placed their four blocks of condos, grouped in clusters of six, three to each side of a common sidewalk leading to the street in one direction and a gated alley in the other toward assigned carport parking. To the south, she added the winding four streets housing the thirty-two garden homes where Mildred and the late Mr. Newman resided. To the east lay the one- and two-bedroom apartment complex in a U shape surrounding a pool and recreation facility. Beyond lay the ten-acre assisted living grounds with a four-story facility to the south of a strip center with a beauty parlor, barber shop, post office, small library, and day clinic. Next, she outlined the tennis courts, two more swimming pools, and the nine-hole golf course, all encased by a meandering walking path which lead to the parking lot where the tell-tale dumpster stood.

Ethel tapped a section of the paper. "Don't forget the club house, Janie."

Janie rolled her eyes. "Yes, the crime scene. I'm getting to it."

"Okay. Good."

She got up and pressed her hands to her lower back. "Done. Now we can each take a section and start interrogating...uh, I mean talking with our neighbors. Find out who saw Mr. Newman last and when."

Ethel sat straighter in her chair. "I'll start with the garden homes on Solar Boulevard and spread out. I want to visit Mildred to make sure she is able to come to Bunco on Thursday. You know how protective she is of Poopsy."

Betsy Ann nodded rapidly. "Indeed she is. Hovers over that doggie. I hear she hasn't left the house since the incident."

Ethel shifted her gaze to the side bureau. "Janie, may I take her a plate of strawberries? I hate to go empty-handed. My mother didn't raise me that way."

Janie opened the bottom door of the hutch and handed her friend a plastic plate which mimicked cut crystal. "Sure. Here you go. Use this so she doesn't need to wash and return anything. I'll get the plastic wrap."

Betsy Ann raised her hand. "I've got a beauty appointment in forty-five minutes. I'll see what I can find out. Tongues like to wag while under the hair dryer or waiting for their perms to set."

"Getting a rinse?"

"No, of course not." She spoofed her russet curls. "This is my natural color. My grandmother went to her grave at eighty-nine with hardly any—"

Ethel and Janie finished in sync, "—strands of gray."

"We know, Betsy Ann. Just ribbing you." Janie had her doubts though. Yet Betsy Ann's hairdresser, who rented a booth at Sunset

Acres' in-house salon every Tuesday and Thursday for the past three years, couldn't be bribed to state otherwise.

Betsy Ann snitched a third piece of cake. "I'm only trying to help."

Janie reached over and squeezed her shoulder. "Yes. Sorry. You go cock an ear. Great idea." She cleared her throat. "I'll ask if Mrs. Jacobs needs someone to sit at the Newman house until the family arrives. That way, I can do some snooping inside." Janie gave them both a wink. "She trusts me. Her grandmother and my aunt were sorority sisters at the university in Austin. What a pleasant surprise to learn she managed this community. One of the main reasons I agreed to sell the house and move here."

Ethel confessed. "I deemed her to be trustworthy as soon as I learned her name. Angela, like the actress in *Murder She Wrote*." She lifted an arthritic finger. "Not a coincidence. Providence, I say."

"As the hymn says, 'God works in mysterious ways, His wonders to be performed.'" Betsy Ann dabbed her mouth with a napkin. "Do you think she'll let you?"

"I imagine Blake ordered uniformed men to search through the vic's things. But, it's worth a try." Janie thumped the eraser against her chin.

Betsy Ann nabbed another strawberry before Ethel covered the batch in clear wrap. "Aren't we going to finish drawing the crime scene?"

Ethel wriggled her brow. "We need to scoop and snoop while the murder's still fresh."

"Right." Janie snatched her house keys. "We'll meet up again at the dining hall for lunch, 12:30 sharp. Come on, ladies."

Janie ushered the women out the door. A brisk breeze whipped in from the north, along with a near-distant rumble. Springtime in Texas. The weather changed with a snap of the fingers. She dashed back in to grab her umbrella, just in time to catch her ten-year-old cat crouched on the dining room bureau licking the lemon frosting from the last slice of poppy seed cake.

Janie shooed her off. "Shame on you, Mrs. Fluffy."

The tabby sauntered out of the room with her tail high.

CHAPTER FOUR

Ethel stood on the sidewalk, scanning up the street and then down. Which way to go? She sighed. Should she bring her pug along for a stroll? People always seemed to be friendlier when her Pugsy panted alongside her and wagged her back end to show off her queued stub of a tail. Nonsense. She had every reason to meet her neighbors instead of always having her nose in a book. After all, they called this a community, right?

Janie's correct. People do open up to me when given the chance. I can do this. She adjusted her blouse and walked on, her chin up. The sun enveloped her shoulders like a heating pad on high despite the thunder rippling on the breeze off to the east. Time to get summer booties to protect Pugsy's tender pads from the hot concrete. She'd buy them when the community van went on the weekly Outlet Mall excursion on Friday—if she remembered.

She decided the garden home with the pink petunias would be a good place to begin. With a tippy-tap on the knocker, Ethel waited and practiced her most neighborly smile. No answer. She dropped her shoulders a half inch and strolled to the next home.

Again, no one came to the door. A ruby-colored cardinal landed with a chirp on the dangling limb near the front porch. Betsy Ann addressed him with a pout. "Don't bother, little one. No one's home to sprinkle bird seed."

Oh, how she wanted to do well and prove her love for sleuthing to be more than a mere reader's hobby. She felt somewhat outside the circle, having not witnessed the body. However, she'd never seen real blood and guts before. With a shudder as if she sucked a lemon, Ethel shoved the memory of the gruesome gurney image away. *Perhaps I'm lucky I didn't.* The pecan syrup-drenched blueberry pancakes she pampered herself with for breakfast would have ended up on the pavement. Even now, the remnants turned to concrete in her stomach, along with the extra helping of strawberries and lemon poppy seed cake.

A slight creak broke her thought pattern. "May I help you?"

Ethel turned to spot a white-haired couple peering through the half-cocked door. They resembled Tweedle Dee and Tweedle Dum. Married for decades, no doubt. She read in a magazine husbands and wives begin to look more and more alike after years of marriage. Proof the Book of Genesis proclaimed the truth. The two do become one. Now why did she think of that, and why did she stand on their stoop? Oh, yes...

"Hello. I'm Ethel MacDaniels. I live a block over." She indicated with her hand in the direction of the condos. "Did you hear about the, er, dumpster incident this morning?"

The two eyed her, glanced at each other, and shrugged.

"Oh, well. Maybe you never met Edwin Newman. He only moved in last Friday. Do you own a dog?"

The man raised his bushy eyebrows. "What?"

Ethel tucked her lip into her lower teeth. This hadn't begun well. She acted as klutzy as a one armed juggler. "He—Edwin that is, was—well...murdered. And people said, or rather hinted, he hated dogs. Mine is a pug. Cute little thing. Name's Pugsy. Always well behaved, except she likes to bark at..."

"And you are here because...?" The man's face puckered. His wife slid a few inches behind his shoulders, though her eyes never left Ethel.

Ethel mopped her brow with the back of her hand. "Oh, never mind. We are hoping someone spotted something early this morning. But," she scanned them up and down, noticing their protruding tummies still tucked under their bathrobe sashes, "I guess you haven't been out and about yet today."

The man started to close the front door when his wife's hand wrapped around the edge. "Wait. Is he the one who threw a mug at Poopsy?"

"Who?" The man turned to face her.

"Mildred's Yorkie."

His face softened. "Yes, that's right. Cute pooch. Wouldn't hurt a fly."

His wife edged though the triangular opening, her other hand clutching the crisscross folds of her cover-up. "I know the man you are talking about. Mrs. Jacobs introduced us when she showed him the library. Rude man. Jumpy, with shifty eyes as if he robbed the U.S. Mint and feared someone would find out."

The man sighed through his nostrils, making a slight whistle. "Now, sugarplum..."

His wife ignored his gesture. "I'm Eleanor and this is Jonathan. We're the Franks, and we moved in a few months back." She extended a still elegant hand with elongated, slender fingers despite the slight bulges of arthritic knuckles and liver spots. "Come inside and have a cuppa. I made some raspberry tarts earlier this morning."

Frank moved out of the doorway and motioned for Ethel to enter.

"Oh, how kind. Don't mind if I do." She gave the couple a sugary smile but her starch-laden stomach screamed, *No. No more sweets.* "I guess one tart couldn't hurt."

Eleanor's face brightened and a pixie grin slid across her thin lips. "Come, come. Kitchen's this way."

Ethel followed, making sure to mention how that painting or this knick-knack enhanced their decor perfectly.

When she sat at their kitchen dinette set, her elastic waistband tugged. I can walk it off as I canvas the rest of the block—unless, of course, each household offers me food as well. Oh, dear.

Betsy Ann sighed with pleasure as the blast from the air conditioned salon slapped her face. "Whew. It's hot enough to fry an egg on the asphalt."

Nancy, one of the assisted living residents, crinkled her nose. "Who'd want to do that? Don't y'all like the food around here? This morning, they served eggs Benedict and waffles."

Sue Lin, the hairdresser, shook her head as she teased another strand of silver curl. "Nancy, it's only a saying."

The octogenarian bounced her head, loosening another hot roller. "Oh. I get it."

The stylist arched an eyebrow. "Hope we get some rain. Looks promising off to the east."

Nancy jutted her chin. "Better not. I paid good money for this hair-do. I don't want the damp air to ruin it."

Betsy gave Sue Lin a sympathetic grin. "I'm early. I'll read up on the latest Hollywood glamour gossip." She browsed through several magazines, most of them dog-eared, and decided on one with a pregnant supermodel in a Brazilian bikini on the cover. "Humph. Back in my day, you wore mu-mus. If you left the house in your third trimester, that is."

Another condo dweller—what was her name, now?—leaned in, swirling Betsy Ann in fumes of permanent curling mixture. "Scandalous how they parade their bodies these days."

Betsy Ann nodded and slapped the tabloid closed. "Speaking of. Did ya'll here about the body in the dumpster today?"

The salon became silent. All heads, whether permed, shaped, teased, or dripping wet turned toward her. Only the soft whoosh of the hair dryer broke the stillness. A giddy shiver slithered up her spine. Proud of her segue into the topic at hand, she wiggled forward in her chair. "Seems his name was Newman. Edwin Newman. A new resident in the garden homes."

Murmurs ensued.

"I recall who you mean." Sue Lin untwisted another roller from Nancy's head. "I heard he hated animals. Liked to beat them."

Gasps echoed through three salon stations. The one with perm fumes—Betsy Ann held her name on the tip of her tongue but couldn't quite grab it—spoke up. "I passed him coming back from the Get 'em and Go, and he ignored me when I called out a friendly howdy. Glared me in the eye before turned his head away. Rude, don't you think?"

The other salon attendant, Maria, piped up as she pumped the chair higher to comb out Becky Smith's curls. "I saw him walking along the road back to the garden homes. He seemed in a hurry, almost as if he had to, well, you know..."

Nancy bobbed her chin. "Maybe he did. None of our bladders are as strong as they used to be. My daughter bought me some of them adult diapers..."

Sue Lin flopped a few strands over Nancy's face to make her stop talking, lest she swallow a mouthful of hair. "You were saying, Maria?"

Maria spun her customer to the left. "I think a touch more off the sides, don't you agree, Becky? Good." She took a pair of sheers out of the disinfectant jar. "Well, he seemed…oh, I don't know. Off, to me. I remember saying to myself, 'Why would Mrs. Jacobs lease to a sour puss when everyone else here is so friendly?'" Maria stopped in mid-snip. "He dressed rather shabby-like, too."

Betsy Ann took out a small notepad from her satchel and began writing these things down as inconspicuously as possible. Her memory often dissipated like a spritz of those over-priced automatic air fresheners. Hawaiian orchid, lemon fields, clean laundry. Pfft. Lemons grew on trees, not in fields. And who wanted a kitchen to smell like Hawaii or laundry? Whatever happened to plain old vanilla? Or cinnamon. Her mother used to boil some on the stove to vanish the musty odors. Now what had she been writing? Oh yes, he dressed shabbily.

"One thing for sure. He was in dire need of a haircut and a beard trim." The lady with the perm jerked her head up and down, releasing more ammonia-laden plumes of odor.

"You don't say…" Betsy Ann paused as she scrounged for the woman's name in her memory banks. Ah, her husband's named Bob, right? Bob and…and…Sheila! "Sheila."

"Uh, huh." Sheila crossed her arms over her bosom. "Not at all like the rest of us."

Betsy Ann drummed her pencil, proud one grey cell functioned at last. She scribbled, *needed a haircut and bears trimmed?* She made a sour face as she scratched it out. *No beard.*

Sue Lin released Nancy from the chair and motioned to Betsy Ann. She smiled, slipped the tablet in her bag with ears cocked to determine if anyone else would divulge pertinent information. But the conversations turned to the upcoming half-off sale at the department store in the mall and someone's granddaughter taking first place in her senior high school's debate contest.

No matter. Janie would be proud of her.

Janie swiveled her hips in a power walk toward the Newman residence. Yep, an Alamoville police car parked next to the curb, shaded by the canopy of an oak tree in the front yard—if one called the twenty-foot stretch of ground cover a proper lawn. But then, not having to maintain property remained the garden homes' biggest selling point, along with their single-story handicapped accessibility. Like the condos and apartments, the extra-wide door frames and the spacious bathrooms easily accommodated durable medical equipment.

The county deputy sheriff's cruiser sat nose to nose with the patrol vehicle. No sign of her son-in-law. *Did he make Ellie's game after all? Doubtful.*

Mrs. Jacobs stood half-way up the walk, talking to an officer. Midday sunlight, shafting through the thunderclouds, shimmered in a soft, auburn halo around the crown of her hair, which she'd secured into a bun. Fly-away wisps curled her neck. Her size-four frame sported a shirt-dress in denim with an embroidered belt in mauve and blues. This season's bone-colored, rubber-soled sandals adorned her long, narrow feet. The popular Texas-based, orthopedic innersole shoe manufacturer had opened a discount outlet down the highway four years prior. On any given day, one could spot at least twenty pairs donned by community members. Janie owned four styles herself. Now why did her mind wander in that direction?

"Good morning, again." Janie shuffled to the sidewalk, her shoulders soldier-straight. She showed them her knitting bag. "Thought I might be of help. I can house-sit a while until the relatives come. Figured I'd help ward off the gawkers."

Mrs. Jacobs opened her mouth, but no words escaped. Instead, she turned to the deputy to respond.

"Well, I guess it would be okay. I think the investigative team is about through inside."

Janie's hopes lifted like a helium balloon.

His attention returned to the property manager. He ripped off a sheet of paper and handed it to her. "We've confiscated his laptop, cell phone, and personal papers, though not much was found other than the lease and your filers on the amenities. How long did you say he lived here?"

Rats. Janie's plans started to deflate.

"Oh, only a few days." Mrs. Jacobs pursed her ruby lips. "He signed the rental agreement on Wednesday, and I think scheduled the moving van to arrive last Friday."

"Van? For what?" He jerked his thumb toward the front entrance. "The only thing in there is a folding card table with two metal chairs and a blow-up mattress."

Janie's hope balloon flattened further.

Mrs. Jacobs scratched her head. "I'm certain he told me last Friday."

Janie narrowed her eyes. *So he lied?*

Another uniformed man exited with a trash bag and a small rolling suitcase. "Here is all his worldly possessions. Just a few changes of clothes, all previously worn, a razor and a comb."

"Whoa. All of that been dusted for prints?"

The underling set the luggage down. "Yes, sir. None found. Bagged some hair follicles from the comb, though."

"Think that's important?"

"Well, sir. From what the coroner said, he had grayish hair, right? The comb had black."

The scene investigator arched one eyebrow so high his forehead resembled the mud-cracked creek at the back of the property before the spring rains.

Jane and Mrs. Jacob shared a blank expression.

The officer continued. "Nothing in the fridge except a half-drunk bottle of O.J. The rest of this junk we found on the counter-tops and in the sink." He lifted the sack.

Janie peered at the garbage. Inside the slightly opaque bag she eyed two plastic wedged containers for sandwiches and a local delivery pizza box bulging to one corner.

Hmmm. Had Mr. Newman's movers been delayed? And why did he never go to the mega grocery store during those three days? Even if he didn't own a car, the community minibus went to the discount super store every Saturday, Monday and Thursday. Surely Mrs. Jacobs pointed that out in the brochure during her welcome-to-the-neighborhood spiel.

Well, it's not too unusual for a man who lived alone not to cook. Janie, herself, didn't piddle about the kitchen as much as when her hubby walked this earth. Still, something seemed askew.

As the officer dragged the trash down the sidewalk to the curb, Janie detected quite a few sixteen-ounce cans of lite beer—the kind always on special across the highway at the Get ' em and Go. Crimson lipstick stained the edges of several cans.

Either Mr. Newman drank a good amount of brewsky and liked to cross-dress with makeup and a black wig, or he entertained a lady visitor over the weekend.

CHAPTER FIVE

Janie drummed her fingers on the tabletop in the dining room. Though she tried to communicate with the officers at Mr. Newman's home on Solar Boulevard, they remained tight-lipped. As well they should. At least her son-in-law trained them well…too well. She needed to come up with another angle. She hoped Betsy Ann and Ethel had better luck.

She glanced at the wall clock. 12:32. Ah, here they came.

The two meandered around the scattered seating with their lunch trays. Betsy Ann's contained three plates in various sizes. Chicken and rice, fruit salad, and a wedge of chocolate pie. Ethel's sported a glass of iced water and a small garden salad.

"Not hungry, dear?"

Ethel puffed out her cheeks. "Everyone on the block offered me a mid-morning snack. Tarts, donuts, brownies."

Janie nodded. "You had some success, I gather?"

The murder-buff's face glowed like the sunshine outlining the rain clouds outside. "I did. Anyone else?"

Betsy Ann opened her pocket-sized tablet. "A little. Everyone agreed he scowled and dressed in a shabby manner. Becky Smith stated he snubbed her at the library with a sour expression."

Ethel relayed her findings from the Franks. "Did you ever meet them? I think we should invite Eleanor to join us at Bunco. We need a twelfth now that Peg Williams is in rehab."

"What about Martha Andrews?"

"She and Bob are snowbirds. They'll be headed back north in a few weeks. Especially if this hot weather sticks around."

"Yes, they stay with the grandkids in Michigan until October, don't they?" Janie stabbed her green beans.

"Well, they used to own the house up there. Sold to their granddaughter and her husband for $455,000. The amount they needed for moving expenses to Texas, a new SUV, and the mortgage on their condo. Quite generous if you ask me." Ethel took a sip of her water.

"Anyway." Janie shot glances at them both. "What else did you discover?"

Ethyl pushed the cherry tomato off to the side and forked a leaf of lettuce. "Josephine and Eduardo Rodriguez had a run-in with him. He nearly shoved poor Eduardo off the sidewalk as he whipped by with hands loaded with beer and junk food from the convenience store. And with Eduardo still on a cane after his fall last month, no less." She bit into the sprig dangling from her fork tong, chewed a few bites and continued. "Eduardo asked if he planned to have a party. Mr. Newman whipped around with an evil glare, cursed at him to mind his own business, and kept walking."

Betsy Ann gasped. "You know, Sheila mentioned how grumpy he seemed."

"Sheila?"

"Yes. The reddish-blonde with a curly perm and thin figure. Husband is Bob. They live in one of the garden homes over on Sunnyside Way. Anyway, she said when he signed the lease, he appeared slicked back and city-fied. But when he walked by on Sunday afternoon, he acted ill-tempered and wore disheveled, army surplus duds. And Sue Lin mentioned he needed a haircut and beard trim." She gestured to her tablet. "I wrote that down, too."

Janie winked. "Good work, ladies. And yes, Mr. Newman organized a party, all right. At least for a lady friend. I spied ruby lipstick marks on a few of the cans as the police hauled out his trash. And..." She bent over her tray and whispered. Her friends did the same to hear over the buzz of conversations around them. "His house contained only a couple of pieces of furniture. Reeked of stale cigarette smoke, too."

Betsy Ann pinched her nostrils. "Yuk. Who smokes anymore?"

Ethel thought for a moment. "Old military? Some of them picked up the habit in Nam and never kicked it."

Janie wrote what they said on her notepad. She stopped, pen in mid-air. "Makes sense, Ethel. Especially if he wore army surplus clothing. You know, the moving van may still arrive. Often times, if they are coming from out of state, they will combine hauls. It can take up to a week. Did for my son and his family when they moved to New Jersey."

Ethel grinned. "Which means we need to keep an eye out."

Janie winked. "Uh, huh. Mildred might help. She lives next door."

Ethel slapped her own forehead. "I didn't get by to see her."

"No worries. I'll go see her tomorrow morning." Betsy Ann gave her friend's hand a squeeze. She'll be napping after lunch today."

Ethel scoffed. "After what he did to Poopsy, I'm sure she'll be more than willing to become involved in this investigation. Find out who his beneficiary is. If I were her, I'd sue his next of kin for the vet bills."

Janie crossed her arms. "Surely Mrs. Jacobs recorded the information in his profile. I overheard her say just the other day she wanted the Board to hire a temporary employee who could help her clean out the old files. Think I'll volunteer."

"Oh, me, too. It'll be fun," Betsy Ann replied in a loud voice with her hand raised, which caused a few heads throughout the dining hall to swivel in their direction. She lowered her arm and hunched over her chicken and rice casserole, her face resembling the tomatoes on Ethel's salad plate.

"Discretion, ladies. Discretion." Janie's whispered tone took on the seriousness of a schoolmarm. "Okay, Betsy Ann, you and I will volunteer in the office tomorrow, and Ethel, you talk with Mildred and continue to canvas the neighbors."

Ethel rubbed her belly and groaned. "If you say so, Janie. But I will have to power walk four times this week instead of two. I'll meet you two in the morning at seven sharp."

Annie Schmidt slipped into the empty chair next to them. "Is your son-in-law leading the investigation into Edwin Newman's, er, demise?" She glanced around the room and motioned the three to move in closer. "I thought he looked a tad familiar when I picked up a package in Mrs. Jacob's office. I ordered an indoor-outdoor thermometer. My air conditioner thermostat is never right and my bill last month, whew!" She fanned herself. "Anyway, Mr. Newman sat with his head bent, signing the lease agreement. She introduced us and as he shook my hand, I recognized him from somewhere. His eyes stood out in my mind, which nagged at the back of my brain all weekend. Then last night, I recalled where I'd seen him."

"Where?"

She reached in her pocket and pulled out a yellowed newspaper clipping. "This is from my great nephew's wedding ten years ago." She turned the article over and pushed the newsprint toward Janie. "See, it's him. Part of a gang convicted for armed robbery of three banks in Austin. Except his name wasn't Edwin Newman."

The faded article depicted a mug shot of a man, though younger, with similar features to their new, now dead neighbor. The caption identified the man as Edward Norman.

All three women gasped.

CHAPTER SIX

Janie and Ethel met at the corner as the breaking day peeked over the horizon in a splash of purple and orange. Ethel stretched her hands behind her back. "Morning. God did good, today, right?" She motioned with her head to the skies.

Janie smiled. "Masterful canvas. Ready?" She began to jog in place. Today, she wore a lime green jump suit which matched the laces in her tennis shoes—her normal Wednesday morning outfit.

The two trotted in sync for a few blocks in silence. A mockingbird sang his repertoire for some unknown feathered lady. Two squirrels wound in a playful dance up an oak tree trunk. The puddles left over from the previous evening's rains shimmered in the early morning glow.

Except for the gruesome crime scene, which still hovered over the community, it might be a peaceful glimpse of paradise.

"Where is Betsy Ann?"

Janie answered without missing her stride. "Her tailbone is bothering her. After all, it's only been three weeks since her mishap." She mopped the first beads of perspiration from her brow. "I told her she pushed her luck yesterday."

Ethel nodded. "I missed because I had to get some blood work done. I wanted to go early since you're supposed to fast after midnight. Afterwards, I was starved, so I stopped off at the Pancake House near the highway and treated myself to a triple stack." Her face took on a penitent expression. "With blueberry syrup. I go see the doc later this morning and I know he'll tell me to lose a few pounds, so I decided to indulge one last time."

Janie chuckled. "Are you going to knock on doors again this afternoon??"

"Not really. After lunch people nap." She patted her now flatter stomach. "Which, despite our investigative efforts, is a Godsend. I doubt my mouth would open to another home-baked goody. Especially after Dr. Weber lectures me."

"For heaven's sake, Ethel. You're only a size twelve."

The two rounded the corner.

"Any word on your secretarial volunteering?"

"Yep. We start today, working from one to four. Same tomorrow and Friday."

Ethel slowed. "What about Bunco at six?"

Janie swiped away her friend's concern like a fly buzzing her face. "It'll leave me plenty of time to get home, freshen up and fix a fruit salad. Don't worry."

"Why don't I pick up one from the store in the morning when the van heads to the supermarket? I'm thinking of getting a rotisserie chicken. They're on special for $4.99."

Janie's silver curls bounced. "Okay. Deal. I'll pay you back. But remember, no strawberries. Bab's allergic."

"Right."

The two slow-jogged past the condos, beyond the strip-mall and up to the clubhouse. Yellow police tape flapped in the breeze, encircling half the parking lot and the now-empty dumpster. The women slowed to a stroll, eyes fixated on the scene. A few others milled around, giving the area a wide berth. Mrs. Jacobs stood on the stoop, talking with Janie's son-in-law and another plain-clothed detective Janie recognized but couldn't recall his name.

"Are you going to go over and say hello?"

"Hmm. Not now." Janie squinted as the morning sun reflected off the patrol car's hood into her pupils, as if God warned her pride to not venture forth until she had all the facts.

Ethel laid a hand on her friend's arm. "But shouldn't you tell him about Edward Norman?"

"Not yet. I need to drive into Austin and scour the microfiche at the newspaper archives first. Don't want him barking up the wrong tree and wasting time."

"Makes sense."

"Do you want to come with me?"

Ethel's eyes took on a gleam. "Oh, yes. Please. I should be back from my, ugh, medicinal lecture by ten."

"Well, we better finish our workout so you can shower and change." She took off in a swivel-hipped strut, making sure her lime green outfit caught her son-in-law's attention. After a quick wave, Janie Manson fast-walked toward her condo with a smug grin inching over her lips.

Soon, I'll have this case solved, dear Blake. Then, they'd pow-wow, but not before.

Ethel tagged along behind.

At 10:00 a.m., Ethel knocked on Janie's door. She'd changed into a cream blouse and maroon and cream skirt. Janie dressed in black slacks with a black, white, and red paisley-patterned top. Red earrings dangled a tad below her earlobes. "Ready?"

Ethel hugged her purse. "Yep."

Janie snatched her keys as they headed to the back door which lead to her designated carport.

"So, how'd it go?"

Ethel stuck out her tongue. "Not as bad as I thought. Need to cut back on sweets."

"Don't we all? I think the commuter traffic will have died down by now. So we should arrive by ten-thirty. That gives us an hour and a half before we must head back."

"Right, so you can eat lunch before you begin your temporary duties."

Janie nodded. "So why don't you search for articles up to the date of Annie's clipping. July 15, 2005, if I recall right. Start with that day and work backwards."

"And you?" Ethel clicked her seat belt.

Janie shut the door and turned the ignition. "I am going to begin with last Tuesday."

Ethel swiveled to face her. "Why Tuesday?"

"Ah." Janie raised a finger as she turned down the main street leading out of Sunset Acres. "Because that's the day before Mr. Newman signed the lease. If he is really Mr. Edward Norman, I should find some report of his release date."

"Unless he escaped."

Janie smirked. "Well now, we would have heard about it, wouldn't we?"

Ethel turned to face her. "Remember the fifteen tornadoes last week which ravaged a good portion of north central Texas up into

Oklahoma? They took the spotlight. So did the backlash from the State Supreme Court's decision about displaying the Ten Commandments on public grounds. One escaped criminal story might slip through the news media's attention. After all, he didn't murder anyone, only drove the getaway car."

Janie thumped her fingers on steering wheel. "True." An icy chill slithered down her spine. Could their manager have been so blind as to lease to a convicted felon? Surely not. She hoped this newspaper article of Annie's represented their first— how did the detective movies phrase a trick to lead them on another trail?— Oh, yes. A red herring.

Betsy Ann sipped chamomile tea at Mildred's. Poopsy sat on his owner's lap, his once black nose red and oozing with salve. Bloodshot squiggles raced through one of the pup's eyes. He kept winking and never quite opened his lid all the way. She stretched out a hand to pat the dog's head.

"How is he doing?"

Mildred's eyes swam. She gathered the pooch to her chin. "Mean old man. I'm glad he's dead."

"Mildred Scott Fletcher."

She wiggled in her chair. "Well?"

Betsy Ann lowered her voice even though they alone sat at the Fletcher's kitchen table. Mildred, though widowed for six months, still set a place for her husband. Betsy Ann had made sure not to sit there.

"The police may deem you a prime suspect if you go around talking like that."

The woman chewed her lower lip. "They called and asked to come by today to speak with me."

Betsy Ann took advantage of the wedge in the conversation door. "Be brief, tell the truth, but leave any emotion out of your responses. That's what Janie says they take note of first."

"Oh, okay."

"Mildred, Janie is—well, let's just say she's helping her son-in-law on this case. In an unofficial capacity, that is. Since Mr. Newman's demise happened here in our community, it makes sense for her to do so, right?"

The woman gave her half of a head wag.

"Do you want to help us identify his killer? She could use your eyes and ears since you live right next door."

Mildred set down the dog and glared into her friend's eyes. "Absolutely. I don't want anyone to accuse me." She gulped a small sob. "I've only received one parking ticket in my entire life. But I've done my fair share of jury duty, and I'm aware of how those high-falutin' lawyers can twist a witness's words around. They do on TV all the time." Her lower lip wobbled. "Besides, who'd take care of Poopsy?"

Betsy Ann patted her hand. "Great. Janie said to tell you not to reveal your anger, not even to the police, okay? You may raise red flags and cause the killer to run."

She sucked in her breath, hand to mouth. "You think he is still lurking about?"

"Nobody is certain." Betsy Ann explained about the clipping and the not-yet arrived moving van. "Here's what Janie says you should do..."

CHAPTER SEVEN

Betsy Ann sashayed up the steps to the leasing office, two minutes before one in the afternoon. Janie perched on a side chair in the lobby, waiting for Mrs. Jacobs to finish talking with Mr. Calloway about the hot water heater in his condo clanking all night long. Last month, his air conditioner whined, and the month before that, the automatic sprinklers came on at the wrong time on the golf course.

Through the opened office door, the ladies saw him lean across her desk. "What kinda cheap joint do you run here?" His crooked finger pointed at Mrs. Jacob's face.

Betsy Ann slipped into the other chair, motioning at the disgruntled man with her eyes.

Janie mouthed, "Whew." She picked up a travel magazine about Central Texas.

"So did you and Ethel have any luck?"

"Not really. Need to schedule more time there. I didn't realize how long it takes to scan one edition."

"Sorry. Mildred is in, though. More than happy to help. I explained it to her just like you said."

"Good." Janie put her finger to her lips. "Here she comes."

Mrs. Jacob's expression remained solid, professional, and unreadable as she walked her disgruntled resident to the lobby. "Yes, sir, Mr. Calloway. Why don't I send Jose over in…let's say, an hour? You can explain everything to him. He is head of maintenance and can get to the bottom of your complaints."

The man's mottled complexion faded from red to a muted pink. "Very well. He needs to learn his crew are a bunch of a lazy, no good…"

She spread her hands, palms out, and plastered on a saccharin smile. "Now, now. No need to slip into name calling, is there?"

He sputtered under his breath and shuffled his feet. "Well, okay. One hour."

The bell on the door tinkled on his way out. Mrs. Jacob pressed her fingers together and sighed. "Are you sweet ladies ready to help out?"

The old files, much to Janie's dismay, did not reside in Mrs. Jacob's office but in a separate store room where she kept cleaning supplies and other items. The temperature climbed at least ten degrees warmer and the air stilled. Janie eyed the ceiling. No intake vents. The three cabinets lined one side of the eight by seven room, and metal shelves crowded the other.

"I'll prop the door open for airflow. You start with "A", Janie, and Betsy Ann, you begin with "M." All files older than seven years can be put in that box to be shredded. Files over three years old place in these boxes to be digitized. Please keep them in alphabetical order, ladies. If you find any misfiled, refile it correctly if you don't mind."

She turned to leave but stopped at the door jamb. "Oh, restroom is to your right and cokes and bottled water are in the fridge in the break room. Help yourself."

Janie huffed through her silver locks. "Now, how are we supposed to get a glimpse at the current resident files or her computer records?"

Betsy Ann sneezed as she opened the first drawer. A whiff of dust motes escaped from their long-locked prison between the folders. A blend of disinfectants and other chemicals from the supply shelves clung in her nostrils. "My allergies, ugh."

Janie dug in her pocket for a hankie. "Here, take this."

"Achoo." She draped her arms across the open drawer and dabbed the handkerchief under her nose. "Thanks."

"All in the name of sleuthing. Do you think Mrs. Jacobs will leave for a few minutes so we can sneak a peek at the recent folders?"

Betsy Ann sniffled. "I'm not sure this was such a grand idea."

They proceeded to sort through the files.

A half-hour and four more sneezes later, Mrs. Jacobs popped her head into the storeroom. "Ladies. I need to go to the office supply store. Can I leave you two here for a little while? If anyone drops by, tell them I will be back by three. If they are looking, several condo units are available, six efficiency apartments, plus three vacancies in assisted living." She hung her head for a moment. "And now, of course, one garden home." Silence filled the room. Exhaling a sigh, she thrust a trifold at Janie. "Hand them a brochure, I guess."

A huge grin splayed across Janie's face. "No problem. And we'll answer the phone, too."

Mrs. Jacobs clasped her hands together. "Oh, that would be such a help. I won't be long."

When the tinkle of the bell announced her exit, Janie said under her breath, "Take as long as you want." She slammed the drawer closed and traipsed across the hall to the leasing office.

Betsy Ann hissed. "Wait. Stop. This isn't right."

Janie halted, hands on her hips. "I'm just going to take a peek. Perchance his folder is still on her desk."

"And if it is, you will open the flap a tad and glance inside?" Her voice held a disciplinary tone as she tapped her foot.

"All right. I get it. Privacy act and all." Janie rolled her eyes, hands folded over her paisley blouse. "I swear God put you in my life to be my conscience."

Betsy Ann's eyes glimmered. "It is tempting, I grant you."

"So how else are we going to find out about Mr. Newman—if that's his real name?"

"Well, Blake can. He has more resources. Did you talk with him?"

Janie cast her gaze to the front window. "No."

"Why?" Betsy Ann's voice shrilled. "Ah, ha. He doesn't know you are helping him in this investigation, does he?"

Janie plopped her rear into one of the upholstered lobby chairs. "Of course not. He won't allow amateurs to become involved. But, when we bring him real evidence which cracks this case wide open, he'll wrap this up with a bow in time to attend Ellie's play-off game next Saturday morning and Jamie's end of the year concert that night." She slapped the arm rest. "So, we have ten days. You still in?"

Betsy Ann slumped into the seat next to her. "I guess. But I think we should rally the troops. Tonight at Bunco, we tell everyone the game plan." She twisted her torso to meet her friend's eyes. "You do have one, right?"

The two amateur sleuths scurried through the dusty files like ants rebuilding a kicked-over hill. By late afternoon, they had sorted half of the cabinets. Mrs. Jacobs returned with a huge smile on her face. "My, my, you two are industrious. You have no idea how much of a load is lifted from my shoulders."

Janie's face produced the sweetest, most innocent smile Betsy Ann ever witnessed. "Well, I don't compare to my son-in-law. Detective Blake Johnson. Never seen a man work so hard. He is so swamped, he never gets to spend time with my grandchildren."

"Tsk, tsk. The way of the world nowadays. Everyone so busy."

"Yes, well." Janie paused.

Betsy Ann saw it coming. She held her breath.

"I sort of agreed to help him out on this case." Janie lifted her hands in front of her. "Unofficially, you understand. But since we all live here, we are privy to more than he could find out in a month of Sundays. So any help we"—she motioned back and forth between the three of them—"can give to expedite this process would be of tremendous service to the community and the police."

"Such as...?" Mrs. Jacobs slid into her official lease manager's ergonomically designed chair and leaned back.

"I, um, gather he took Mr. Newman's file?"

"Of course. First thing he asked for."

Betsy Ann let out an elongated sigh.

Janie elbowed her in the ribs. "Can you divulge anything about his background? I mean without breaking any rules." She brushed away the thought like a pesky mosquito. "All of these privacy laws now are so restrictive."

Mrs. Jacobs leaned over her desk. "Tell me about it. More and more paperwork to fill out, plus they make being able to screen residents hard as granite. I purchased a special program through an agency to do thorough background checks. Costs a bundle. But the thing often produces quirky results."

"You don't say." Janie scooted into one of the two faux leather, armless seats facing the desk. Betsy Ann followed suit.

Mrs. Jacobs stretched her torso further across her desk, signaling the ladies to draw closer. She darted her eyes back and forth as she lowered her voice as if afraid someone would eavesdrop. "Just between you two and the walls, when I keyed in Edwin Lewis Newman's name and Houston, Texas, where he declared he last resided, the search result claimed he died six years ago."

CHAPTER EIGHT

Ethel dashed through Janie's back door at twenty after five, with her rotisserie chicken in one hand and fruit salad in the other. "Okay, I'm here. What's up?"

Betsy Ann chopped celery and carrot sticks while Janie dumped the plastic take-out container of potato salad she'd also brought into a cut glass bowl. "We found out something rather alarming at the lease office today."

Janie tossed the container in the garbage container under the sink.

"Isn't that recyclable? You should rinse it out." Ethel reached into the trash and pulled the tub out. She washed away the remaining mayo-soaked remnants and placed it on the counter, sans label, to dry. "Here's your fruit salad. I need to slice up the chicken if you don't mind. Now what were you saying?"

"Mrs. Jacobs disclosed some information about Edwin Newman." Betsy Ann waved the knife.

"Well, not quite..." A sly grin slid across Janie's mouth. "The agency found hardly any information on him. At least not for the past six years after he died!"

Ethel gasped. "Ooh, this is good." She shriveled into her shoulders. "I mean, as far as mysteries go, this is turning into a classic, don't you think? Reminds me of one I read last summer, but I don't recall the name. Can visualize the cover..."

"Ethel. I'm sure you cross-cataloged the book, crime, and motive. You can find it later. Anyway, we wondered why Sunset Acres would let him rent a garden home if his history is so sketchy."

"Well, yes. That is rather disturbing. What did Mrs. Jacob's say?"

Janie carried the salad to the serving bar. Betsy Ann followed with her fresh veggies and Ethel brought up the rear with her chicken.

"She asked him about the findings and he said a computer glitch at the Harris County records caused confusion, and he'd tried for two years to get everything cleared up only to become entangled in a bureaucratic web of paperwork. Then, he handed her cash for a full year's rent along with his social security card and driver's license."

"Both of which can be faked." Betsy Ann added with a nod.

"Ahhh. And she snatched the dough right up, didn't she?" Ethel laced her arms over her bosom.

"Uh, huh. After the turn in the economy, a good many vacancies came up and the corporation needs the revenue."

"Oh, dear. So it's back to the records room?"

"I think tonight after Bunco, I will pull up the Houston Obits from 2009 on the computer. If his name is not listed, that either confirms the glitch or he's not from where he stated."

Janie added the fruit salad to the array of food.

The doorbell rang. Within minutes, Janie's living and dining area filled with eleven chatting Bunco Biddies who, after a quick blessing, shared the potluck entrees before settling into some serious dice rolling—only for fun of course. No cash ever exchanged hands. Instead, the ladies doled out mild gossip, clean jokes, and a few prayer requests. The main topic of the evening filtering through the tables as they changed partners naturally hinged on the mystery neighbor and his ghastly demise.

Before they rolled for sixes, Janie whistled with her fingers in her mouth to get their attention. "Ladies. Don't leave after the next Bunco." She glanced to Ethel and Betsy Ann. "We have some important news to share."

Murmurs floated around the room. The bell dinged to begin the final round for each person to toss as many sixes as possible until someone at the head table rolled three sixes to declare the game over. By providence, or perhaps the corporate wish to end the session, Annie Schmidt landed the Bunco on the second round. Roseanne Richards won the most overall Buncos and Josephine Rodriguez scored the highest points.

After the applause died down and second helpings piled the paper plates, Janie took the floor. "Ladies, I need your help. Actually, my son-in-law, Detective Blake Johnson, does. He is over-tasked at the moment with his lead partner out on medical leave. I am sure all of you want this recent tragedy resolved quickly. Face it. A murder happened here in our midst at Sunset Acres. Until this person is apprehended, can any of us feel safe?"

Negative responses and head shakes floated around the living room.

"I propose we help expedite matters and assist the police in discovering what we can about Edwin Newman..."

"Who did ya say?" Betty Lou Simpson crinkled her brow.

"Didn't he create Mad Magazine?" Babs cocked her head.

Ethel sighed. "No, Babs, you're thinking of Alfred E. Neuman. The freckled cartoon character featured on the covers."

"Oh, I recall those. Mother never let us read them, but I sneaked them into the house. I loved the Spy vs. Spy antics." Norma Rodgers giggled.

Janie clapped her hands. "Ladies, please."

Josephine whimpered. "You think the murderer is still around?"

Betsy Ann patted her arm. "We can't be sure, and I am positive the police are doing all they can."

"Yes, but so can we. This is our community. Simply because our hair is white..."

Betsy Ann arched an eyebrow and harrumphed.

"Okay, most of us." Janie rolled her eyes. "This doesn't mean we are helpless victims. I suggest we rally our men to organize a neighborhood watch. Mildred, who lives next door to the house Mr. Newman rented, will keep vigil and inform me of any strange goings on."

"You never heard a thing?" Rosanne peered into Mildred's eyes before spooning more raspberry gelatin in her mouth.

"Well, I was so worried about poor Poopsy, my mind raced. So Monday night, I took a sleeping pill. An atom bomb could have gone off and not woken me."

More murmurs.

"Who lived on the other side of him?"

Janie lifted her finger. "His home sits on the corner lot. So nobody."

Several women responded with an, "Oh."

"What can we do?" Josephine wound a paper napkin in her fingers.

"Trace his movements from last Wednesday. Oh, not yesterday but the week before after he signed the lease, you understand? All the way through to Tuesday morning when Betsy Ann and I discovered the body."

"*Ya'll* did? I assumed the sanitation driver did. Oh, how horrid for you." Babs clicked her tongue.

The other ladies mumbled sympathies.

Carole Jamison stood. "Of course we will all help. Tell us what we need to do."

Janie pressed her hands together. "Good. I took the liberty to write up some instructions. We will divvy the duties by the three Bunco tables where we are sitting. Betsy Ann will lead the first one. I, the second, and Ethel, who we all know is a murder mystery aficionado, will organize the third table."

Everyone located their score pads and pens, prepared for their assignments like diligent students in a prep school classroom.

Janie scanned the room, a determined smile on her lips. "Ladies. Let's begin. Operation Bunco Biddies commences now."

CHAPTER NINE

Betsy Ann's team received the assignment of canvassing the neighboring stores and businesses, both inside Sunset Acres and along the highway, in particular the Get 'em and Go where witnesses reported seeing him. Ethel's group took to organizing the hubby-led neighborhood watch, and knocked on every door within two blocks around Newman's house to find out if anyone noticed anything out of the ordinary. With fading memories of what people ate for breakfast so prevalent in a retirement community, time remained their largest determent. Janie headed the group in charge of researching the computer and county records for any information on both Edwin Lewis Newman and Edward Norman.

After every one left, Jane was surprised at how easily she pulled up records from the Houston obituaries. She once again marveled at the endless realm of cyberspace technology. Alas, her search proved unfruitful. No Edwin Newman or Norman died six years prior. She checked 2008 and 2010, just to be on the safe side. Nada. The same result in the Austin, Dallas, Fort Worth, and San Antonio newspapers.

Frustrated, she decided to go to bed.

In the wee hours of the morning her eyes popped open. She scooted her chair to the laptop monitor perched on her dressing table and squinted into the bright light emitting into her dark bedroom. Doing a general search, she typed in his alleged name. Within a nanosecond, several entries surfaced. Only one matched in age, but that person passed away in California in the 1990's. Next, she tried Edward Newman, but too many articles popped up to research. Maybe with more manpower... She decided to print out the first five and review them later over her morning coffee.

On a whim, she entered her name in the query box and nothing surfaced. With a humph, she turned off the machine and crawled back under her covers. Well, so much for her cyber footprint. If she solved this crime she would surely appear on the internet all over the place, at least for a day or two. Her Bunco Biddies wouldn't only be the talk of the town, but the world.

A new determination clouded her sleep the rest of the night.

The next morning, the three from her table rode into Austin in her sedan. Annie inched forward from the back seat. "What are we looking for again?"

Janie eyed her in the rear view mirror as she merged onto the interstate. "We're searching for any information on those two names I scribbled on index cards for you. The first is our neighbor's supposed name. The second name is a convicted criminal who resembles the younger version of him. Part of a gang of robbers who hit three banks in Austin years ago, according to the articles I read last night. They may not be the same person and the name similarity a total coincidence, but it is worth a try. We have more time to research this than my poor son-in-law does." Her lips curled into a pout.

Her last comment rallied the troops with revived gusto as the biddies crawled through commuter traffic on the way to the newspaper archive department. Since Austin, the nearest largest city to Sunset Acres, happened to be the state capitol, they also planned to bop over to the library in the Capital Complex after a scrumptious lunch at a downtown bistro.

Betsy Ann's militia met at the club house at 9:00 a.m. She and Babs rode bicycles so they could visit the convenience store, diner, and antique collectibles which dotted the farm to market road near the entrance to their retirement community.

Roseanne and Mildred waited for the Sunset Acres shuttle to take them to the Outlet Mall, armed with a police sketch of the deceased from a newspaper clipping. Betsy Ann pulled her cycle to a halt. "I hope you have some luck. I'm not sure he did much shopping. From what Janie told me, he didn't own much of anything at all."

Mildred nodded. "And no van's arrived yet. I figured after a week..."

Betsy Ann ran her fingernail over her lip. "I'll tell Ethel's group to keep an eye out as they canvas the neighborhood." She punched in her jogging buddy's number into her cell phone.

"Hello." Ethel's gruff voice always reminded Betsy Ann of her junior high Physical Education Instructor, who'd once been a sergeant in the Air Force. She swallowed a giggle. "Ethel. Good morning. We need a favor. I'm here with Roseanne and Mildred. They're headed to the mall then Babs and I are canvassing on bikes."

"Okay. Everyone at my table is gathered over coffee in my living room. Seven husbands, including Jonathan Franks, are here as well. They're more than willing to form a neighborhood watch. Says we should have years ago."

"True. Perhaps poor Mr. Newman, or whoever he was, would still be alive." Betsy Ann paused for a quick, silent prayer. "Anyway, please tell everyone to watch for a moving van, okay?"

"Sure, I'll tell the men to be alert to it."

"Thanks."

"Oh, Betsy Ann? Do me a favor. Tell Roseanne to get some puppy paw pads for Pugsy and I'll pay her back. Size small." Ethel prided herself on remembering.

"I'll do it."

"Roger Wilco, over and out." Ethel clicked off after delivering the old military walkie-talkie euphemism.

"Psst. Janie." Annie slid into the wooden chair next to her as Janie peered into the cream and black microfiche images.

"Yeah? You find something?" She kept her voice low out of respect for the other researchers who littered the archives, a vast majority being university students.

"I believe so. Come check this out."

Janie walked over to Annie's station to read her computer screen. In the flicker of the illuminated monitor, she scanned the same newspaper article Annie showed them earlier.

"Yes, so. You showed us this on the back of the wedding clipping."

Annie whispered in a hurried tone. "I know. But because we cut out my nephew's announcement, the rest of this article didn't appear. See what I mean?" Her finger swiped across the screen to reveal the sentence making her breathing rate increase. She mouthed the words as they both read. "Police have yet to locate the stolen money from any of the three robberies."

Janie's spine tingled. Could this be why someone diced him into pieces?

That evening, Janie arrived at her daughter's house for dinner with a chocolate pecan pie she'd purchased at the bistro in her hands and a photo copy of the news article tucked inside her purse.

"Oh, Mom. Looks delicious. What a treat."

"Will Blake be joining us?"

His size twelves pounded over the hardwood floors, followed by a peck on Janie's cheek. "Unless the phone rings again I am. Yum. Pecan pie."

Janie handed the desert to her daughter but clutched her handbag. "May I speak with you about the murder at Sunset Acres, Blake? It has rattled a lot of us."

Melody hugged her mother's shoulders. "I have been so worried about you, but Blake states the police are sure it is an isolated incident and no one there is in any danger."

"Even so... Can we talk?"

Blake's face warmed. "Of course, Janie. Let's go into the study while Mel and Ellie finish setting the table. Jamie is upstairs, no doubt spraining his thumbs as he texts on his cell phone."

They walked into the only distinctly male room in the house. Not the pure definition of a man cave, but the wood paneled walls and built-in bookcases exuded a masculine feeling along with the evergreen leather chairs cloistered in one corner and mahogany executive desk with computer credenza flanking the other wall. A deer head mounted on the wall and the frosted glass-front rifle case depicting geese in flight rounded out the effect. He perched on the edge of the desk. "What do you need to know? Without breaking protocol, I will be as forthcoming as I dare."

"Well," Janie dug into her purse. "Anne Schmidt, one of the ladies I play Bunco with..."

"Hold on. You stirred up the Bunco Biddies, too?"

"They all live in our community, so of course it affects them. She found this on the back of an old clipping from her great nephew's wedding in 2005. They trimmed a good portion away because of the one about the nuptials lay on the other side. So we went to the newspaper archives to retrieve the full article, you see."

Blake snatched it from her hands and frowned.

"See, the resemblance is rather uncanny. And check out at the name."

He rubbed his chin. "Well, Janie, I am not so sure. I recall this case. The court sentenced them to twenty-five years in prison and no one reported any all point bulletins on an escape."

"Yes, except for Edward Norman. He got the lesser sentence because he only drove the getaway vehicle." Her slightly arthritic finger tapped the paper. "The judge awarded him ten years with parole, which means he could have been released by now, right?"

Blake's right eyebrow lifted into a sharp point. "Hmmm. We'll check into this. Thanks, Janie. You were correct to bring this to our attention. Somehow, the state data search on his likeness failed to flag it."

A thought splashed Janie's septuagenarian brain like refrigerator-chilled water as she noticed the header on the newspaper copy. "Perhaps because the article is from the Tulsa, *Oklahoma*, newspaper?"

Now why didn't she pick up on that before?

CHAPTER TEN

Dinner dragged. Janie kept eyeing Blake at the head of the table. He chewed as if every morsel might hold a clue, the way one seeks the baby hidden in a king's cake during Mardi Gras. Ellis chatted about her volleyball team's victory which assured them a place in the finals next weekend. The band director awarded Jamie to be first chair saxophone for the end of the year concert. Yet their father's enthusiasm waned. Had she been right about bringing him the news clipping? Would it jeopardize his chances of attending both these pivotal events in his teenage children's lives? Yep, the Bunco gals needed to step it up and solve this thing soon.

An hour later, Janie couldn't stand the intensity in her son-in-law's jaw another second. She announced she felt exhausted, dug her keys from the side pocket of her purse, and walked to her car. Her daughter followed with arms wrapped around her waist. "Will you be okay, Mom?"

"Yes. Just need a good night's sleep and I will be right as rain, as they say." Janie started her engine and waved goodnight. However, as she rounded the curb, she pulled over and dug her cell phone from her bag. First, she dialed Betsy Ann, who picked up on the third ring.

"Hi, it's Janie. Any luck today?"

"Well, witnesses spotted him at the Get 'em and Go, but we already knew that. In fact, they recalled him being in there twice. Once on Saturday and again on Monday afternoon. But the second time when another man entered the store, Edwin Newman seemed, hmm, how did the clerk put it?"

Rustles of paper sounded over the receiver. She surmised Betsy Ann thumbed through her spiral tablet.

"Ah, like hot grease on a griddle."

"So he appeared nervous?"

"Yes. Apparently so. The clerk described the other man as burly and he wore a scar on his left cheek. He didn't recognize him but didn't think much of it until Babs asked him about it."

Janie restarted her car. "Thanks. I know it's late, but can you call Ethel and meet at my condo in a half hour?"

"Okay. Did Blake tell you something new?"

Janie chuckled. "Not exactly. I think we are the ones who gave him something to ponder." She put the car in gear and checked her mirror to make sure no other traffic came in either direction. "I'll explain when I see you. Meet you in twenty minutes."

The mantle clock bonged ten chimes. Ethel yawned. She tucked her shawl around her torso and rubbed her eyes. "Sorry."

Betsy twitched her foot as she dangled it over her knee. Her thigh, encased in her polyester purple pants, resembled a giant eggplant in motion.

Janie paced the floor, forearms crossed in front over her torso. "Oklahoma, ladies. Not Texas."

Betsy Ann stopped wiggling. "Then why did the Austin papers carry the story?"

Ethel shifted in the winged back chair. "Because that's where the robberies occurred."

"And, one of the other thieves hailed from Bastrop, only a half hour east of the city. But, get this. I looked him upon the internet. The news photo shows a scar on his cheek!"

Betsy Ann perked up. "Oh, like the man in the Get 'em and Go."

Janie snapped her fingers. "Correct."

Ethel squirmed. "I think we need to turn this all over to the police. We may be good at ferreting out clues, but there are dangerous criminals involved."

Janie peered at her over her readers. "We will, eventually. You say the Willises reported they heard a car backfire in the wee hours of Tuesday morning?"

Ethel gave her head a fast nod which loosened a few tight bobby-pinned curls under her scarf. "That's what they said and they live behind Mildred on Radiant Way. Their carport shares an alley with hers."

Betsy Ann sat forward. "It could have been a gunshot?"

Janie scoffed. "Someone chopped him into pieces, Betsy Ann. Knives don't go bang."

She pouted. "Maybe they shot him first."

"Well, true. It makes sense to kill him first." She gave her an apologetic smile. "But, where did they perform the butchery? Trust me, the house looked vacant but also pristine. That would be a lot of blood to clean up. And nobody reported a noise such as a chainsaw.

I don't care how many sleeping pills Mildred took. Surely she'd hear it."

"I read a novel where the villain used a saber from his stint in her Majesty's service in India and butchered the girl in the bathtub." Ethel now seemed wide awake. "I could go get it for you so you can read the scene."

Janie shook her head. "I seriously doubt anyone in this part of Texas owns a saber. This is 2015."

Ethel slunk back into the cushions. "True. But surgeons, well at least forensic doctors, use electric saws to cut bone. I've seen those crime shows on TV."

"Not too easy to acquire would be my guess."

"I'm trying, Janie."

"I know, dear. Sorry." She wandered over and rested a hand on Ethel's shoulder.

Betsy Ann raised her hand. "Would a turkey knife work? I remember getting my son, Edgar, one for wedding present. He could slice through a thanksgiving bird in seconds flat."

"Electric knife? Betsy Ann, do they still make those?"

"I'm sure so, Janie, but come to think of it, I don't know if it would carve a human. The turkey was cooked, and people are, well, raw." She stuck out her tongue and shuddered.

Janie swatted the air with her hands. "We are getting off the track. We need to print out a picture of the robber with the scar. We can ask the clerk if he thinks it's the same man. If so, I'll call Blake. What was his name, Betsy Ann? Did Babs say?"

"The scar-faced guy?"

"No. The clerk."

"Um, yes." She dug in her purse for the trusty tablet. "Travis. He works the daytime shift, I believe."

"Great. Let's see if we can locate one on the computer. I think finding it on the internet is easier than scanning the microfiche at the newspaper again. You and Babs take it over there tomorrow."

"If he's there. It's Saturday. He may only work during the week."

Janie sat for the first time. "It's a chance we'll have to take."

Leaves scrunched outside the side window near the air conditioning compressor. Janie dashed to her back door and called out, "Who's there?"

Her friends peered over her shoulders to get a look as well. A heavy-set but tall dark figure sprinted toward the side street and hopped over the hedgerow onto the golf course. The new moon offered enough illumination to catch him hurrying out of sight.

Betsy Ann's fingers quivered over her cell phone's dial pad. "I'm calling 911."

Janie closed the door, flipped the dead bolt, and leaned against the jamb. "Good idea. Guess we've rustled the bushes."

"I think you mean ruffled feathers? One beats the bushes."

"Whatever, Ethel. Whatever."

CHAPTER ELEVEN

A patrol car's red and blue lights pulsated through the sheer curtains. Janie huddled with the officer taking her statement. Out of the corner of her eye, she detected a small crowd gathering on the sidewalk. Betsy Ann had been correct. Her neighbors flocked to emergency lights like children to an ice cream vendor. The policeman's voice brought her attention back to him.

"Um, no. Nothing stolen. He didn't actually break in. More like a Peeping Tom."

Another uniformed man stomped in, leaving muddy tracks in his wake. Janie sighed. She paid professionals good money to clean the area rugs right before Easter. "Found footprints outside the window, sir. Getting pictures and molds of them now."

"Male?"

"Most likely. I'd say the size is at least an eleven."

"Okay. Dust the windowsill for prints. We might get lucky."

Janie hated to be ignored. "Ahem."

"Oh, yes. Sorry, ma'am." He touched his Stetson rim. "You were saying?"

"My son-in-law is Chief Detective Blake Johnson. He's investigating the dumpster murder last Tuesday. This may be related."

The Alamoville officer raised an eyebrow. "And how do you figure that?"

Betsy Ann spoke up from her perch on the sofa. "Because we sort of helped him gather evidence." She lifted her shoulders to her ears and batted her lashes.

"Excuse me?" The policeman shifted his weight to the other foot.

"Well, unofficially, of course." Janie poofed her curls with her hand. "We decided this is our community and we understand how overworked ya'll are. So in order to expedite the process, we've been doing some background checking." She cast her glance to the floor. "I told Blake all about it tonight at dinner, but I don't think he was pleased."

The office tapped his pen. "I imagine not. You ladies can get him in trouble for sticking your noses where they don't belong."

Ethel shot to her feet. "Now just a minute young man. We are not a bunch of senile old biddies even if we do call our Bunco gathering that name in jest. Janie's late husband was a renowned police detective, Betsy Ann was a reporter for the newspaper for decades, and I am one of the leading authorities on murder mysteries in modern-day literature."

He exhaled and plastered on a sweet smile. "My mother watched Mrs. Marple capers and Murder She Wrote on TV, too. But this isn't Hollywood, ma'am. Or an Agatha Christie novel." The officer gazed into each of their faces to drive home his point.

Ethel's cheeks flamed.

Betsy Ann wrinkled her nose.

Janie crossed her arms.

None of them spoke.

The officer's expression morphed into the same one little Josh Beaumont produced when he broke Janie's front window with his baseball while visiting his grandparents last fall. He coughed into his fist and broke eye contact. "So, if I am understanding correctly, you believe your Peeping Tom may have something to do with your, um, unauthorized snooping?"

Janie gave him a terse "yes" in response.

"Couldn't have been a nosey neighbor?"

"The men in this community are not the type to traipse through bushes in the night. In fact, due to the latest incident, they are forming a neighborhood watch."

The policeman exchanged glances with his underling who slipped back into the room. "No prints, sir. Sill is clean. But there are scratches in the paint, and they appear to be new."

He rubbed his temple with the clicker end of his pen. "All right. We have your statements, ladies. I suggest you bolt your doors, stop your, um, sleuthing, and leave this and the murder investigation to us. We are here to protect and serve you. Let us do our job."

He ripped off a goldenrod-colored carbonless copy of his report and handed it to Janie. "I'll notify Detective Johnson of this occurrence. Goodnight, ma'am."

"'Night."

He pivoted on his police-issued boots and sauntered out the front door to his patrol car, his deputy in tow.

Janie bolted the door. "Hmph. He bordered on downright rude. Blake will hear about this in the morning." She read his signature. "Connor Gonzales. Badge number 134A68."

Betsy Ann squeaked. "Maybe he's right. I mean a man has been brutally murdered. I'm sleeping with my beloved husband's—The Lord rest his soul"—she crossed herself—"Louisville slugger next to my pillow."

Ethel crossed her leg and sat back. "He didn't ruffle my feathers in the least. But our beating the bushes possibly spooked a pigeon or two. Why else would someone be peeking in your window?"

Janie let the segue into the confused metaphors reference go to the wayside. "And right when we are gathered to compare notes. Almost as if he eavesdropped." She crossed the rug and sat in a side chair angled toward the couch. "Well, ladies. Whoever our intruder, my bet is he's long gone. Too much commotion. So let's adjourn and regroup tomorrow over brunch."

"Sounds good to me." Ethel rose. "Saturday morning spreads are always the best. Nine, then?"

Betsy Ann and Janie agreed.

Janie's cell phone sang out the theme from Dragnet at 7:10 a.m. Her son-in-law called. She yawned and reached for the instrument on her bedside table. "Yes? Good morning, Blake."

"I understand you had a bit of excitement last night." His tone sounded gruff.

"Nothing much, my dear. However, I have a bone to pick about Officer Gonzales. Spoke in an uppity attitude in my opinion."

Blake exhaled through his nose, sounding like the ocean waves inside a sea shell. "Janie, I thought I'd made it clear at dinner. This is not a game. You are impeding my investigation."

Janie sugar-coated her response. "But, my darling, sweet son-in-law, it is our civic duty to help in any way we can. We know this community and its residents. We take pride in the reputation of this being a safe and quiet place to spend our last years."

His silence iced her receiver. She bit her lip, picturing his eyebrows morphing into one furry line and the vein on his forehead beginning to turn purple. His next sentence spurted in metered words. "Janie. Back off. Understood?"

"I must go. Saturday brunch begins soon and the Belgian waffles disappear fast." She clicked off and turned the volume to mute.

Janie ran a hand down Mrs. Fluffy's spine who'd hopped onto the bed to encircle her in purrs. "He'll change his tune when we solve this case. I'm making it my personal agenda to put this murder to bed before next weekend so he can spend time with Ellie and Jamie." She picked up the cat and snuggled her. "Mommy will soon be on the internet searches. I'm going to post a query through the social media to see if anyone recognizes him or has any information. If only I'd remembered to take pictures that day at the dumpster. It would have caused a ruckus. Perhaps they would have gone—what is the term? Oh, yes—viral."

CHAPTER TWELVE

Ethel and Betsy Ann sat with plates piled around them. Janie plunked her tray down. "Only one waffle left."

"They opened the omelet station today. I got a spinach, sautéed onion, and shitake mushroom with brie." Betsy Ann scooted herself closer, fork poised and ready.

Ethel peered over her readers. "You seem miffed, Janie."

She stabbed a square of the puffed bread doused in stewed strawberries and powdered sugar. "Blake called. That's why I'm late."

"And?"

She chewed in slow, steady movements before swallowing the piece with a swig of coffee. Her two friends waited in still-frame mode. With a dab of her napkin to the corner of her mouth, Janie answered with a controlled tone. "We are to cease and desist."

Ethel thrust her spine into the chair spindles. "Oh, gracious."

"Are we?"

"Of course not, Betsy Ann. We must be more stealth, that's all." Janie forked a piece of turkey sausage. "Stay under Blake's radar until we obtain compelling evidence."

Ethel pointed with her spoon. "Or involve more people. Rally the troops. They can't arrest all of us."

"Yes, they can. Remember the peace riots in the seventies?" Betsy Ann waggled her finger.

The image of her silver-headed neighbors throwing rocks and Molotov cocktails at swat teams while chanting, "We shall overcome," almost made Janie choke on her waffle. She wiped the condensation from her orange juice glass to regain composure. "I found the photo of the robber with the scar after surfing the internet. I put the print out in my purse so I'd remember to show y'all." She reached for her shoulder bag and rummaged through the organized pockets. "Ah, here we go. Betsy Ann, you and Babs go to the store and ask if that clerk, Travis, is working today. Find out if this resembles the guy who made Mr. Newman edgy."

"And me?"

"After breakfast, you and I are making fliers to place on everyone's door. I want all concerned Sunset Acres residents to meet here at 4 p.m. for a town hall meeting. We will ask them for any observations over the last week, no matter how trivial, in one fell swoop. It'll save time, and as Sherlock Holmes said, 'Time is of the essence.' It will also be our first neighborhood watch sign-up."

Ethel swirled her napkin. "Tally ho! However, my friend, I believe his famous line was, 'The game's afoot.'"

"Whatever you say, Ethel."

Blake snapped the morning newspaper, a sure sign something bothered him. Melody pushed it down to stare into his face. "Grumpy, sweetheart?"

He drew a long breath and folded the sports section. "You need to have a heart to heart with your mother."

"About?"

"Trying to solve the murder of the man in the dumpster. She and her Bunco cronies are running all over town interviewing people and gathering false clues."

"But, Blake, this awful thing happened in their retirement village. They are part of the 'pull up your straps and do it' generation. And they are bored. No one takes them seriously anymore."

"Even so..."

She scooted into the dinette chair next to him and squeezed his forearm. "Look, let them have their fun. What's the harm? Frankly, I haven't seen Mom so alive in years. Last evening at dinner, her eyes danced."

He rubbed his temples. "I understand their intentions are good, but they are getting in the way and the Mayor called me on the carpet about it."

"When?"

"Just now. On the phone. Honey, you must rein her in. She only bucks and bolts when I try to talk sense into her."

Melody shoved the heels of her hands to her hips in jest. "My mother is not a horse."

Blake snickered. "More like a stubborn ol' mule." He got up from the table. "She encountered an intruder last night, Mel, which may be related or not."

His wife gasped and clutched the small silver cross necklace she always wore. "Is she all right?"

"Yes. Turns out he didn't actually intrude. The ladies caught him peeking in the window. But the jamb showed marks as though someone tried to pry the sill open. And the officers at the scene collected some decent footprints in her flower beds thanks to the recent rains. Forensics is analyzing them."

"I'll go over right now." Melody snatched her shoulder bag and keys.

Blake whispered a prayer, eyes to the ceiling. "Dear Lord, knock some sense into these women so we can do our job. Encourage them to go back to their Bunco or knitting or whatever they do. Oh, and keep them safe from breaking a hip or having a heart attack. Amen."

Melody arrived to find her mother and Ethel, along with Norma and Betty Lou, printing and sorting fliers. Paper stacks with sticky notes attached littered the mahogany table for eight. "Mom, what are you doing?"

"Organizing a small rally, dear. In the dining hall at four this afternoon. The men wish to organize a neighborhood watch and we women are not going to feel secure in our own homes until whoever chopped up poor Edwin is caught."

Melody clutched Janie's elbow, realizing anew how thin and brittle she'd become. All Melody's life, her mother displayed the symbol of strength, her embrace a shelter to ward off all evils. Now, frailty oozed through her sagging muscles. She sensed a role reversal in the near future. "Mom, come into the living room. We need to talk."

Janie snatched her arm away. "If this is about Blake, the subject's closed. We are under the gun to get these distributed as soon as possible."

She sighed. "Okay. If I agree to help, then can we sit down for a chat?"

A shrewd smile etched the corners of Janie's lips. "I thought you'd never ask."

A bang ricocheted through the room.

Ethel jumped and Betty Lou squealed.

Babs and Betsy Ann dashed in, holding their chests, out of breath. "Sorry. Didn't mean to slam the front door into the wall."

Babs waved the photocopy of a mug shot. "Travis is almost sure this is him. The guy who made Mr. Newman jump like a bull frog."

Betty Lou fanned herself. "As I almost did just then?"

Melody turned to Janie. "Oh, now we must talk, Mom. Immediately."

Blake sighed when the call tune signaled his wife on the line. He walked a few paces away from his crime team. "Hi. What's up? You speak to your mom?"

"Yes. And some new developments popped up. Can you and perhaps two other officers be here at three-thirty today? It's important."

He pushed up his sleeve to check his watch. 1:28. "I guess. Why?"

The sound of Melody scraping a chair across linoleum made him pull the phone from his ear. Whenever she sat down to relay the news, he learned to expect the worse. What now?

He waited until her voice came through the receiver. "Well, the ladies uncovered more evidence and called a town meeting of sorts in the dining hall at four. If you are present, you may be able to diffuse some of the anxiety."

Blake scratched his eyebrow. A tension headache began to tighten against his temples. "What new evidence?"

"The manager at the convenience store near the entrance to Sunset Acres thinks he recalled one of the armed robbers from those bank heists a decade ago buying two sodas and chips. He states the man who they found in the dumpster, who happened to be in the store at the same time, recognized him as well. He became unusually nervous."

"The clerk?"

"No, hon. Mr. Newman. He purchased some snacks and tall cans of beer last Monday afternoon when this occurred."

Blake motioned to his crew seated at their desks in the large open room. "We'll be there."

CHAPTER THIRTEEN

Chief Detective Blake Johnson and two detectives, Phil Edwards and Connor Hemphill, entered the dining hall at Sunset Acres at three twenty-five. A backdrop of light blue-draped windows shed a soft, filtered glow over the hall, shielding it from the harsh afternoon sun. They made the room look almost celestial, as if a foreshadowing of the residents' next home beyond the pearly gates. He shook off a slight shudder as he perused the sea of silvered heads already seated around a cluster of round tables. His wife, mother-in-law, and several other ladies milled together at the front of the room behind three long tables jutted together. He caught Melody's glance and she waved him over.

He turned to his underlings. "This way, gentlemen." A lanky young man scurried to match his stride. "I didn't expect such a crowd on short notice, sir."

Blake kept walking but cupped his mouth toward Phil's ear with his hand. "They're all retired. Nothing better to do, I guess. I imagine they've awakened from their afternoon naps with a half-hour to kill before dinner is served."

Phil chuckled. "Yes, sir."

The trio weaved their way through the tables and chairs as whispers and murmurs increased around them. One elderly man with a large forehead and a shaky hand motioned to them with his cane and exclaimed in a loud voice to a birdlike woman next to him wearing a silvery-white bun, "Them be the cops, eh, Margaret?"

Blake tipped his cowboy hat and moved towards Janie who grinned like a house cat after downing a plate of chicken livers.

"Well, well. What a thrill for you to join us. Here to update us on the investigation?"

"I came to calm you folks down, let you in on a few facts we can divulge at this point, and to emphasize this is a serious crime and not something for amateurs to meddle in."

"I'll have you know we unearthed some important information." Janie tippy-tapped her foot.

"So I understand. Why don't you tell me then, hmm?" He pulled out a chair and motioned for her to be seated. He sat on one side and his mother-in-law on the other. Behind him stood his two associates. Around her huddled Ethel, Betsy Ann, Mildred, and another mousy lady who wouldn't quite look him in the eye. Blake almost planted an elbow to the table and challenged Janie to a round of arm wrestling, winner buys drinks. The thought made him chuckle.

"What's so funny?"

"Nothing Janie. Just relieving the tension, I guess. Whatcha got for me?"

Betsy Ann and the mousy woman, introduced as Babs, began to chatter all at once about the Get 'em and Go clerk, the man with the scar, and Mr. Newman's reaction. Blake swiveled his head between them as if following a tennis match as he tried to absorb their information. When the last wrinkled mouth closed, he motioned to his men. "Connor, go ask the manager for the surveillance tapes for Monday the fifteenth around the time of the sighting. Also, get the ones for Saturday around two to four. Phil, take this photocopy back to the clerk and get his written statement."

Ethel snapped her fingers. "Why didn't we think of that?"

Mildred gave her a small pat on the shoulder. "You can't think of everything, sweetie."

Blake bit his tongue and focused on Janie's face. "It's almost four. Will you introduce me?" He elevated his chin and motioned with a wave to a uniformed officer who slid through the door. "I invited Lieutenant William Everett to go over the details for organizing a neighborhood watch. He will go over the rules and procedures."

Janie bounced her chin up and down, first to her cronies and next toward him. "Oh, good. Good."

Blake caught his wife's wink. He returned the gesture. For a halted split-second in time, their eyes locked and the years of mutual love signaled a desire to make tonight a late night. How long since that happened? Not since his partner went on medical leave. Where had his head been? She still outmatched any woman on the block in the looks department, not to mention her ability to melt his heart with one soft touch.

He broke the stare with a quick, apologetic grin. Melody returned the facial gesture as she moved to one of the side chairs and sat, her purse perched in her lap. The Bunco biddies followed suit.

Janie tapped a spoon against her glass of artificially sweetened iced tea. The murmuring didn't subside. She clunked it again. The chattering continued.

Then a shrill whistle blasted throughout the room.

Blake jumped and turned to view Ethel's fingers jammed in her mouth. Did that ear-piercing screech come from her?

She flashed him a wide grin. "Used to volunteer at the Y's after-school program. Only way to get the kiddos' attention."

Blake made an "O" with his mouth. He shook his head and leaned into the officer's car. "These women do beat all."

Lieutenant Everett's shoulders jiggled as he stifled a laugh.

Janie cleared her throat. "You all know why we're gathered here. This is my son-in-law, Blake Johnson, Chief Detective of the Alamoville police. My dear, late husband, as many of you recall, was a renowned detective in Austin PD for years, and Blake is almost as good. So that's saying a lot."

What? Blake swept his gaze to catch Janie's facial expression, and in his peripheral vision he spied his wife place a hand over her mouth. His mother-in-law continued without missing a beat. "He is in charge of the investigation into the demise of one Edwin Lewis Newman, if it was his real name..."

Blake stood. "I'll take over from here, Janie. Thank you." He placed both hands upon her elderly shoulders and pushed her downward to her chair with care. "This is Lieutenant Everett, who's organized at least eleven neighborhood watches in Alamoville in the past three years. In a few minutes, I'll hand the floor to him to explain what steps need to be taken to get one going here. Even though this is a gated community, establishing one would be prudent and wise."

Many white-haired heads bounced up and down in affirmative response.

"But first, I want to update you as best I can as to our progress in this investigation. Most importantly, we believe Mr. Newman's death is an isolated incident by a person or persons unknown."

One man raised his cane. "Well, you better get cracking, sonny, and find out."

Blake swallowed what he wanted to say in response and continued. "We are checking into his background history to determine if anything might lead to the reason for his violent end." He paused, cleared his throat, and swallowed a long swig of iced water. "We do not, I repeat, do not believe the perpetrator is still in this village or that any of you are in danger at this point. However, patrol vehicles are assigned to monitor this community and cruise through your streets. This is for your peace of mind as requested by your manager, Mrs. Jacobs. We are more than happy to oblige."

Mumbles waved throughout the crowd.

Blake spoke louder. "Now, while I cannot go into detail, I can relay a few facts gathered so far. The coroner examined the body — that is the parts found in the dumpster. The forensic team has ruled a gunshot to the back of the skull as the cause of death."

Gasps echoed throughout the hall. Janie leaned toward Ethel and Betsy Ann's faces and dropped her voice. "Well, well. The Willises didn't hear a car backfiring after all."

Blake spun to her with his brow furrowed. "You didn't tell me about that."

Jamie glared at him over her glass of tea hovered near her mouth. "You didn't let me."

Blake reached for his cell phone. "Phil, get back in here as soon as you can. Tell Connor to do the same."

He faced the crowd. "I want everyone here who thinks they may have any information pertaining to this case to step forward and write down your name and phone number." He opened his notebook and set it on the table in front of him. "Be prepared to give statements."

Janie tugged his sleeve. "Blake, tonight is buffet night, so the crowds usually spill over into the lounge for Wheel of Fortune while waiting for the lines to open."

He spoke close to her ear. "Where can we set up, then?"

Betsy Ann tapped his other shoulder. "How about the rec room down the hall where they show movies on Friday nights?"

Janie nodded. "Perfect, and we can ask them to sign up for further information about the watch as well. Okay?"

Everett gave her a smile. "Works for me. But first, let me explain the process, if there is time."

Janie gave him a slight bow. "You have the floor. We have forty minutes until dinner. Meanwhile, my son-in-law wishes to talk with me in a more private capacity." Her eyes focused on Blake's face. "At last."

She jutted her chin and rose from her seat, with Betsy Ann, Babs, Ethel, and Mildred traipsing behind like cows following the lead one with the bell to the trough.

Blake shook his head. Better to keep that image to himself.

Over the next hour and a half, only a few brave souls stepped forward to sign up for the neighborhood watch training. To his dismay, even fewer reported anything worthwhile. Most came for the show, so to speak. From what his team gleaned, a strange noise possibly woke a neighbor who lived behind Newman, but her weak bladder often nudged her eyes open, so she couldn't say for sure. Marge and Ralph Walters recalled, as they rounded the corner after a day visiting the grandkids, that their headlights illuminated a large man wearing dark-colored clothes in the dusk of Monday evening. He possibly got into a black van parked in the alley by

Newman's home. Then again, the vehicle might have been one of those brown parcel delivery trucks.

"Wait. You said the alley?"

"Oh, yes," Marge and her husband replied together.

She went on to explain. "Many of the delivery drivers come around back to the kitchen door. The door knocker's louder so we residents can hear it from the bedrooms."

Blake cocked an eyebrow at his underling who jotted the responses onto the report. "Well, I guess it makes sense."

The couple shuffled out, murmuring to each other.

Blake stretched and turned his gaze to Janie who toggled a pen back and forth. "Well, worth a try."

She humphed. "I figured somebody spotted something. You can't just shoot and then cut up a person without making noise."

"You'd be surprised. Often we find neighbors of little help. A too loud TV show drowns out the ruckus, or they took a sleeping pill, or weren't home at the time." He lifted himself from the chair and pushed his hands to his lower back. "Nowadays, everyone keeps to themselves."

"True enough. Plus, half of these folks are hard of hearing. I'm getting there, I know. Not putting it off because of vanity. It's the expense. If only hearing aids weren't so ghastly expensive. Why Medicare doesn't pay for them..." She shook the rabbit trail thought away. "What do we do now?"

"You go home. I will assimilate this with the other evidence we gathered."

Her eyes widened. "Such as...?"

His eyebrows scrunched in sternness, but a smile etched the edge of his mouth. "Now, Janie..."

She swatted his comment away like a horse's tail shooing a pesky fly.

He took her spindly hands in his and bent to her seated level. "Why are you so gung-ho to get involved? I always thought you to be a sensible woman."

Janie dashed her eyes to her lap. "Perhaps because this happened in my own backyard, so to speak. Plus, I am the one who discovered the body, after all. Well"—she sighed and lifted her gaze—"parts of him, that is."

His face softened. "I'm sorry I came on so strong. But the Mayor's boot is on my neck."

"Blake. This is not new to me, you know. Remember who your wife's daddy was."

"Mel tells me your husband often discussed his homicide cases confidentially with you. Is that true?"

A glint of pride lit in her eyes. "Yes, whenever he became stumped. Using me as a sounding board gave him clarity. I often visualized an angle he didn't."

Blake stroked her cheek. "You are an amazing lady. And you raised an equally amazing daughter."

Janie stuck her finger towards his face. "Who, lately, you can't find the time to be with, or the kids."

He sat back down next to her. "Ah. So now we get to the core of the matter. You think if you help me solve this case I can ease up a bit, eh?"

She fiddled with the pen again. "The thought did cross my mind."

"That borders on meddlin'."

"Well, I do possess some expertise, and Betsy Ann worked as a reporter. Ethel is a murder mystery aficionado par excellence. She still offers a keen viewpoint."

Blake chuckled. "Janie, even if you did crack this wide open, I guarantee next week a new case will pop up, then another.

Alamoville is booming, which unfortunately means crime is on the rise." He shrugged. "Nothing I can do about it. But, Bob should be back on the beat by June."

"That's good news, isn't it?"

"Yep. I plan to take at least a week's vacation and go to the coast with the family. I booked a cottage rental on South Padre Island."

Janie's face lightened. "Oh, how wonderful. Did you tell Melody?"

A chuckle gurgled in his throat. "She bought a brand new bathing suit two weeks ago." His eyebrow wiggled. "Even modeled it for me."

A rose tint flushed his mother-in-law's crinkly cheeks, which made him laugh. Then he cleared his throat and attempted to knit his brow in a serious, professional manner. "Now, I want you to back away and let me do my job. However, if you happen to come across anything important, you tell me. Got it?"

She fluttered her eyelashes. "Of course, Blake. Happy to do so."

He caught a suspicious gleam in her pupils as he raised up to leave. *What swirled in her head now?*

CHAPTER FOURTEEN

The next morning Janie heard a titty-tat-tat on her door. Ethel and Betsy Ann stood in their Sunday bests. "Ready for services?"

Janie peered into the hallway mirror, ran a finger over her lips to erase any smudges from the coffee cup, and lifted her purse from the peg. "Yep. Let's go."

They scooted into her sedan and buckled up. As Jane started the engine and adjusted the air conditioning, Ethel groaned. "Well, are you going to tell us what happened or not?"

Janie gazed at her passengers. Betsy Ann tilted her head in the back seat. "Yes. What did Blake say?"

"Not much to tell. No one came forth with a breaking testimony. Marge thought they recalled a delivery van in the alley near the Newman home Monday evening."

"Well, that may be worth looking into. I don't remember Mildred saying anything about receiving a package."

"True." Janie twisted to peer for any oncoming traffic before turning right. "When we return from church, we can ask her to knock on a few doors. Claim she's been waiting for a parcel and thought they possibly delivered to the wrong place."

Betsy Ann clucked her teeth. "You'd be asking her to tell a falsehood. And on the Sabbath."

Janie's chest heaved. "Yes, of course. You're right."

While the traffic light glowed red, she punched in a search for the parcel company, tapped the number, and put the cell phone to her ear. "Yes, I am hoping you can help me. Were any deliveries dispatched to Sunset Acres, specifically Solar Boulevard, last Monday?"

Silence.

Ethel punched her shoulder to tell her the light switched to green.

Janie glanced at her with a quick nod, and pushed the accelerator a split-second before the person behind them honked.

"Why? Oh a neighbor of mine may have been expecting a package but she is rather hard of hearing, you see. Yes, Sunset Acres, the retirement village... Oh, will you? That would be so kind."

Betsy Ann humphed and crossed her arms as she turned to view out the side window.

"Oh, okay. Well, thank you for checking." She clicked off the phone and accelerated up the ramp to the highway. Her eyes fixed on the rear view mirror she announced. "I didn't lie, Betsy Ann."

"I guess not. But you fudged, and in the eyes of the Lord..."

Ethel cut her off. "So no deliveries, huh?"

"One earlier in the day, but to the leasing office. Another to one of the condos on Sunray Terrace, which is three blocks away. A third on the same route went to the assisted living center, and the last to the Butterfields, but Babs doesn't live anywhere near Mildred."

Betsy Ann scooted forward. "Wow. Isn't that a lot for one day?"

"Evidently they deliver from the cable shopping channel all the time. You know? The one with all the bargains?"

Ethel agreed. "Hmm, yes. My sister tunes in all the time. Quite addictive. One month, she couldn't pay the rent because she bought so many Christmas presents."

"Well, it happens."

Ethel scoffed. "In February?"

Janie tapped the steering wheel with her hand. Her eyes narrowed. "So a van would be rather inconspicuous, right? No one would think the wiser. Marge didn't. Perhaps they cut up Edwin Newman in the back while cruising through the community and dumped him on the way out."

"Ewww." Betsy Ann shivered.

Ethel moved her shoulders up and down. "Makes perfect sense. Are you going to report it to Blake?"

Janie shook her head. "Not yet." She pressed her lips as they pulled into the parking lot to join the other worshipers. "Time for church."

Later in the afternoon, Janie leaned across her dining room table eyeing the makeshift map of Sunset Acres sprawled over the top. She put an "X" on the now-empty garden home. Next, she wrote in all the names of the people she recalled who lived within a three block radius. The area resembled a smile with several teeth missing.

She frowned. Once upon a time, she knew all of her neighbors. But, over the past two years, several passed on or moved into the assisted living or advanced nursing facilities. A conviction splashed her like a cold shower blast when the toilet is flushed. She didn't visit any of them who had moved to the facilities nearly enough. Perhaps because the idea of her ending up there as well gave her the willies.

Janie clucked her tongue and hung her head. "I'm sorry, Lord. I've been too caught up in my own little world and my selfish attitude. Well, that will change now."

On a separate sheet of paper, she scribbled their names and vowed to call on each one over the next week or so. In fact, she would organize a monthly schedule. That way, she would force herself—no that was the wrong attitude—encourage herself to spend time with them on a regular basis. Pay it forward so when her time came…

Erase that scary thought. Back to the business at hand. In smaller letters, she jotted down what each of her neighbors witnessed, heard, or suspected was something out of the ordinary. The delivery van with a large man driving, the car backfiring. The whack to Poopsy's nose. How Edwin had been so rude to people. The trash, especially the beer cans.

A tingle iced up her arms. She picked up her cat and spoke to it as if the animal could understand every word. "Wait. How did Mildred surmise the man who tossed the mug to be Edwin Newman? What if she just assumed? If she never met him before that day…perhaps someone else lurked in the house on Saturday. Blake didn't tell me how long the coroner determined Edwin to be dead. Perhaps the killer spent the weekend with someone who had black hair and ruby lips."

The police sketch from the newspaper, along with the print-out of the scarred robber, lay on top of the pile of notes. "I'll take them over to Mildred and get a positive I.D."

The clock chimed two. Mildred's nap would be in full swing. Better wait until four. Tea time. She'd take her a plate of butterscotch brownies left over from the social hour at church.

Janie returned to her original task. Rosanne Richardson mentioned during Bunco she eyed something peculiar in the wee hours of Tuesday morning. A strong white light flashed through the bedroom curtains into her eyes. Much brighter than the street lamps' soft illumination casting over the neighborhood. She lived catty-cornered to the Newman residence. A flashlight, perhaps?

Of course! Headlights of a van backed up to the house might cast the same strong beam. But it didn't make sense. Marge eyeballed the van at dusk Monday evening, a good seven to eight hours prior. An inkling of a headache pulsed in her temples. Janie sighed, pushed off from the table, and grabbed a bottle of aspirin from the kitchen cabinet.

Perhaps a nap could do her good as well.

Blake shuffled the reports once again. Someone, somewhere in the village, observed something. His wife came up behind him with a tumbler of sweet iced tea. "Must you work, sweetheart? It's Sunday afternoon."

"I know. But this case is baffling me. How can a man be chopped into pieces and no one suspect a thing?" He glanced at her paled face as she dropped her gaze. "Oh. Sorry, honey." He shoved the bloody crime photos under the stack.

"That's what my mother witnessed? How awful. I had no idea." She clasped the gold and pearl necklace he'd given her for their tenth anniversary, the one she always wore to church.

He reached and took her hand. "Yes."

Melody perched on the edge of his desk. "Her bravery amazes me. I'd probably throw up or swoon."

"She's a tough old bird. I've told you so."

She bopped him on the top of his head in jest. "Did mother's unauthorized snooping lend any clues?"

"Not really. Vague innuendos and a few bunny trails at the most." He tapped the pen. "Any clue as to why she talked all of her Bunco friends into sleuthing?"

"No."

Blake scooped her off the deck onto his lap. "Because according to Janie, I am a neglectful father and husband." He pressed his forehead against hers.

She reared back. "Mother said that?"

"Uh huh. Well, not in those exact words, but she made her point."

She huffed. "What a meddlin' old coot." But her eyes twinkled with mirth.

"I do love you, Mel. You know that, right? And the kids, more than all the tea in China, as my grandmother used to say."

She brushed her lips over his cheek. "Yes, my sweet. We all do." She clicked her fingernail over the stack of reports. "Now go get this maniac. Okay?"

As she sashayed out, Blake whistled through his teeth. His wife still maintained her figure after two kids and walking this earth for almost four decades. Plus, her giant Texas-sized heart oozed the sweetest disposition a man could ask for. How had he become so blessed? He raised his tea glass to the ceiling and whispered, "Thank you, Lord God."

CHAPTER FIFTEEN

"Well, now I'm not sure." Mildred placed another morsel of blond brownie in her mouth as her eyes shifted from one print out of a man's face to the other. "No, I never met him before. And I didn't get a good look at him. I was more concerned about Poopsy. Much of him lay hidden behind the privacy fence separating our patio areas." Her gaze darted between the two photos one more time.

"But he made me so angry I called Mrs. Jacob's and asked her my new neighbor's name as soon as I came back from the vet. $182 for x-rays, antibiotics, salve, and then the vet's fee. I wanted him to reimburse me. I just assumed it was him."

"But you didn't speak to the man again?"

She lowered her eyes. "No. I tried to muster the courage all day. He is...er, was quite a few years younger. Muscular like. From what I could tell." She took a breath. "I mean he'd have to be to chuck a coffee mug so hard, especially one of the ceramic ones they sell at the Get'em and Go. You know, the ones with your horoscope on it. I tossed it in the trash."

Janie nodded. "Of course. Caution is always wise. He did display a hot temper. Um, you don't recall the specific astrological sign do you?"

"No. I don't follow that stuff." Mildred lifted her chin. "But, Sunday afternoon after church and lunch with the grandkids, I put on the armor of God and marched to his door. Rang the bell, ready to give him a piece of my mind. No one answered. Never spotted any car in his designated spot, so I couldn't tell when he came and went. No lights came on at night, but then movers never arrived, did they? I figured he rented a motel room or something." Her face paled. "Do suppose he was already dead?"

"Not with lipstick on those beer cans. No, he decided to entertain in, at least part of the weekend. Probably just didn't want to answer the door." Janie pressed her finger to her chin. "I wonder why the movers never came?"

"Well, I'd venture to say when Mrs. Jacobs notified the next of kin, they intervened and diverted it."

"I suppose. If any family exists."

Mildred knitted her brow. "Doesn't everyone have relatives? Even ex-cons?"

"I'm sure I can find out who claimed the body. I got somewhere with the delivery service using my helpless, elderly voice."

Mildred laced her arms over her chest. "That's a thought. But I still don't get why Mrs. Jacobs would rent to such a grumpy person."

Janie rubbed her fingers together. "He offered a year's lease in cash."

"Wonder where he laid his hands on that amount of dough?"

Janie's eyes twinkled. "Exactly my question."

Later that night, a rapid pounding shook Janie's back door. She wrapped her robe tighter around her waist and peered through the peephole. Carole Johnson stood on the stoop, glancing up and down the alley. "Janie, let me in."

She wedged open the door. "My word. You're acting as nervous as a calf before a rodeo scramble. Come inside."

"I recalled something. Hit me in a dream as I snoozed in the recliner. The new public channel program didn't hold my interest."

"The one set in Africa in the early 1900s?"

"Yes. I hoped to view fantastic scenes with exotic animals. Instead, they reported on all the poverty and the atrocities of apartheid." She pulled out one of the kitchen dinette chairs. "Then I remembered the package I got from my niece. She thought my birthday fell on the 5th not the 25th. The gift came wrapped in wadded newspaper."

Janie sat across from her. "And?"

"Well, she lives in Skiatook, north of Tulsa."

Tulsa…why did the city sound familiar? Janie smiled as her brain cells kicked in. Yes, where Edward Norman lived.

"This is one of the pages." Carole slid a crumpled piece across the Formica tabletop.

Janie picked up the newsprint. "Half-price sale at Sole-full Shoes?"

Carole snatched it back and flopped it over. "Other side." She pointed with her ruby-coated fingernail to a faded photograph of a man. "Check out the headline."

"Local Tulsa man to be released today after ten years wrongfully imprisoned."

Janie read the report to the right of the picture out loud, which looked quite familiar indeed. In a bizarre twist, mislaid records confirmed Edwin L. Newman was falsely identified as Edward Norman, a gang member in burglary case concerning the robberies of three Austin, Texas, banks more than a decade ago. The police didn't lift any fingerprints from the three scenes but two eye witnesses, plus one of the bank's security camera, confirmed a man bearing the likeness to Edwards sitting in the getaway car. Maintaining his innocence all along, Newman could produce no proof of his identity. His birth certificate became misfiled in the Houston records due to a clerical error. The hospital transposed the numbers in his records to read June 10, 1972, the exact birthdate on Norman Edward's driver license, instead of June 01, the same year. Newman's niece located the original church baptism certificate, dated July 15, 1972, tucked in in her aunt's, Newman's mother's, bible stored in an attic trunk while taking estate inventory after her funeral on April 25, 2014."

She glanced at Carole who pointed to article. "Go on. Keep reading. It gets juicier."

Janie smoothed the newspaper print and squinted to better decipher the typeset through the crisscrossed creases.

"Mrs. Edith Newman, a widow, had suffered from severe depression and agoraphobia following her only son's imprisonment. Concerned neighbors discovered her body in her bed after nobody detected lights in the house for almost a week. The coroner stated she'd been deceased approximately five days. Prison officials released Mr. Newman today from the Wallace Unit near Navasota, Texas, and issued a cashier's check for $250,000.00 to compensate for their error along with profound apologies from the Texas Attorney General."

Janie lifted her gaze from the article. "Is that so?"

Carole nodded. "Check the date. Published three days before Mr. Newman signed the lease."

"So that's where he got the loot to pay for a year's lease."

Carol's voice softened to a quivery whisper. "You think someone bumped him off for the money?"

"People have killed for less, I suppose."

A sudden chilled blasted through the small kitchen.

CHAPTER SIXTEEN

"Yes, dear. I know what time it is. But Blake needs to get over here now. I cannot sleep a wink until I show him what Carole uncovered."

"Okay, Mom. Give him a half-hour."

The rustle of bed sheets sounded in the background. Janie glanced at her clock. Twelve minutes until ten. Pretty early for people their age to hit the hay. Unless...oh.

Her cheeks warmed against the receiver. "Thanks, Melody. That's fine. Take an hour if need be. No rush. I'll wait up. Tell Blake I'll put a pot of coffee on."

Carole wiggled her fingers in goodbye as she slipped out the kitchen door.

Janie waved and mouthed a thank you to her. She rinsed out the carafe and scooped three spoonfuls into the paper-lined drip basket as she fanned the blushed heat from her cheeks.

For mercy's sake. Her daughter and son-in-law bore two children. Of course they...well, still, she didn't care to think about such an intimate of a detail in their marriage. Everyone realized marriage meant the squeaks of springs now and then, but in her day and age, such things remained a taboo topic. She never pictured any of her friends and their husbands...oh gracious, no.

She pushed the image away and puttered about. Scrubbed the sink, mopped the floors, and rearranged her spices. At last, Janie heard a soft knock on the door and Blake's face gleamed through the peephole.

He brushed her cheek with a kiss. "What's this all about?"

She handed him a mug of steaming brew and motioned to the kitchen table.

He scanned the article as he rubbed his chin. "We learned about this four days ago."

She plopped into the chair next to him. "You did? Why didn't you say so?"

The vein on his forehead began to change color. "I am not in the habit of discussing the details of a case with my mother-in-law." He shot from the table and thrust his finger at her face. "Janie, so help me, God. This nonsense must stop. You understand me?"

Her lip quivered.

The angst in his expression melted. He came and placed his hands on her hunched shoulders. "I'm sorry. I know you mean well. So do your friends. And I can understand why recent events disturb you. You feel helpless and wish to do something." He knelt down and lifted her chin to meet his eyes. "But, Janie, that's my job."

She nodded and dabbed her eyes with a paper napkin.

He placed her deep, blue-veined hands in his. They trembled like a baby bird's heartbeat. Her age and fragility hit him in the stomach. This strong, pioneer-spirited Texas woman had been a rock his family clung to for almost two decades. She lost her husband way too early in Melody's senior year in college, shot during a stakeout gone bad while negotiating the release of three hostages. She and her daughter still carried his banner with pride, as did Blake. Despite the fact they fell in love at first site, he figured Melody became enamored by his police uniform. A rookie straight out of the academy. Seemed ages ago. Though it tore Janie up when Mel married a cop, she never once held it against him.

Yet in so many ways, Janie remained sharp as a tack and stubborn as a mule. Qualities he admired and found endearing. Her generation jolted from the serene fifties into an age of drugs, sex, and violence, yet still managed to endure numerous economic crises, political unrest, and war in order to secure the American dream for his peers. Now, society forced many of these late Baby Boomers into "out-to-pasture" communities like this, out of sight and out of mind. They huddled together and once again carved out a life as best they could, something they'd always done. You had to admire them. Their parents' may have been called the Great Generation, but the Boomers were the most durable. They deserved respect.

"Okay, Janie. I will tell you what I can. But you can't make this the gossip of your village, understood?"

A tiny sparkle flickered in her eyes. He reached for the coffee pot and topped off both their mugs. After taking a deep sip, he set his cup down. "Here is what we can confirm so far. Yes, the authorities assumed Edwin Newman to be Edward Norman. However, why would Norman's old gang pay for him to be knocked off? First off, they are both still secured in the state pen in Abilene. We checked to make sure. Secondly, from what we unearthed, the real Norman died of a heart attack eight years ago in

Guatemala. I'm thinking he hightailed it and spent all the dough from the heists on wine, women, and song."

"But the man with the scar?"

"A lot of men have them, Janie. In particular, large, burly types. Comes with the lifestyle."

She waggled her head and more wisps from her silver and gray-streaked bun escaped onto her neck. "But Mildred isn't sure Newman attacked Poopsy. She only assumed so. When I took her the police sketch from the papers she couldn't identify him with any certainty."

"Which means the man may have been the killer instead? But it happened on Saturday. You and Betsy Ann discovered the body in the dumpster on Tuesday morning."

She took a sip from her mug. "True. And folks identified him on both Saturday and Monday at the Get 'em and Go."

Blake clunked his wedding ring against the coffee cup. "So, that leaves us still with the big question. Who would want to kill Edwin Lewis Newman, a man with little or no family, locked up under false pretenses for close to a decade?"

Janie sighed. "Exactly." She titled her head to the side. "It may have been simply a robbery gone wrong. Someone read in the paper he had gotten a wad from the government and wanted it instead. Edwin busts in on them and it turns ugly."

"Hmmm."

Janie sighed. "It does sound like a plot from one of Ethel's novels."

Silence fell between them.

Then Blake saw his mother-in-law's eyes grow as wide as the rim of her coffee cup.

"Perhaps someone who feared what he would do or say once they released him? You can learn a good many secrets in prison, right?"

Blake winked. "And perhaps make a few enemies as well. It's possible. Very good, Janie. Very good."

CHAPTER SEVENTEEN

Janie's speed walking was missing a gear Monday morning. Betsy Ann almost passed her twice. Ethel slowed down several times to stay in sync. "You feeling okay, Janie?"

"Yes, Janie. Are you? Should we take a detour to the clinic?" Betsy Ann reached over to check the temperature of her friend's forehead.

Janie pulled away. "Stop."

Betsy Ann halted.

Ethel did too.

But Janie kept going.

The two eyed each other, then their friend's strutting backside. Ethel called out. "We thought you said you needed to stop."

Janie began trotting backwards. "No. I meant stop worrying over me."

"Oh," her friends declared in unison and picked up their pace again.

At the clubhouse turn, Janie motioned toward the park benches across from the parking lot and dumpster. She sat down and wiped her face with the towel around her neck.

Betsy Ann slumped to her left, Ethel on the right.

Janie pointed with her head. "Hard to believe only a week's passed."

Ethel nodded. "Are they any closer to solving his murder?"

Janie pulled up one of her socks. "Nope. Guess I better catch you up. Blake and I talked into the wee hours in my kitchen." She squinted at the sun rising over the village. "About a lot of things. So I'm kinda pooped today."

"Why did he come over? Did he and Melody fight?"

Janie laughed. "Um, no. In fact, you might say they're right as rain." She wiggled her eyebrows.

Betsy Ann's face flushed. "You discussed that?"

"Not in detail, for heaven's sake. I called and asked him to come over after Carole paid me a visit to bring new evidence. Caught them, well...later, I apologized. Blake told me they'd finished so no big deal. Anyway, let me bring you up to speed."

As they sipped their power water, Janie told them about the article. "But Blake is insistent this is all in confidence. He doesn't want any of the other Bunco gals to find out."

"Even Carole?"

Janie nodded. "I told her this morning I spoke with Blake about the article but the investigative team already uncovered the mix-up. However, I assured her she did the right thing by bringing the newspaper to my attention."

"So where does the investigation stand?"

"Blake will send one of his men to interview Edwin's roommate at the Wallace Park Unit to ask if he's aware of any reason why someone on the inside would want Newman killed once he stepped on the outside."

Ethel slapped the bench. "Wallace Park Unit? Why does the name sound familiar?"

"That's where the Kairos team Ralph Butterfield leads goes. Remember? We all baked cookies for them a few months ago to hand out to the prisoners who attended the program. Used the kitchen at the church and made a day of it."

Janie's spine straightened. "Oh, of course. They lead Bible studies and prayer retreats on weekends for the inmates. Wonder if Ralph ever met Edwin Newman?"

"Possibly. They asked Ralph to lead because of his age. Most of the convicts are in their later years. Wallace Pack is mostly a fifty-five and above prison."

Ethel scoffed. "Sounds like this place."

The three women chuckled and resumed their morning exercise.

Ethel invited them to brunch the next day. "I thought after the week we've encountered, we deserved to be pampered. So I stopped off and bought a dozen kolaches at the bakery on the square in Alamoville. Just don't tell Dr. Weber, okay?"

"Won't hear it from me." Janie smiled as she set the tray of fruit-filled Czech pastries on the table.

"Take your pick. Peach, cinnamon-apple, or raspberry."

Betsy Ann plopped one of each on her plate. "Why choose?"

Janie licked her fingers. "Yum. Thanks. As I went over all the people I know in Sunset Acres, I realized several have moved to the assisted living center or nursing facility recently. In fact, a total of eight did. And that revelation convicted me. So"—she re-positioned herself in her chair—"I am going over in the early afternoon the rest of this week. I'll meet with two a day. I plan to visit with two of them every Tuesday from now on, so that way, I will call on each of them once a month. Do either of you want to come along?"

Ethel spoke up. "Great idea. Peggy Williams is in the rehab wing and her husband is in the Alzheimer's Unit. We can wheel her down to see him."

"I have her slotted for Tuesday."

Betsy Ann wiped a crumb from her lap. "I have an appointment with the cardiologist Tuesday so I'll have to miss." Her lip protruded a bit, but then her eyes grew larger. "Oh wait. That's in the morning, I think." She perked up. "Hey, my tea roses are blooming. I can bring along a bouquet for her. Peg loves roses."

"Who are we calling on today?" Ethel cocked her head to read Janie's list.

Janie scratched drew an arrow from Peg's name to Daphne's. "Let's go see Peg today and take Betsy Ann's roses to her while they are in fresh bloom. I can see Daphne on Tuesday instead."

Betsy Ann clapped her hands. "Goodie."

When they got to the orthopedic unit, Peggy's bed lay empty. The nurse on duty said her physical therapy lasted an hour, after which she'd be too tired to chat.

"Okay, we'll come again soon. We'll leave her a note."

Betsy Ann traipsed alongside, her rubber-soled shoes squeaking on the high-shined, polished floors. The roses began to droop underneath their aluminum foil wrap, matching her mood. "I so wanted to see Peg. I miss her at Bunco."

"What if we drop by after our jog and breakfast on Wednesday? Might be a better time."

"Well, while we are here, let's try Angela in 208. Not everyone can be in physical therapy." Ethel led the way to the next wing.

Three hours later, the trio strolled across the vast green lawn separating the need-care folks from the independent living side. Janie threw back her shoulders. "What a marvelous afternoon. I'd forgotten what a hoot Angela is."

"Yes, and Mary in 214 appreciated our visit. She liked the roses a lot, Betsy Ann."

"I think we made her day, Ethel. Such a sweet soul. I enjoyed our chat with both ladies."

"It felt good to talk about something other than Mr. Newman's demise for a while, that's for sure." Janie's breath quickened. "Life does go on, and none of us are privy to how much longer, right?"

Betsy Ann leaned into Ethel's ear. "Is she throwing in the towel on the investigation? What else did she and Blake discuss?"

Ethel shrugged.

CHAPTER EIGHTEEN

Janie answered on the second ring. Or should she say stanza, since her grandson Jamie reprogrammed her phone with different song tunes for each person on her speed dial. He explained she could then decide which ones to answer. This time, the phone played Unchained Melody, which meant her daughter called.

"Hi, dear. What's up?"

"Blake tells me you two had quite a talk a few nights ago."

"So we did." She sighed into the receiving speaker. "He reminds me more and more of your dad every day."

"Is that why you called him a neglectful father and husband?"

Janie sputtered. "I did no such thing. I simply told him I worried because he never seemed to have any time off for his family."

Her daughter's pitch jumped an octave, the way it did as a girl when she discovered once again life wasn't fair or she couldn't get her way. "Mom, how could you?"

Janie sat on the sofa. "Mel, you sniveled to *me*, remember?"

A more subdued response followed. "Yes. But it didn't give you the right to tell him."

"Humph. Well, obviously you didn't."

Silence.

"Look, Melody, dear. I remember how much I balked at the idea of you marrying a policeman. I understood the hard life ahead of you. I lived it. But Blake is a fine man, and he loves you and the kids very much." She paused before slinging the next arrow. "However, his priorities are muddled and he now is aware of that. I'm glad you are going to the coast as a family. Before long, Jaime and Ellie will be out the door and then what will you do?"

"Oh, I don't know. Breathe. Sleep. Relax."

Janie chuckled. "More like worry."

"You're right. I'll stay on my knees asking God to watch over them because they are no longer under my control."

She angled into the back cushions. "Or in view. I did the same thing for you and you turned out okay."

"There is one more thing, Mom."

The slurp of her daughter sipping more coffee came through the receiver. *Now we get to the meat of the call.*

"Have you decided not to pursue the reason that body ended in the dumpster?"

"I gave your husband a few good nuggets to investigate. If I gather any more by happenstance, I'll tell him."

"I see, and the same is true for your Bunco friends as well?"

"They only did it for me, Mel. Except now, I think they find being sleuths rather exciting. Not much else happens around here."

Another noisy sip. "Mom, you moved to Sunset Acres because of the activities. You didn't want to—how did you put it?"

Janie sang song the answer. "Rot in that big old house by myself."

"Yes, that was it."

"Ha, ha." She traced the piping on one of the sofa cushions. "They do try to keep us occupied. But some the events they organize are, well, so lame. Which is why we gather to play Bunco."

"Mom, you're in your senior years. You are supposed to slow down, not take up a new career in detective work."

"I only tried to help. I figured if we gathered evidence, they might find the killer sooner than later. This is my community, dear. I don't want this being shoved in the back of a filing cabinet drawer."

"Blake wouldn't do such a thing."

"Ah, but when a new murder surfaced, or a robbery, that would steal his time and attention away while the trail grew cold over here. I've seen that happen time and again."

"But with modern technology they can work on several cases at once."

"I know. I watch those crime investigative shows with Ethel. I am not that far under the rock. Oh, look at the time. I must go. My love to Ellie and Jamie."

She clicked off as Melody responded with a "Now, Mom...", and tossed the phone in the direction of the winged-back chair. Oh, how she wished she and Betsy Ann never discovered that leg, and then arm, and head...but they did.

Her thoughts shifted to the victim. Poor Mr. Newman. Disgraced, lonely, and cheated out of a decade of life. He came here to start anew and ended up diced into pieces like a tomato into salsa. He deserved justice as well.

Why did someone do it? Janie began to pace her living room as her mind churned. Had it been simply a random act of violence or did the wrong person recognize him from the papers? Maybe another con felt threatened by Edwin's time in the limelight? Or had he, similar to the faulty eye witnesses ten years ago, once again became a victim of mistaken identity?

She retrieved her phone and laid it on the side table next to the lamp. Her Bible passage of the day calendar glared at her. She flipped to Wednesday, May 6.

Proverbs 14:25 - A truthful witness saves lives, but a false witness is deceitful.

As her lips moved when she silently read the passage again, new resolve coursed through her veins. Edwin suffered from too many false witnesses. The truth must come out so his life and suffering made sense.

She tied on her tennis shoes and exited to meet the other two ladies for their daily power walk. However, she jolted to a stop at the curb. A notion began as a tingle in the back of her brain. Staring into the rising sun, the query formulated into a full blown quandary. Why did Edwin end up like leftover cuttings of raw steak?

First, she must pinpoint the reason for his death. If she found that out, discovering who killed him would be easy. The answer to the choice of method would logically surface.

Janie strutted to the end of the block. In three breaths, Betsy Ann waltzed up to her side and Ethel waved from halfway down the street as she quickened her pace.

"Good morning, ladies." Janie's smile widened. "Guess what the passage was on that day calendar you gave me, Betsy Ann?"

"Now, how would I possibly know, sweetie?"

She recited the verse.

They stared.

"Don't you see? This murder is no longer just about us and our security. It is up to us to right the wrong Mr. Newman suffered. Did someone mistake him for the bank robber Edward Norman who disappeared from sight? Or did Edwin die because of another secret he held? Until we can answer that, we are spinning our wheels. Now, let's get going. I can't think on any empty stomach."

Ethel trotted to catch up with her. "I knew you wouldn't give up."

Betsy Ann thrust her palm in the air. "For the truth."

Two more elderly hands clicked against hers. The three zipped down the street, hips encased in bright colored velour swiveling in perfect tempo.

CHAPTER NINETEEN

Betsy Ann, Ethel, and Janie huddled over their breakfast tacos and juice. They batted ideas around in a circle until Janie finally waved her hands in front of her chest. "Wait a minute, girls. Blake and his men are going to interview Edwin's roommate in prison. We can't follow that lead. But there may be others. What if someone had an ax to grind against Norman and mistook Edwin for him."

Ethel shuddered. "Appropriate metaphor, my friend."

Janie hid her neck in her collar, but her eyes glistened as a smirk etched her lips. "So it is."

Betsy Ann raised her hand.

Janie scoffed. "This isn't a classroom. Speak up."

She wiggled in her seat. "Well, how can we find out? I mean, didn't Blake say the man at the Get 'em and Go with the scar might not be the robber named Lopez?"

"True, both Smithers and Lopez are still in the state pen. I verified the info online."

"You can do that?"

Janie indicated yes as she bit into her egg and chorizo breakfast burrito.

Betsy Ann sat back. "Well, I never."

Janie swallowed. "Public Records Act, or whatever it is called. Amazing—and scary—what information you can glean over cyberspace these days."

Ethel sat straighter. "Takes sleuthing to a whole new level."

A frown curved Betsy Ann's lips. "Seems almost like hacking."

Janie pitty-patted her hand. "Except it's legal. Now, where were we?"

Ethel inched forward. "Who besides the burglars would want Edward Norman dead?"

"The bank presidents?" Betsy Ann giggled.

Janie snapped her fingers. "You know, that may not be far off. Very good, Betsy Ann."

A wide grin spread over Betsy Ann's face. "Thanks."

"You're welcome, dear. Let's search online for the names of the presidents, or at least the branch managers. There may be a connection as to why the trio chose those institutions."

They downed the rest of their breakfast in a few seconds and rushed through the dining area's double doors as several of their village neighbors shook their heads or clucked.

Janie overheard someone whine as she maneuvered through the tables. "Always in a hurry, those three are. We're supposed to slow down in our golden years, aren't we?"

He's been talking to Mel, no doubt.

The trio gathered around Janie's laptop, iced tea glasses sweating onto folded-over paper napkins. Mrs. Fluffy hopped in the middle and rubbed against the monitor as she purred loudly enough to imitate a lawnmower. Janie lifted her over the keyboard and onto the floor. "Not now, cat. We're busy. I'll give you hairball prevention tasty treat later."

"So what are we looking for?"

"Well, Betsy Ann. We can request the court transcripts of Edwin Newman's trial, as well as the records of other two, Smithers and Lopez. If we read them, something might show up."

"You can order them?"

Ethel gestured to the screen. "Even better. Says right there you can download them. Let's print them out and then each of us can take one to read."

Janie agreed. She entered the names and dates into the search box and clicked for the documents to be sent to her desktop printer. Within a few minutes, it began to churn out the first request.

"This will take a while. I hope I put in plenty of paper. Betsy Ann, will you make some more sun tea? Today promises to be a scorcher, and I'll be parched by the time we're through visiting our friends. That's a dear."

Ethel snatched her cell phone. "I'll call and check when Peggy will be available for visitors."

"Great." As Janie walked toward her bedroom, she spoke louder. "Check on Beatrice as well. She is next on my list."

"Will do." Ethel screeched at the same decibel, sending Mrs. Fluffy under the coffee table.

A jug filled with tea bags and water perched on her sunny windowsill by the time Janie returned with a stack of papers.

Betsy Ann grinned. "Brewing as we speak."

"Ah, thanks." She flopped the printouts onto the kitchen table. "This is only one of them. The copier is starting on the next one now."

Betsy Ann's eyes enlarged. "How many pages is that?"

"124. Front and back."

She whimpered. "It'll be like plowing through Moby Dick. You realize I'm a slow reader."

Ethel placed a hand on her back. "We'll make sure you get the shortest one."

A half hour later, the printer spat out the last page. The ladies divvied up the transcripts. Janie took Edwin's, Betsy Ann chose Lopez's, and Ethel gathered together Smithers'.

Betsy Ann fanned the pages. "102? Can we scan through these?"

Ethel weighed her stack in her hands. "What are we searching for anyway?"

"Anything that pops out." Janie placed hers on the dining room table. "A disgruntled witness. Angry family members. A bank employee who received a reprimand or a pink slip. Anyone who possibly wanted Edward Norman dead."

When Ethel called, the nurse informed her Peggy didn't feel well. The orthopedic doctor changed her pain medication which made her nauseated and dizzy. The trio asked her to deliver a note stating Peggy remained in their daily prayers and they would visit her in a few days.

"Well, I guess we call on Beatrice." Janie dug in her purse for her list. "Maybe Amelia is up to company."

"I don't recall her." Betsy Ann pouted.

"Sure you do. She volunteered in the library and read stories to the grandchildren during the celebration on Grandparents Day."

Ethel clicked her fingers. "Didn't she act on stage?"

"Yes, summer stock in the Texas Hill Country. Mostly Rogers and Hammerstein's musicals."

"Oh. I remember her now. She sang "Can't Help Lovin' Dat Man" from *Showboat* at the talent contest last summer." Betsy Ann's eyes glistened. "I still have that program."

"You do?"

"Do you think she might give me her autograph?"

Janie gave her a sugary smile. "Of course, dear. Would make her day if you asked, I'm sure." She leaned toward Ethel's right ear and whispered, "If she recalls her performance." She tapped her left temple and mouthed the word dementia.

Betsy Ann dashed to Janie's kitchen door. "I'll be back in two shakes of a lamb's tail."

That evening after she chomped on her Cobb salad, Janie settled into her sofa to read the transcript of Edward Norman, a.k.a. Edwin Newman's, trial. After fourteen pages, she yawned, and petted her cat who had curled next to her thigh. The animal opened one eye and upped the volume of her purrs.

"Not what I call a page turner, Mrs. Fluffy."

The feline snuggled closer to her, using her small, furry body weight to expand the way her species often does in order to shove her master off the end cushion. Janie conceded the battle and decided to make herself a cup of coffee. As she gazed out her kitchen window, the memory of the shadowed figure tickled her brain.

Who had it been? Male or female?

She shut her eyes and visualized the scene. The person appeared masculine in physique, but the darkness skewed her vision. Perhaps a tall, athletic woman? One thing for sure, he or she was nimble and quick enough to dash away. But why peep in the window?

Janie shook the image from her thoughts as she stirred some stevia and hazelnut flavored creamer into her mug. Two long sips revitalized her enough to tackle the court proceedings once again. With legal pad and pen in hand, she settled at the kitchen table for what promised to be a long night.

At 10:05 p.m., the phone rang. Ethel's excited voice blasted through the receiver.

"Turn on the news. Channel Five. Hurry."

CHAPTER TWENTY

Janie clicked the remote to view the reporting team. The anchor lady spoke. Behind her, a familiar mugshot gleamed in digital glory.

"The total bizarre story of Edwin Newman may never be fully discovered, though police are still investigating his ghastly murder last week. His niece, Marjorie Newman Spellman, informed us a memorial service will be held at Thompson's Funeral Home in Alamoville tomorrow at 11:00 a.m., preceded by the viewing at ten. In lieu of flowers, donations can be made to the Misidentified Criminals Foundation, who help the falsely accused assimilate back into society."

Ethel's voice came through the receiver. "I think we should go, don't you?"

Janie tapped the remote to her thigh. "Yes. Can't believe the next of kin wanted a viewing, though. Guess they found enough pieces to put Humpty Dumpty together again, huh?"

Ethel's scoff echoed in her ear. "Janie, really."

But a sputter told Janie Ethel tried hard not to laugh.

"I'll call Betsy Ann first thing in the morning. She's usually in bed by nine, you know."

"True. But I think it would be wise to wake her and tell her now."

"You think so?"

"She hates last minute changes in plan. You know that."

"Well, we better go on our walk at six-twenty instead of six-forty-five so we have time to eat breakfast, shower, and change. What ya figure? Meet back at your place at nine?"

Janie nodded and then realized her friend couldn't decipher the gesture over the phone. "Yes, shouldn't take us more than forty-five minutes to drive there. Okay, I'll give Betsy Ann a ring now."

"Okay."

But, Ethel?"

"Yeah?"

"Let's meet up at six. That'll allow her a good hour after breakfast to decide which black outfit to wear."

The blast of stale air conditioning hit Janie's cheek as the women slipped into the low-lit funeral parlor. Mildred came as well, stating it to be her pious duty to forgive and forget.

A white, satin-lined guest book sat in the vestibule on a pedestal. The four women signed in their names with the snowy plumed pen, identified themselves as neighbors on the adjacent line, and tiptoed down the ramp into the viewing room. Soft, piped-in organ music filtered from speakers hidden in the ceiling. The mahogany casket sat half-open in the back of the room, centered under pink pocket lights. At least ten flower arrangements, several on easels, dotted the surrounding area as forty-plus people occupied the room, some standing and whispering, others clustered in seated groups.

Janie spoke in a library-hushed voice. "Can't believe so many folks turned out for this."

Ethel bobbed her short, steel-colored curls. "Well, call me morbid, but I am curious to take a peek. The restoration must have cost a bundle."

Betsy Ann shuddered. "Wonder which one is his niece?"

Janie removed her glasses and rubbed them on her blouse. "Darn photo-chromic lenses. I can't see a thing." She sighed and cradled them back onto the bridge of her nose. "Well, let's pay our respects and mingle. We might be able to pick up a clue in conversations."

Three heads bounced up and down without making a sound. With a collective breath to steady their nerves, the ladies traipsed past the grouping of bystanders with respectful nods and pursed smiles.

Betsy Ann whimpered. "This is eerie. The last time we saw him was...well, in pieces."

Ethel shushed her. "Don't think about it."

"You didn't discover him, Ethel." Her voice quivered. "Janie and I did."

Janie held her hand to her waist. "I admit the Danish I ate for breakfast is churning in my gut."

The three gazed into each other's eyes and whispered in unison, "We can do this."

Ethel heaved a deep sigh. "Let's go."

As they shuffled closer to the casket, Mildred stopped. She put out her arms for the other to halt as well. "Wait."

"Mildred? If you don't wish to come, we understand."

She shook her head. "That's not the problem, ladies." She pointed with her head at the body laid out in estate. "Are my eyes deceiving me or is that a...?"

Ethel whispered the startling revelation. "A woman!"

Janie began to back step. "Oops. Wrong viewing."

Dozens of eyes peered as the quartet scurried away, hands to their mouths. Outside on the stoop, they burst into laughter.

Betsy Ann wiped the giggle-tears from her face with a tissue fished from her pocket. "Should we go in and cross our names off the guest book?"

Janie stared at the other three blush-cheeked women who gazed back at her for the answer. "Nah. It would look tacky. No one ever reads those things, now do they? At least, after my late husband's funeral, I never did." She swatted the thought away with a raspberry sound, causing another episode of nervous chuckles.

They propped against the pillars in the porte-cochere as they tried to stifle their giggles of embarrassment. However, as soon as everyone took a breath, one of them would sputter again, sending the rest into fits of suppressed laughter again. A group of people entering the parlor cocked their eyebrows at them and frowned.

Janie motioned with her hand. "Come on, let's go find out where *our* corpse is."

Betsy Ann slapped her back. "Janie!"

They all burst into laughter one more time.

Mildred wiped under her eyes. "Let's locate a receptionist. Who knew there'd be two viewings?"

The four entered the glass doors on the side where a young lady in an austere-tailored navy blue suit and hair tucked into a tight French bun greeted them. She motioned down a narrow hallway. "Past the restrooms and water fountain on the right."

The biddies edged down the oriental runners and peered in. A middle-aged woman shriveled on the edge of a love seat, a linen hankie clutched in her hands. A vase of roses, a winged-back chair in faded, maroon brocaded upholstery, and an easel depicting Edwin Newman as a younger man comprised the only other items in the room. Janie knocked on the door jamb.

"Ms. Spellman?"

She jolted with her hand to her throat. "Oh, hello." She extended her other hand but didn't rise from her seat.

Janie clutched her purse to her stomach. She plastered on a sympathetic, matronly smile. "My name is Janie Manson, and these are..."

Marjorie's eyes enlarged. "You are the ones who...who..."

Betsy Ann sniffled. "Yes. We did. So horrid." She clucked her teeth and dashed her gaze to the flowers which showed signs of wilting in the sunbeam. "Let me draw those drapes. The heat will wither those blooms in no time."

Mildred perched next to the niece. She placed a hand on her knee. "I was his next door neighbor, if only for a few days."

The grieving relative swiveled towards her. "Oh, you must be the one with the dog. Mrs. Jacobs told me about that. I am so sorry. Edwin never liked dogs. One attacked him as a small child. A Schnauzer, if I am not mistaken. He still carried the scars on his arms and neck. Any barking set him on edge."

Janie slunk into the occasional chair. "Why didn't this come out in the trial? Such evidence like physical markings would have proven he wasn't Edward Norman."

Marjorie shook her head. "My guess is the prosecution thought they had their man and the bank officers wanted a quick closure."

"Yes, all three are branches of the same financial institution, correct?"

"That's true. Any hint of the theft being an inside job would damage the bank's reputation. I'm sure the shareholders and board wanted to squelch any notion. They made Edwin their scapegoat." She swallowed a sob and gazed at her clutched fingers. "His court-appointed rookie lawyer proved no match for their well-respected and learned attorneys."

A moment of uneasiness draped the small room. Janie followed the dust motes as they swirled in the sunlight streaming through the opening between the drawn drapes. It landed onto Edwin Newman's photo-glossy, framed-in face. Even as a younger man, he held a far-away look in his eyes as if a deep pain refused to surface. "Tell us about him. We never got the chance to know him and he went through such an ordeal."

His only living kin took a deep breath before beginning her tale. "His father died in a car accident a few months before he turned twelve. His gambling debts left Edwin's mom penniless. My mother, her sister, took them in. I was in pre-school at the time. I recall him being sullen and moody, and he often spent hours locked in his room which they converted from half of the garage. He ran away five years later. Joined the Army. Never finished high school."

She paused and sipped a glass of water which she had perched on the carpet next to her shoes. After a couple of sips, she continued. "Three years in, he caught shrapnel in the leg and they discharged him after several months in rehab. After quite a few dead-end jobs over the next twenty years, he became a janitor for one of the banks Norman, Lopez and Smithers robbed. Worked for that financial institution for twelve years."

Ethel spoke up. "Ah, I understand."

Marjorie's eyes narrowed. "Yes. He never possessed one reprimand on his employment record, but they always blame the cleaning crew, don't they?" Her lips curved to one side as her eyelids drooped.

Janie softly touched the woman's arm. "I gather your parents have passed on?"

She gave her head a quick bob. "Dad died of heart failure at only fifty-nine. Smoked several packs a day, but didn't everyone in his generation? Mom suffered a stroke within two weeks of Edwin's conviction. She never recovered. She's been gone ten years now. Edith, Edwin's mother, remained in the house as a recluse until the neighbors discovered..."

"Yes, we read that in the papers. I am so sorry." Janie gave her a sweet smile of sympathy.

"I should have visited her more often." Marjorie's voice caught in her throat.

The four Bunco Biddies glanced at each other. Ethel leaned in. "We better get going. Funeral is in fifteen minutes, correct?"

Marjorie pushed back her sleeve to read her watch. "Yes." Her voice remained flat. "Will you stay?" She lifted her gaze to each one, an unstated plea reflected in her dark brown, red-rimmed pupils.

Since the service began soon and no one else milled around, Janie doubted anyone else would attend. "Of course. We will meet you in the chapel." Janie gave Marjorie's arm a gentle squeeze and rose from the cushion.

The other three followed her into the hallway in a stiff, silent parade. Betsy Ann spoke first. "I want to freshen up." She motioned with her eyes toward the door marked for their gender.

Everyone murmured in consent.

The whole thing lasted twenty minutes. A generic preacher expounded on judgment being in God's hands and how we are called to love and forgive. Mildred sniffled. Betsy Ann crossed herself, and Janie and Ethel stared at each other with renewed resolve.

"This poor man did nothing to deserve his demise." Janie put her hands to her hips. "I agree judgment belongs to the Almighty, but we can ensure justice is done here on earth."

Ethel arched her eyebrow and scribbled her response one of the information pamphlets. "Remember, Marjorie is now about two-hundred-fifty thousand dollars richer."

Janie's eyes became as large as the spider mums in the floral arrangement on the closed casket. She glanced up a row across from them to Edwin Newman's niece. Ms. Spellman seemed meek enough and her sorrow genuine. However, she recalled what she had told Blake. People have killed for less.

CHAPTER TWENTY-ONE

"What if Edwin Newman died because he wasn't Edward Norman after all?" Ethel made her point with an erect finger.

Janie gripped the steering wheel. "Well, I guess that's something to think about, though it seems unlikely."

Betsy Ann scooted forward from the back seat to be heard over the hum of the tires. "Not if Edward Norman wanted to remain incognito. Remember, they never found the money. Once people learned the authorities mistook Edwin for Norman, it only stands to reason the feds would be searching for the real robber now."

"Blake told me the real Edward Norman died in South America or somewhere years ago."

Ethel twisted to face her from the front passenger side. "Maybe sweet Marjorie wanted the compensation money more than a reunion with her sad-sack uncle. Two-hundred-fifty thousand is nothing to sneeze at."

Mildred humphed. "We never learned what she did for a living."

"No, no, no." Janie shook her head back and forth as she refocused on the traffic ahead of her. "I can't believe such a sweet woman could be so dastardly. Let's hope Blake uncovers something about Edwin from his prison mates. I get a nagging suspicion Edwin crossed the wrong people after he became incarcerated."

"But will he share that with you?"

"I'm having dinner with them after church on Sunday. I'll tell him about our conversation with Marjorie Spellman and perhaps in exchange...well, I can try."

Ethel pressed her spine into her car seat. "Why do I feel as if we are back at square one?"

"Again." Betsy Ann folded her arms and flopped back to stare out the side window.

Mildred sat in quietness, biting her lower lip. Cupped in her hand lay a crumpled photo of her Poopsy.

Later in the afternoon, Janie made her appointed Good Samaritan rounds at the assisted living center. Her cohorts opted out, both stating weariness from today's outing and needing time to review their court transcripts before they met an hour before the rest of the Bunco Biddies arrived for the weekly Thursday evening fun.

"All right. Meet you for our walk tomorrow morning." Janie waved as both strolled down the street to their abodes.

After changing into walking shorts and a layered top, she chomped a tuna fish sandwich, washed down with a glass of two-percent milk, and headed across the expanse to the four-story building she dreaded one day would be her residence. Anyone who lived in the community's independent housing claimed first dibs on vacancies in the more monitored units.

She chatted with a couple who shared quarters on the third floor. They had been one of the first residents to buy a condo in Sunset Acres. However, over the winter, their health declined so drastically, the family became concerned about their ability to live self-sufficiently.

"I don't miss cooking and cleaning." Mrs. Joseph winked at her husband. "He won't admit it, but he doesn't either. In fact, the doctor says he gained a few pounds since we moved in here."

Mr. Joseph clasped a shaky hand over his ear. "What you say?"

She erased the thought with her hand. In a higher decibel voice, she addressed him. "Never mind, honey. Go back to your nap." She turned to Janie. "He takes three a day now." Worried lines crinkled her brow line.

Janie closed the door to their room as her heart fluttered. She went to the ladies' room and stared into the mirror. Suddenly, her hair appeared whiter and her wrinkles more numerous.

She chided her reflection. "There but for the grace of God go you." Visiting these old neighbors weighed upon her spirit more than she realized. "But you've got to do this, Janie, old girl. Who will visit you when the time comes?"

Blake and Melody and the kids would try, when they found time. But lonely long days stretched out in her mind. However, as she continued to chat with her peers who resided in the monitored facility, the boulders in her stomach became pebbles. Well-cooked meals, caring staff, and the ability to bring some personal belongings to make the small efficiencies your own eased the angst. The staff offered activities for all levels of competency, from ice cream socials to Bingo and movie nights. Wonder if they organized a Bunco get-together? Well, they would when she arrived.

The thought put a slight bounce in her step as she headed back to her condo.

She spent the evening with a cup of chamomile tea and the transcripts, more confident than ever of the futility of her efforts. Still, this stone must be overturned and Blake didn't have the time, not with his hectic schedule. Perhaps Betsy Ann or Ethel would uncover a clue in their documents.

Yet something in the back of her brain tugged at her. No one killed Edwin until after the courts discovered his true identity. As long as he remained incarcerated as Edward Norman, he stayed safe. Why?

She gathered Mrs. Fluffy and shuffled off to bed. Perhaps a good night's sleep would un-muddle her grey cells.

A rumbling through her bedroom jolted Janie from her dream state. The kitty burrowed under the covers against the crux of her knees, a sure sign foul weather loomed on the horizon. Stark white light pulsed through her curtains followed by another elongated boom. Within seconds, the tapping of rain pounded above her head.

She glanced at the illuminated dial of her alarm clock. 5:48. Janie flopped back on her pillow with a groan. Hopefully this would be over in an hour. Texas storms often breezed through at fifty miles per hour, rattling and shaking everything in their path. Which meant jogging in muddy puddles later this morning.

Janie folded the sheets back, causing a disgruntled growl from her furry companion. She waddled into the kitchen and put on the kettle as bright, flickering shafts blasted through her mini blinds along with rhythmic tumbles of thunder.

As Janie filled her cup with boiling water, a loud crash from the heavens vibrated her walls. A streak of gray stripes dashed in and wrapped herself between her mistress's legs. In an effort to sidestep the feline, Janie lost her balance.

She cried out as Mrs. Fluffy leapt to the kitchen counter and then cowered on top of the refrigerator.

Her right ankle twisted out of her bedroom slipper. Sharp needles zipped up her ankle and down across her toes. Her elbow whacked next, breaking her fall before her face met the linoleum.

Janie struggled to a sitting position on the floor. Her foot throbbed. Pulsating pain emitted from above her baby toe, across to the big toe and up to her ankle joint. She knew better than to try to stand. "Well, at least I didn't break a hip."

Fighting tears, she scooted on her behind, foot aloft, down the hall to her bedroom table where her cell phone sat recharging. Each inch shot more pain into her injured joints. But with gasps, a thumping heart, and tears streaming down her face, she stretched her fingers to snag the recharging cord tethering her ability to contact to the outside world via the electrical outlet.

Speed dialing her daughter, Janie waited for the rings to be answered.

A groggy hello followed after the third one.

"Melody, dear. I know it's storming, but I fell and twisted my foot. It hurts like the dickens. I need you to come take me to the emergency clinic."

Sheets rustled through the speaker along with Blake's mumbling in the background. "Mom. Hang tight. I'll be right over. Do *not* move."

"I already did in order to reach the phone. But I'll stay still now. I'm in the bedroom. You'll have to use the spare key."

Janie listened as drawers pulled open and shut. Her daughter's voice muffled.

She must be cradling the receiver with her chin.

"Be there in twenty minutes, max. I promise."

"Thank you, Mel. Drive safe, now. The roads will be slick."

Melody's exasperated response came through the receiver. "I will, Mom."

Janie hung up and gulped back a series of sobs. She may be in the assisted living center earlier than she anticipated.

Dear Lord, what will I do then?

CHAPTER TWENTY-TWO

"Well, these came out nice and clear," the emergency tech told her as he hung the x-ray on the white screen. "The doc will be in a minute. He'll study these and give your foot a more thorough examination."

Janie heaved her chest as she propped on her elbows. Melody paced, her hair skewed in a hurriedly wrapped ponytail. From the multiple creases, her shorts and T-shirt had been worn earlier in the day. "Daughter, stop fidgeting. It might be much ado about nothing."

Melody's eyelids reddened. "Nothing? Mom, you fell. Don't you understand this is every grown child's worse nightmare?"

Janie lay back on the examining table and stared at the acoustic tiles. She blinked back the tears before they showed on her cheeks. *Every elderly person's one, too.*

The on-call physician tapped on the door and entered with a warm smile and kind eyes. "Well, now. They tell me you took a tumble. Has this happened before?"

Janie lifted herself to a sitting position with his assistance. "No. First time."

"Hmmm." His hands slid over her foot as he studied the swollen and discolored area. "Tell me when it hurts."

"I could've told you that a half hour ago." Janie winched as his fingers probed the muscles.

He chuckled. "Any place worse than another?"

As his thumb pressed, she jerked. "You found the spot, Doc." She jammed her lips together as a tear slid down her face.

He patted her calf. "Sorry. Let's take a look." He turned to the bluish-white box illuminating the x-ray. He peered over his readers and leaned in with a frown to scrutinize one particular area.

Jane cut her eyes to Melody who tucked her lower lip into her teeth. The silence thumped in her ears.

"Well...." He swiveled to face her with a quick grin. "I don't detect any signs of a break."

"What luck." Melody's shoulders slacked.

"Not exactly. From the swelling and bruising now forming, I venture to say she strained several muscles in the outer foot."

Melody's face paled.

He peered into Janie's eyes. "That sometimes takes longer to heal. We are going to construct a splint for you and give you crutches."

"Is it really necessary?"

"Absolutely." He waggled his finger as if she had diminished in age by sixty years. "You are not to put any, and I mean any, weight on your foot for seven days. Understood? If you re-injure the ligaments, you may tear one, which would not be pleasant."

Janie looked down at her hands and nodded.

The doctor turned to Melody. "Someone should stay with her for first forty-eight hours. They make a device on which she can rest her bent knee. Works well for older patients. I think Medicare covers the expense as durable medical. The girls up front will provide the name of an orthopedic equipment company in Austin who carries them. I suggest you get one for her tomorrow. It'll make compliance a lot easier."

Janie narrowed her eyes, miffed that he spoke as if she were deaf as a doorknob or not even in the room. "Now, she is to rest. Elevate it and apply ice for ten minutes every hour for the next day. Do not let her get up without assistance. Okay?"

She cleared her throat loudly and arched her left eyebrow high.

He turned toward her and winked. "If the swelling or pain doesn't subside after a few days, return to the clinic. If your foot becomes reddened, hot to the touch or spongy, come back. Okay?"

His patronizing, stern tone made Janie recall her kindergarten teacher. Humph. *Does he assume I am senile as well?* Even so, she spoke through gritted teeth. "Yes, sir."

The tech will be in with the splint in a minute. Questions?"

"How long will this take to heal?"

"Four to six weeks. My guess is the latter. In ten days, you can remove it and try wearing one of those athletic wraps they sell in the drug stores. Get one with supporters on either side which secures with Velcro strips, not the one you slip on, okay? Tugging may damage the muscles. And if you don't own a cane, buy one. I want you using it for support for at least a month after the splint comes off." He wrote on a piece of paper, ripped it from his tablet, and handed it to her. "Return here a week from Monday and let me see how you are progressing. If I'm satisfied with your recovery process at that time you can switch to the cane. But don't try it on your own. I will send you to physical therapy so they can instruct you on its proper use. Too many people use them the wrong way and end up with knee and hip pain."

Mother and daughter bobbed their heads in unison.

The physician shook both their hands and exited.

Another tear cascaded down Janie's cheek. "I am so sorry, Mel. I know how busy you are with the kids. I can see if one of the Bunco Biddies can babysit me. Perhaps in shifts?"

Melody rested her hip on the gurney. She took Janie's hand. "Mom, after all the years you cared for me, now it's my turn. Blake can handle getting the kids to school. I can stay the rest of the night and until tomorrow afternoon. But I am going into Austin to get that contraption for you, so can one of them keep you company for an hour or so mid-morning?"

"I'm sure they won't mind. I'll give them a ring first thing in the morning." Janie slapped her forehead. "We need to let Betsy Ann and Ethel know I won't be jogging with them."

Her daughter laughed. "No, I guess you won't."

Another tap. The tech returned with a towel, a bowl of water, and a long strip of felt. Rolls of stretchy, flesh colored bandage were tucked under his arm.

"What's that?"

"Your splint. We mold the plastic to fit your foot." He put the towel over the counter top and dragged the felt strip through the water. Next, he formed the warmed material under and over Janie's foot like a stirrup and held it in position. The fabric soon cooled and stiffened. "Minuscule fiberglass pellets inside this covering melt in the hot water then begin to harden as they cool."

"Well, I'll be."

He gave her a quick smile as his hands gingerly pressed the mold against her ankle and calf, halfway up to her knee. "You can take this off for fifteen minutes each day as you bathe. But no standing in the shower. Do you own a bath chair?"

"I can locate one. Besides, all the tubs at the village are equipped with handicap rails."

"Sunset Acres? My great aunt lives there. Rosanne Richardson."

Janie's facial muscles eased. "I play Bunco with her."

He nodded in approval. "Tell her hi from Evan." His cheeks took on a rosy tint. "And I will get by to visit her soon."

Melody and Janie exchanged glances. *Sure he will.*

He cleared his throat. "This will take about another five minutes to set. I'll return with your pain medication prescription, instructions, and the crutches. Stay put, now." He winked in the same manner the emergency doc did. Must be part of their training in bedside manners.

Twenty minutes later, Janie emerged, wrapped in Velcro bandages around the fiberglass splint and wobbling on crutches. The tech followed behind, his arms wide to catch her if she toppled backwards. Melody back stepped in front of her, ready to grab her if she tilted too far forward. In Janie's mind, the trek to the car—parked in the closest space—seemed at least two miles long. Down the handicapped ramp she tottered and puffed. Her face inflamed with heat and sweat dribbled down her back, even though a post-rain, post-rain summer breeze rustled the nearby tree leaves.

At last, she plopped her rear end in the front seat as the orderly swung her leg around to the mat. Melody placed Janie's purse on the floorboard to prop the heel and clicked the shoulder harness over Janie's torso.

As they drove off, Janie's heart tap danced inside her chest wall. She placed her hand over it. "Okay. First thing in the morning, you are getting that device. I'm too old and out of shape to manage these confounded things." She slapped the steel sticks resting against the door beside her. "My armpits already ache like crazy."

Melody squeezed her hand before returning her attention to the road. "I love you, Mom."

Janie's lips quivered as her eyes dampened. "I know, dear. I know." She turned away.

How can I help your husband solve this case now?

CHAPTER TWENTY-THREE

"You did what?" Betsy Ann's voice shrilled over the speaker phone. "Oh, my goodness. What can I do?"

Janie rolled her eyes to keep from sighing. Betsy Ann hung the moon as far as sweet, good-intention friends came, but she had a tendency to hover and be dramatic. "Hmmm, some of your tomato bisque soup would be lovely. Make enough for Mel, she is staying with me through the afternoon."

Her voice elevated. "Glad to, and I'll bring those little round crackers you love. How about some chicken salad with pecans, celery, apples, and grapes?"

"Perfect, thanks. Don't bother ringing the bell. Come on around back. The door to the kitchen will be unlocked. I'm sequestered on the couch."

Melody handed her a steaming cup of vanilla chai tea as she bent toward the phone. "Howdy, Betsy Ann."

Janie pulled it away from her ear. "She says 'hi' back."

Next, she called Ethel, which started the avalanche of calls, casseroles and clucks as word spread through the Bunco Biddies.

Melody withered after the first hour of answering the door and acting as hostess to all the well-wishers. At last, only Betsy Ann, laden with soup and salad, and Ethel with fresh, warm-from-the oven banana bread remained.

"Mom, you rest. It's been a busy morning. I'm heading for the durable equipment shop. They show one for only $79.99, and he will bill Medicare since the doctor wrote a script." She slung her purse onto her arm, and from the tight pull on her forehead muscles, appeared anxious to exit.

Janie waved. "These ladies will keep an eye on me. Promise I won't let them take me dancing."

Ethel and Betsy Ann nodded.

Melody scrunched her mouth to one side. "Okay. Remember to take your pain pill at eleven." She swiveled to the visitors. "And one or both of you help her if she needs to go to the restroom. She is still wobbly on those crutches."

With a chin-jerk for emphasis, she left.

Ethel let out a nervous chuckle. "Wow, is she ever a tough nanny!"

Janie smoothed the quilt draped over her leg. "She's worried. Afraid this is the beginning."

The other two exchanged looks.

Betsy Ann reached over and took her hand. "We all fear that, hon. However, this was just a stupid accident. Could happen to anyone with a pet."

Janie scanned the room. "Where is my nemesis anyway?"

Ethel crossed her arms. "Hiding under the bed in penitence?"

Her mistress knew better. "Not in a million years. Mrs. Fluffy most likely blames me for being in her way."

The three fell silent for a moment as the mantle clock ticked away the time. After a while, Ethel broke the stillness. "What do you want to do about the investigation?"

Janie scooted up on her pillows. "Continue, of course. Despite my injury, the game's still...ahem, afoot." She wiggled her eyebrows.

A sly grin curled Ethel's lips. "Well said. So how do you wish to proceed?"

"Since I'm laid up, why don't y'all hand over your court transcripts along with any notes. I'll take over the task while you, who can walk, continue to figure out Edwin's last two days on this earth. Surely someone sighted something." She yawned.

"Take a wee cat nap, honey. I'll go get mine and be back in a jiffy." Betsy Ann stood and bent over Janie to wipe a curl from her brow.

Ethel reached in her bag. "I'll sit here quiet as a mouse and read. Gotta new mystery from the library where the woman's been stabbed twenty-two times, one for each year she's been alive."

Janie sighed and closed her eyes, thanking God for her quirky and loving friends.

Tummy filled with tomato soup and chicken salad, Janie took her second nap of the day as Melody did a load of laundry before leaving later that afternoon. The bent-knee thingy worked oh so much better than crutches, which helped Janie prove she could maneuver without anyone hovering over her. A bonus? Mrs. Fluffy dashed under furniture each time the contraption came within five feet of her.

Melody shook her mother's shoulder with tender care, rousing her from a dreamy, drifting state.

"Mom, I gotta go. Ethel says she will drop by about four with some reading material you wanted. I'll leave the back door unlocked for her in case you want to nap some more."

Janie stretched her upper torso and reached for her covered tumbler of iced tea, complete with straw. "Thanks, again, Mel. For everything. How would I have managed without you?"

"Mom, hush. You'd figure out a way." She kissed her cheek and left.

At the sound of the click, Janie reached under her pillow and pulled out the report of Lopez's trial. She balanced her reading glasses on her nose and licked her finger to flip the first page. "Okay, something worthwhile jump out at me."

Within fifteen minutes, the papers tumbled to the rug as her eyelids grew heavy again.

A shadow passed over Janie's face. In her dream state, she swatted as if a fly buzzed her nose. Then the thing darkened and grew wider. A pressure pushed onto her mouth. A hand with a faint odor of...no? Raw meat?

She thrust her eyes open. A hooded figure dressed in black hovered over her. "Hush. Don't make a sound. Back off of this body in the dumpster stuff, okay? If you don't, you will be next."

He—she assumed it a male from the low cadence of his voice—released his hand and slapped her hard across the face before she could call out. Shaking and dazed, she lay still while he dashed out of sight. The kitchen door slammed, and the echoing vibrations tinkled the goblets in her dining room hutch. She reared up on her elbows and scanned the room. All seemed in place...except for her psyche.

First a whimper emerged through her lips. It bubbled into a yell, and burst over her tonsils in a high-pitched scream. She waited. No one rushed to her aid to hug her and tell her everything would be all right. Oh, how she missed Jack. She needed him.

Her hand trembled as she stretched toward the coffee table for her cell phone and punched in 9-1-1. "Help. A man broke into my home." Her sentence quivered as the reality seeped into her brain.

The calming and in-control voice on the other end asked a few questions, such as was he still there? Did she feel safe now? Could she give her location? And did she want the police to be summoned?

"Yes, my-my son-in-law is Blake Johnson," She inhaled a deep breath to steady her nerves. "He's Alamoville's Chief Detective."

The operator relayed the message and assured Janie help had been dispatched. "Do you want me to stay on the line with you until they arrive?"

Janie edged up into a sitting position. "Would you? I'm injured so I can't walk."

"He hurt you?"

"No, I fell. Yesterday." She gulped back the lump at the base of her tongue. "Not related. I have this contraption to hobble about, but I feel a little woozy right now."

"That's understandable, ma'am. Just take deep, slow breaths."

"Tell them to come around back. I can't answer the front door because it's locked."

The responder soothed her as they chatted about her foot, her home, and friends. In minutes, sirens wailed, growing in volume as they zoomed closer. They reached a piercing decibel, then shut off with a whoop, whoop. She listened as car doors shut and footsteps scrunched across the miniature lawn. Shadows zipped past her curtains.

"The kitchen door's open," she called out as loud as her parched throat allowed.

The door whammed open and male footsteps stomped into her house.

"I'm in here. In the living room."

As soon as Blake's concerned face appeared in her range of vision, the sobs took over.

CHAPTER TWENTY-FOUR

Blake knelt next to her and enveloped her in his arms as she shook, slobbering on his shoulder like an infant. After a few minutes, she took a gulp of air and patted her eyes with a tissue from a box one of the uniformed officers located. Her son-in-law sat on the edge of the sofa, his eyes on her face.

"Okay, Janie. Tell me what happened." He handed her the water glass and helped guide it toward her lips. The cool liquid slid down her throat, diminishing the lump of emotion lodged there.

"Melody left the back door unlocked because Ethel would be coming in a little while. I took a pain pill so I dozed off, I guess. Next thing I know, this large hand clamped over my mouth and nose."

"Go on. Take your time."

She told Blake what the gruff voice said. "He slapped me, I imagine to make his point." She sucked her sore lip and tasted blood.

He cocked an eyebrow and glanced up at his underling. "Add assault to the charges." His gaze shifted back to her as his eyes grew cold. "Janie, I thought we agreed you'd let the police handle this. What have you been doing?"

"Nothing. We went to Edwin Newman's funeral and spoke with his niece."

He held up a shuffled a stack of papers, now half dispersed onto the area rug. "And this?"

She batted her eyelashes. "A little light reading while I am convalescing."

His jaw line hardened. The air became frigid as he thumbed through the court report.

Janie winched.

Blake smacked the documents down on the table. He rose off the couch and paced, hands rubbing down his face. After a moment, he stopped and turned to her. "Give Connor as full a description as you can. A patrol car is making rounds, but we will step it up a notch."

"Okay, thanks." She stared at her hands as they clutched her quilt. When did they start to get so old and wrinkly?

"In the meantime, Janie..."

She lifted her glance as his finger aimed at her face.

"...you are to stop this nonsense immediately. You understand me?"

She gave her head a quick nod.

He thrust his thumb into his necktie. "I'm the detective. Let me do my job."

Her lips quivered as his image shimmered through new tears.

Blake shifted his weight. "Don't start the water works again. Please. I'm sorry, but you do yank my chain."

The officer, pen poised over his notebook, let off a snicker. His expression returned to a stone-faced one when Blake's gaze shifted in his direction.

"Connor, gather what evidence you can and fill out the report. Bradley, check for footprints in the yard."

"Yes, sir."

Blake knelt to Janie's eye level again. "I gather he wore gloves?"

Her eyes widened. "No, he didn't. I just remembered something."

"What?"

"His hands smelled of truck stop soap and raw hamburger meat."

Blake's expression tightened. "Branson, get the fingerprint kit, too."

Ethel tapped on the backdoor jamb. "Hello? Janie, are you okay?"

Blake called to the kitchen. "In here, Ethel. All is fine. But do not touch the door knob, okay. We need to dust for prints."

"Fingerprints? Oh, gracious. May I watch?"

"As long as you stay out of the way. My officer is getting the kit now."

She tiptoed across the dining room rug and stood in the threshold of the living room, her arms laden with her stack of court papers and two grease-seeped sacks from the fast food joint down the road.

Janie groaned.

Blake eyed the papers, humphed again, and patted her shoulder. "Remember what I said, now." He half-bowed to Ethel on the way out.

Janie motioned for her friend to sit and wait until the officer finished asking her questions. When he ran out of them, he handed

Janie the golden copy of the report and said they would be in touch. "We will dust the back door. Did he touch anything in here?"

"Besides me, no. I don't think so."

The cop grinned. "I'll close the door on my way out." He touched the tip of his hat. "Ladies."

Ethel stopped him. "Blake…er, Detective Johnson, said I could observe ya'll as long as I stay out of the way."

Connor's eye twitched. "Okay. Bradley is outside taking pictures. We'll call you when we start."

Ethel gave him a sugary smile, opened the bag, and pulled out a large box of fries, batter-fried chicken sandwiches, and fruit cups. "Figured you might want comfort food after your accident. Little did I know…" She jutted her thumb toward the kitchen. "What happened? Are you okay? You're pale."

For the third—or was it the fourth?—time, Janie relayed her harrowing adventure.

"Wow." Ethel sat back and took a bite from her whole wheat bun. "Guess we've ruffled a few feathers, huh?"

"I don't see how." Janie gathered the quilt to her neck. "I mean, who figured out we've been snooping?"

"About everyone in a five-mile radius of Sunset Acres. You know how fast gossip travels."

"Hmm."

"So," Ethel pointed with a French fry to the stack of papers. "Discover anything?"

"No. Something tells me I won't. Keeping my mind occupied, though. How about you?"

"Well, maybe I shouldn't tell you after the expression on Blake's face." She motioned with her head to the underling who combed the room with his eyes looking for anything out of the ordinary.

Silence fell between them. They locked gazes.

Ethel took another bite of her meal and chewed like a cow taking its time to graze. She wrapped her lips around the straw of her iced tea and took a long, slurpy draw.

Janie arched her left eyebrow and tapped her fingernail on her take-out cup. Connor moved toward the dining room, his head bent to the ground as if searching for a lost contact lens.

Ethel set down her food and dabbed the napkin to the corner of her mouth. In a quieter voice she resumed. "I went to visit Peggy Williams today. She says 'hello' to you by the way. We had a nice chat, and I caught her up on all the news." She crossed her leg. "Can you believe she never heard about the, well, about Edwin? I gather they are more or less isolated so news travels pretty slowly around those facilities."

Janie cocked an eyebrow.

Connor glanced at them, gave them a head nod, and continued his search.

In an even softer voice she proceeded. "Guess what she told me? She couldn't sleep one night so she wheeled herself down to the common area. You remember? The one with the big picture windows that overlook the complex?"

"Yes, go on."

"Well, this occurred a week ago Monday, I mean Tuesday to be more accurate since Peggy figures she witnessed the van about two in the morning."

"A van?!"

"Shhhh." Ethel wiped a smudge from her glasses and waited for the police investigator to shuffled toward the kitchen. "She thinks so. A vehicle with its lights on dim moved at a tortoise's pace down the lane."

"She could see it?"

"Oh, yes. Even with a new moon, the street lamps cast a soft glow and the fourth floor offers a wonderful bird's-eye view. The residents often peer out from that vantage point as they wait for relatives to arrive."

Janie re-positioned herself, leaning on one elbow. "I see. And?"

"Well, she described a dark colored van, like one of those delivery ones. Except who gets packages at that hour?"

"She is sure about this?"

Ethel nodded. "Uh, huh."

Janie's eyes lit up. "How interesting."

"She detected a huge dent on the passenger door as if it'd been t-boned in a wreck. What's odd is she remembered seeing the exact same damaged van leaving Sunset Acres about seven earlier that evening. Close to the time the Roberts spotted one near Newman's house. "

"Well, well."

Ethel grinned like a lion spotting a wounded gazelle. "Here's the thing. This time, the truck headed into our community instead of out. And"—she edged closer and whispered into Janie's right ear—"stopped at the club house dumpster."

A jolt zipped up Janie's spine.

CHAPTER TWENTY-FIVE

While Ethel witnessed the fingerprint dusting process, Janie contemplated her latest news. Why would a van leave but come back to deposit the body? Unless the murderer transported the corpse to another location to be dissected and came back to hide the pieces in the dumpster, knowing full well the trash service came early the next morning. That would mean the perpetrator had prior knowledge about the comings and goings in Sunset Acres. So he staked out Edwin's garden home? No, he'd only been there less than a week. That meant the perp lived in the community or had a family member who did. She shook off that thought like a spider web clinging to her shoulders.

Janie's cell phone rang. At the other end, Melody's nerve-racked voice wobbled. "Mom, Blake just called and told me. Are you okay?"

"Yes, besides a cut lip where he slapped me."

Her voice elevated to a high soprano. "He did what?"

"I'm fine, dear. Ethel is here and she brought me supper."

"I shouldn't have left." Her daughter swallowed a sob.

"Now, Mel. Don't be ridiculous. This is a gated community. Most of the time we are perfectly safe..."

Wait a minute. A gated community. The thought struck her as Melody's voice faded into the recesses of her brain. The killer knew the entry codes. But, then again, all the major delivery carriers did. And the pizza and Chinese restaurant drivers. Only God could determine how many people learned the code since the take-out food industry typically had a large turnover of employees. Or so a magazine article she read several months ago stated. Add in the friends and families of the residents, and it easily equaled half of the population of Alamoville. What a false sense of security.

Janie turned on the local evening news as she crocheted a new tea cozy for the church bazaar. Waiting for the weather forecast, she half-listened to the reports from around the city and state until one sentence caught her ear.

"A recent development has occurred in the law suits against Texas prisons for not being air-conditioned. You may recall when several inmates perished from heat exposure at the Wallace Pack Unit near Navasota last summer. Temperatures climbed over one hundred degrees for ten straight days. The unit houses over sixty men in their seventies and many more over the age of fifty-five."

She set down her needlework and reached for the remote. Her thumb pressed the button four times to jack up the volume. The anchor continued.

"Families of the victims gathered testimonies from former inmates, but those still incarcerated are reluctant to speak out. A few, however, proved quite verbal. One such person, Edwin Newman, was recently found murdered in a retirement community near Alamoville. Police have yet to connect his death to his willingness to come forward and testify against the Texas State Prison system. However, the attorney for one family is concerned Newman's death will silence other witnesses."

Janie set down the remote control and picked up her phone. She hit the one to speed dial her daughter.

"Mel, it's Mom. No, I'm fine. Is Blake around?"

Her daughter's voice deflated. "He's gone to get Jaime from practice. He should be home in an hour."

"Okay, honey. Tell him to call me this evening when he gets a chance. I want to let him in on the recent incidents over here. I also want to ask him a question, but I promise not to take long."

After five minutes of placating Melody's ruffled feathers and discussing the grandkids' latest accolades, Janie hung up. She glanced at the mantel clock. 6:22. May as well hobble to the kitchen and heat up some more bisque soup for dinner.

Her mind flopped the news report over and over like a pancake on a not-yet-hot-enough griddle. Could the report and Edwin's death be related? Two theories existed. First, someone opportunistically burgled the wrongly accused man to get his almost a quarter-million-dollar settlement. Or, a shady character angrily silenced him for his whining about prison conditions. But would the killer not shoot Edwin and leave him on the floor of his garden home?

No, this smelled of a clever, premeditated plot. Edwin's murder had all the markings of a professional hit. It took time and effort to dice a body into pieces and dispose of the parts. Which meant someone held a mighty grudge. Not because of his mistaken identity. The notion dead-ended somewhere in South America. Even if he faked his death to stave off the authorities, Edwards would never surface now, nor would the robbery money.

Dollars to donuts, the hitman hijacked a delivery van, transported the body to another location to slice and dice it, and returned to unload the remains in the dumpster hours before the garbage disposal truck arrived. That way, no odor, no flies, and nobody would detect them in a truck container filled with hundreds of plastic bags. Except for two Bunco Biddies who decided to power walk in that direction Tuesday morning and happened to be taking a breather at the right time and place.

Janie sighed. She located a note pad and wrote down her questions.

1. How did the interview with Edwin's old inmate go? Ask Blake.

2. Did the inmate ever suffer from heat stroke last summer? What about Edwin?

3. Why was no money found on the scene? Did a check get deposited into a bank account? There are only two branches in Alamoville.

4. Any delivery vans accidents reported in the past week or two?

5. Where can someone chop up a body? Meat packing plant? Butcher? Surgical unit? Coroners lab? Mortuary?

Janie read over her list and nodded. The memory of the raw hamburger odor tickled her nose. Must be a meat packer or a butcher's. She underlined both. *My still slightly-throbbing foot may be sidelined, but my brain cells will remain in the game.*

CHAPTER TWENTY-SIX

Blake called at seven-thirty.

"Can you come by this evening for a chat. I might have a new development."

Blake didn't mask the tiredness and frustration in his voice. "We're just sitting down to dinner."

"Of course. Which is important. You never get a chance to be with your own family anymore."

The silence iced her phone receiver.

Janie swallowed her words. "This can wait. How about in the morning?"

"Is this about your attacker?"

"I think so, yes. Hindsight being twenty-twenty and all. Lying here mulling the whole thing over, you understand." She decided, since he had not heard the news program, not to mention the special report until he sat across from her face to face.

He grumbled something to Mel in the background. "Okay. Eight too early?"

Janie smiled into the receiver to lilt her response. "Perfect. Thank you ever so much, Blake. Especially since I can't quite come to you."

His tone softened. "Right. Because of your hurt foot. Of course you can't." More murmuring. Then his voice returned to the receiver. "Take it easy and get some rest. We'll talk tomorrow. Shall I bring coffee and donuts?"

"One of those breakfast tacos from the drive-through near the highway would be nice."

He snickered. "Deal. See ya, Janie. Oh, and try not to worry."

She clicked off and stared at her phone. "And I hope you don't choke on your taco, dear Blake, when I tell you what I suspect."

CHAPTER TWENTY-SEVEN

At 8:05, three sharp raps pounded on Janie's front door. Had to be Blake. He never used the doorbell.

Sure enough, she heard a key scrape the lock. He sidestepped through the opening with two coffees and a take-out bag in hand. "Good morning."

"To you, too. Let's sit in the kitchen where I can rest my leg on a chair." Janie wobbled on her contraption, missing the edge of her dining room buffet by a hair. Blake sucked in his breath. Janie glanced back. "It's okay. I'm getting more sure-footed with it."

"Pun intended?" He set the breakfast on the dinette table and turned to the sink to rinse off his hands. "Is your injury doing any better?"

"You mean my foot or my lip?"

With his back to her, he chuckled. "Both, I guess." He swiveled to face her as he dried his fingers on a dishcloth. "You are one tough ol' bird. Told Mel that just the other day."

She cocked an eyebrow, but couldn't hold her stern expression after he winked. "I'll take that as a compliment, then."

"Good." He sat down across from her and bowed his head to bless their meal. She followed suit.

After taking a large bite of taco he began. "So, why am I here, Janie?"

She wiped her mouth with the skimpy paper napkin which came in the sack. "Edwin stayed in Watson Pack Unit, correct?"

He nodded as he sipped from the designated mouthpiece in the plastic cup lid.

"I heard on the news last night some inmates filed a law suit..."

Blake pressed his spine into the spindles of his chair. "Yes, Janie. Their attorneys filed a civil action case. Seems several prisoners succumbed to the heat during the hot summers we've had since 2008. And of course, last summer, the temps hovered over one hundred for weeks on end."

"Why aren't the prisons air conditioned?"

"County ones must be cooled to at least seventy-eight degrees since those who are incarcerated are still awaiting trial. You know. Innocent until proven guilty, so we have to treat them better. They're still viable citizens with rights. But the state prisons which house the convicted are another story. Tax payers never approved the expense. And the more secure they build these facilities, the more air-tight they become. They don't call it the 'hothouse' for nothing." He stretched his chest forward over the table and glared into her elderly, smoky blue eyes. "What is this all about?"

Janie ran her finger along the cardboard holder on her cup. "Did you get a chance to speak to Edwin's old inmate? Did he ever become ill from the stifling conditions?"

"Ah, you think Edwin Newman became a stool pigeon and so someone slapped a contract on him?"

"It's possible, right?"

Blake pushed from the table and crossed one leg over the other. "Hmmm. You know, I'll be honest. I put off driving all the way to Navasota, but I will go there now." The small wrinkles at the edge of his eyes crinkled. "Worth investigating, at any rate."

"I thought I'd send Betsy Ann or Ethel to the newspaper archives again to scan through the articles. The news story stated Edwin had been one of the complainers. Of course, his being falsely accused overshadowed a lot of the other inmates' complaints." She snapped her fingers. "Or, put the limelight on him even more."

"Janie." His tone took on that of a school monitor in detention hall.

"Well, why not use us, Blake? You're overbooked as it is until your partner returns from leave. The murder happened here and we feel helpless. We can spend hours doing grunt work."

His mouth curled up on one side. "Like perusing old court transcripts?"

Janie crossed her arms. "Waste of time."

He reached over and patted her wrist. "Thanks for the info. Now I won't have to plow through them."

Her face brightened.

Blake rose. "Okay. You and your Bunco gals can do some background checking. It's your right to do so and I can't stop you. But, Janie." He bent over her with both hands pressing on her shoulder. "You received one threat already. Be careful."

"We will. Promise."

"Gotta get." He kissed her on the forehead, grabbed his coffee cup, and left.

As he closed the door, Janie slapped her forehead. She forgot to tell him about the mysterious van. Ooh, she hated becoming old and forgetful.

Janie punched speed dial number five to call Betsy Ann. "Can you come over in a few?"

Betsy Ann hesitated. "Well, I threw laundry in the washer ten minutes ago so it should be through in fifteen. I'll be over as soon as I shove it in the dryer."

"Super. Ethel is coming as well."

"What about Mildred?"

Janie pondered how to respond. Mildred said she had too much to do, yet her excuse fell into the lame category. A jitteriness in her manner lately seemed out of character. Something ate at her friend's psyche more than her puppy's snout and Janie didn't understand what. She told Betsy Ann her concern.

"Well, maybe the idea of finding out more freaks her out. He did live, and die, next door to her. Burying your head in the sand can be a form of defense."

At times, Betsy Ann appeared ditzy, but at others, like now, she seemed to be the wisest friend Janie possessed. "I imagine you're correct. See you in a few."

The three friends huddled around the kitchen table, the fourth chair reserved for Janie's swollen foot.

Betsy Ann nodded to her. "Your lip is looking much less like a raspberry stuck to the corner of your mouth."

Janie touched where the cut still hurt. "Thanks. I guess."

"How scary for you. Do you think he's an ex-con?" Ethel's eyes stretched into wide circles.

"He fit the bill. Which is why I called you to come over." Janie rubbed her hands together as her smile widened, despite the sting of pain. "Blake came to his senses and agreed to let us do some background investigating."

Ethel high-fived her. Betsy Ann squealed. Mrs. Fluffy, who rested on Janie's good foot, dashed behind the living room curtains, one of her favorite hiding places.

"Where do we begin?"

Janie scrunched her neck into her shoulders. "The newspaper archives."

"Again?" Ethel blew an elongated sigh through her lips.

Betsy Ann patted her on the shoulder. "I haven't been yet. Let me do that. You're better at sniffing out other clues."

"But Betsy Ann, you are a pro at getting people to talk. People open up to you like a new Ann Landers."

She blushed. "Look who's talking? Besides, I didn't glean much from the conversations. People are tired of talking about it."

Janie templed her hands. "Still seems strange no one saw anything."

Ethel raised a forefinger. "Except for Peggy Williams and Marge Roberts. Both sighted a delivery van."

Janie laid a hand on Ethel's forearm. "Yes, and you are the one who discovered that fact from Peggy. What did I tell you? You are good at gathering info. Take your mystery filing system. I mean, does anyone have anything to rival it?"

Ethel's facial muscles relaxed. "Okay. You're right. So what can I do?"

Janie thought for a minute. "Somehow, we need to find out if such a vehicle has recently been in accident. Take some of the biddies and peruse the public police reports in the newspapers of the surrounding towns over the past month. Most have weekly editions. Talk with the townspeople in and around the cafes to see if they know anything at all. Make it a road trip."

Ethel smiled. "I'll call Ann and Babs. They will make it a fun day."

"If you don't find anything, then have Betsy Ann check the Austin daily papers. The answer could lead us to the van's owner. Also, check to see if someone stole one since Edwin's release from prison."

"Speaking of which?" Betsy Ann tilted her head. "A moving van never showed up, did it?"

Ethel gave her a quick, well-duh smile. "Most likely a man imprisoned for close to ten years doesn't own much."

"That's right. He'd have to buy new stuff, wouldn't he?" Janie crossed her arms. "Maybe Mrs. Jacobs misunderstood him. A smaller truck probably delivered the folding table and chairs and the blow-up mattress."

Betsy Ann's mouth formed a silent "O".

Janie slammed her hand on the Formica, which rattled her visitors. "Well, it's seems likely Edwin waited to lease a condo before he bought furnishings. My guess is he shopped on the web. Furniture and discount stores use delivery vans. Perhaps that is what people saw."

Ethel titled her head up to the ceiling. "Hmm. It's a possibility. But they usually are bigger than the postal delivery ones. Besides, why would come so late in the evening? And then return in the wee hours?"

"True." Janie's body slunk. "And nothing else showed up after his death."

"Well, our little neighborhood crime did make front headlines. Perhaps somebody called to verify and our manager halted the order. Or his niece did."

Janie narrowed her eyes. "If only we had a way to contact her. I wish to ask her some more questions."

Ethel's mouth stretched into a long grin. "There is. I subscribe to a people search site. We can pull up her address and phone number in a snap."

The other two responded at the same time "You do?"

She shrugged. "Passes the time."

CHAPTER TWENTY-EIGHT

Betsy Ann stared into her closet. What did one wear for a day at the newspaper archives? She decided on comfortable, navy polyester slacks, a white shell top, and over that, a three-quarter-length sleeved blouse-jacket in a soft flowered pattern of white, blues, and moss green. Navy flats and her navy loop earrings completed her ensemble. She slipped a tablet into her purse and made sure she took two pens, just in case. What if she got all the way downtown and one of the pens ran dry? With these new felt points, you never knew. Even when they appeared to contain ink, they quit halfway through as you jotted down something important.

With the keys to her trusty compact car in hand, she crossed the alley and clicked the key-less entry button. The friendly beep-beep greeted her. She slid into the driver's seat and patted the dashboard. "Good morning to you, too."

The traffic into Austin trudged slow but steady. Betsy Ann learned long ago if she stayed in the middle right lane all the way in, she'd be in the correct one to exit toward downtown. But the one way streets always muddled her. She found the building she needed but took another fifteen minutes to turn around, head the right way, and find a parking spot. After the third time circling, she settled for one of the hourly lots. Three dollars for sixty minutes? She handed the man a five and a one in case it took her over an hour to glean from the microfiche what Janie wanted her to find. The cost put a damper in her lunch allowance, but no matter. She hated parallel parking and feeding coins in meters.

Now for the two-block traipse through the Texas heat to the main entrance. The bank marquee read ninety-one degrees. And only ten in the morning? They were in for another long, hot summer if this kept up. She fanned herself with her hand as she walked.

The revolving doors swished cold air onto her face. Once inside, she stood for a minute on the marble floor, heart thumping as her core temperature declined.

"Are you lost, pretty lady?"

"Oh?" Betsy Ann swiveled in her shoes to meet a white, wavy-haired man with cornflower eyes. A suave grin touched his dimples, snuggled by a well-trimmed snowy beard. He wore a baby blue polo shirt and khaki trousers. He gave her a dip of his head.

"Name's George McGuffy. May I have the honor of helping you locate what you need?"

"Well, I..." *Why am I stammering?* She placed her hand on her chest. "I'm looking for the newspaper archives."

His smile widened. "As am I. Shall I lead the way?" He offered her the crux of his elbow.

Betsy Ann's cheeks heated. "I, well, I guess so...if it's no trouble."

"None at all. I consider it a pleasure."

"Very well, then." She laced her arm through his.

He gestured with the other hand. "This way to the elevators, unless you wish to take the stairs?"

"What floor are we going to?"

He gave her a wiggle of his eyebrows. "One down. The basement." With a chuckle, he punched the button.

The doors opened as if on command and the couple stepped in. George pressed the B on the panel and the elevator jerked to begin its descent. He patted her hand draped through his arm. "Don't let the noise bother you. It's old but quite reliable. Like me."

Being with him alone in a confined space made Betsy Ann a tad squeamish. She struggled to make conversation. "So, Mr. McGuffy..."

"Oh, no, Please. Call me George."

"All right, George. Do you come here often?" She winced. *Sounds like a pick-up line at a sleazy bar.*

George's demeanor remained the same. "I do. Quite often, as a matter of fact. I am a retired professor of Texas history. With time on my hands, I decided to write a historical fiction about the life and times of the students killed by Charles Whitman in 1966."

"Oh, yes. The sniper who holed up in the clock tower at the university my freshman year."

He turned to face her. "Really? My junior year. English major with a minor in U.S. History."

"Elementary education and the arts."

The door dinged. As it opened, the odor of stale air-conditioning and old papers assaulted her nose.

George chuckled. "Ah, the aroma of times gone by." He motioned down the hallway. "Have you been to the university archives?"

She shook her head.

"No? There's a real treat. Perhaps after we finish here..."

She blushed, again. "My research only goes back a year or so to one incident."

"Wedding or funeral?" He pushed open the glass doors.

She gave him a sly smirk as she slid through. "Prison deaths from heat prostration." As she sashayed up to the information desk, Betsy Ann detected his eyes boring into her. She bet they twinkled with curiosity.

The words began to blur after skimming fifteen articles in the Austin paper alone, plus eighteen more from Dallas, Houston, and Navasota. After the seventh one, her enthusiasm had waned though she kept reading. She discovered the families of the prisoners rallied behind four inmates of Wallace Pack Unit complaining of inhumane conditions. Three, aged fifty-five or older, suffered with health conditions often aggravated by heat. So did a younger one in his twenties. She jotted down their names and then sorted through the other articles to glean any more information. Near the bottom, an article posted February 12, 2015, showed the class action lawsuit still pending in Federal Court. She couldn't locate any more reports after that date. Betsy Ann rubbed her temples and sighed.

"Not finding what you need?"

She jolted and hit her knee on the wooden support of the table.

"I'm sorry. Didn't mean to startle you." George McGuffy slid into the chair next to her.

She massaged her knee. "It's okay. My eyes need a break anyway."

His scanned the screen. "I thought you joked with me earlier about your reason to be here. Now why would such a classy lady like you want to get her nails dirty with something such as this?"

His compliment once again made her blush. "I am helping a friend. Well, I'm interested as well." She edged a tad closer and lowered her voice. "You see, Janie and I found one of the released inmates diced up in our retirement village dumpster. We are helping the police figure out why, and Janie thought perhaps the lawsuit last summer might have a bearing on the case."

George sat back and cocked a bushy, white eyebrow.

Oh, no. My mouth ran like a broken-handled toilet again. She bit the inside of her lip.

"Well, you *are* more than just a pretty-faced gal."

That twinkling wink again. Betsy Ann squirmed in her chair. She eyed him for a moment, trying to determine if he should be classified as a charmer or a rogue.

"Oh, dear. I came on too strong." He bowed his head and clucked his tongue. His attention fell to the mild liver spots on his hands. "My son keeps chiding me about living alone these past six years since Emma passed on, rest her soul."

"Oh, I am sorry."

He raised his eyes to her. They shimmered. "Says I need to get back in the game. But I guess I am a tad rusty."

She gave him a sympathetic grin.

"Forgive me if I intruded upon your generosity. I'll leave you alone." He started to get up.

"Are you hungry? Is there a restaurant close by where we could grab lunch?" The questions blurted off her tongue before her brain realized they did.

The twinkle returned. "I am running on empty, now that you mention it. I frequent an affordable diner a block away. Décor isn't fancy, but they serve everything from chicken fried steaks to chili to salads. Best pecan pie in the city."

Betsy Ann clicked off the microfiche screen. "Lead the way, my good man."

His backbone became arrow-straight as a delicious smile tickled his beard. Arm in arm, the two waltzed to the elevators, though Betsy Ann swore her feet hovered a few inches off the ground.

CHAPTER TWENTY-NINE

"I am afraid I need to return to the archives tomorrow, Janie. The lawsuit is still pending in Federal Court, so I didn't locate much in the current papers. Thought I'd try papers in Washington, D.C. I hoped a computer search would be of more help. But mine is a dinosaur and way too slow."

Janie didn't respond right away. Something in Betsy Ann's voice indicated her friend didn't reveal the whole truth. Besides, the community offered a state-of-the-art computer room. "Betsy Ann? What's going on?"

"Nothing. My eyes became weary, that's all. All the small print. And the legal jargon, ugh. I did get the names of the inmates in Watson Pack who complained, and found one interview which included our dear friend Edwin's name…well, Norman back then. All the others are still incarcerated as far as I can tell. The families of men who died or succumbed to heatstroke in other prisons over the past few years also hired attorneys and filed civil suits."

Janie rapped her pen on the coffee table. Being laid-up scraped the edge of her nerves. "Perhaps I can ride with you tomorrow."

"Oh, no. You shouldn't. The doctor said to rest. It's only been a few days. Besides, I walked a good block and a half. Parking is atrocious." Her words spilled out of the receiver like a rapid fire machine gun.

"All right, calm down. I can browse with my laptop propped up on a pillow as I lay here trying not to be bored. Why don't you see what you can discover about his release and how it all came about?"

"Be happy to. And I can check the Austin paper for stolen vans or accidents while I am there. All this archives stuff is kinda fun." A nervous giggle.

Betsy Ann's bubbly and a tad ditzy personality did lend itself to the sniggers, but to Janie these sounded different. She let it go, for now. "Talk later, hon."

"Byeeeee."

Janie hung up and stroked Mrs. Fluffy. "She acted as giddy as a school girl. If I didn't know better...oh, but that's absurd. She's a year younger than me."

She got up and slid, hobbled, and grunted into the kitchen on her new contraption, hands steadying herself on furniture as she went. Easier than crutches on the arm pits, but she still needed practice. She peered into the freezer and decided on Roseanne's tamale pie for dinner. As the savory casserole swirled in the microwave, she opened one of the salad-in-a-bag varieties, complete with dressing and topping, and prepared a third of it. As she ate at the dinette table, she cocked an ear at the local news on the radio. Nothing exciting happened that day other than the stock market nose-diving again.

After dinner, Janie's eyes scanned the laptop screen as she propped her foot on a throw pillow. She cyber-searched for any articles on Texan prisoners' lawsuits and found a few, the majority dated in June, 2014. Next, she researched by names and places, but only sketchy information came up on the monitor.

Betsy Ann's right. Like finding a needle in the haystack. After an hour of frustration and perseverance, she unearthed an article from the Dallas paper. The report stated one prisoner, released several years back, had been the first whistle blower to come forward about the sweltering conditions in Texas prisons. The action began a cascade of legal filings by families of prisoners who perished during the past few summers. All claimed previous medical conditions, though, from what she gleaned. At last she found one lone article dated last March which relayed the civil suit as still pending in federal court, so no action had been taken by the state legislature despite the fact Texas faced another record-breaking summer of heat. But nothing since. She rubbed her eyes and stretched her hands over her head.

"Well, Mrs. Fluffy." She re-positioned the cat which had confiscated a majority of the pillow at her head by encircling her scalp like a furry tiara. "Guess the public lost interest after a while. Reporters often put things on the back burner for more pertinent headlines to tantalize the American minds and sell papers."

She placed the portable computer onto sleep mode. Rolling on her hip to stretch for her cell phone, she texted a message to Betsy Ann and Ethel. "Found someone we should speak with regarding the heat issues. Trouble is, he lives near Dallas."

And I can't drive.

The screen of her phone revealed 9:42 PM. She yawned and snuggled back into her pillow on the couch, not willing to put forth the energy to wobble down the hallway to her bed.

The next morning, Betsy Ann perused the archives, but for George more than any news articles. At last she found him at the station by the window, leaning forward with his lips pursed as he read the minute print on the microfiche screen. He appeared dashing in a hot pink sports shirt and dark walking shorts. They accented his snowy, white hair and beard.

Takes a man secure in his own skin to wear such a color.

She peeled her gaze from her target and asked the clerk for the files dating from March 2015 through April 30th. Receiving her disc, she strolled in his direction. By happenstance—or perhaps Providence?—a young student packed his notes in a satchel and vacated the monitor catty-cornered to George.

She smiled as the young man edged past her before sliding into the still-warmed wooden chair. Making a slightly louder than normal rustling noise as she flipped to a blank page on her writing tablet, she let out a deep, audible sigh.

George's eyes dashed from his machine. When they landed on her, his countenance brightened. He waved and mouthed the word, "Hi."

She glanced through fluttery eyelashes and gave him a soft smile of faked surprise.

He scooted next to her and whispered near her ear. His breath upon her neckline sent a shiver up her arm. "Well, well. We meet again. Still crime solving?"

Her cheeks flushed in the demure way her grandmother taught her when Betsy Ann turned sixteen.

His eyes took on the familiar twinkle.

Hook, line, waiting for the sinker. He may be rusty, but I'm not, I guess. "This is tedious work, but I am only glad to do it in order to assist that poor family in finding closure."

The man's Adam apple bobbed. "You are a kind-hearted soul." He laid his hand across hers.

She peered through her eyelashes. "Want to help?"

His face lit up. "Sure. Be happy to do so. Perhaps, in a while, we can grab lunch? Have you ever been to the tea room in the historic hotel?"

She sucked in her breath. "No, I got their cookbook for Christmas last year."

"Ah. Your, ahem, friend gave it to you?" He released his fingers from hers.

"We are both widows."

His eyes held a question mark.

She quickly replied, "Oh, but we live alone. She has a condo about a block from mine. We play Bunco together, along with lots of other ladies."

George's expression gleamed. "I see. Well, perhaps we'll order a piece of that cake today. My treat. Though I bet you add a little extra something to yours to make it more scrumptious. I can tell you know your way around a kitchen."

She fanned her hand in front of her. "Is it a touch hot in here today?"

His grin touched his sideburns. "Tell me where to begin, pretty lady. I am your humble servant."

She handed him a disc. "We are looking for any information on Edwin Newman's release and mistaken identity. Also scan for the name Edward Norman."

He wrote both of them down. "Got it."

As he pulled away, the whiff of his cologne feathered her nose, the brand her late husband always wore. A slight tug on a heartstring brought a tear to her eye.

Ethel tapped her teeth as she waited for Janie to answer her call. Ann and Babs huddled next to her in the stairwell of the Red Oak courthouse. Finally, she heard Janie's slightly out-of-breath voice. "Hello?"

"Janie. We hit the jackpot! A delivery van was stolen from the Two Cheap Brothers' Movers. It was a used one, you know. Like the kind you rent to move yourself? They reported it stolen three weeks ago."

"Well, well. I don't suppose it had a dent in it?"

Ethel's grin stretched as she answered. "Yep. One of the movers backed his pick-up into it and it was at the body shop pending the insurance claim adjustor eyeballing it."

"Hmm. And a body shop would be the perfect place to paint it so it looked more generic. But why not repair it while you are at it?"

"Dunno. Rush job?"

"Possibly. Or they hoped the paint would cover it. Great work, ya'll." Janie's tone sounded more chipper than it had in days. Ethel felt her chest swell.

"I have info as well. I found out Marjorie Spellman's cell phone number."

"Really? How'dja do that?"

"I called the Funeral Parlor and told them the Sunset Acres Bunco Club wanted to send flowers but didn't know how to reach her. The receptionist recalled us and gave me the information in a heartbeat, no questions asked. Sometimes, being elderly has its advantages."

"Indeed." That's how she, Babs, and Ann sweet-talked the desk clerk at the police station into revealing the details to them beyond the one sentence report in the Red Oak Reader. Of course, the excitement in the young cop's eyes help to loosen his tongue. Not too many burglaries happen in Red Oak, Texas.

"Now, Ethel. Do you feel up to paying Mrs. Spellman a visit and sweetly pumping her for info?" Janie paused. "I would myself, but…"

"Roger that. Let me get a pen and you can give me her number."

CHAPTER THIRTY

Ethel eyed herself in the rear view mirror. A fresh dab of Reticent Rose lipstick and a poof of the sides of her hair with spray to thwart the ravages of the Texas humidity boosted her confidence. She whispered to her reflection. "You can do this."

149 Sycamore. The house sat in an older neighborhood in Alamoville, one which investors and real estate agents no doubt claimed to be up-and-coming. A modest wood-slat home with a large front porch and attached carport greeted her. It needed a new coat of paint and the lawn a good feeding and weeding. So Edwin Newman's niece resided here now, huh?

She lifted the cellophane-wrapped grocery store bundle of daisies off the front passenger seat and strolled up the cracked sidewalk. She almost lost her footing on the chipped concrete steps but managed to right herself before tumbling onto the welcome mat. With a deep breath, she punched the doorbell.

Click-clacks of shoes echoed inside and the door opened. "Yes, are you Ethel? Please, come in."

Ethel handed her the summer arrangement.

"Oh, how thoughtful. Go on in and sit down while I put these in water." Marjorie Spellman disappeared down a narrow hall, most likely to the kitchen at the back of the house.

She stood in the hall while the niece got a vase. The plastered walls showed spider vein cracks. The scuffed and stained original wood floors needed refinishing. A threadbare oriental runner covered the center of the foyer. To the right, an archway revealed a room with large windows and an age-worn, bronzed chandelier. Nothing else. No furniture in sight. Faded wallpaper in a light green with magnolia blossoms peeled at the seams. To the left, another arched entry led into a small siting room with a settee, two chairs and a bricked-up fireplace. This room had a soft rose wall color which accented some of the colors of the floral area rug. The Victorian-styled couch had been reupholstered in a time-appropriate cream on cream design. Needlepoint pillows in muted tones of pink, beige, and baby blue basket weave stitched squares accented the rolled arms. The chairs flanking the fireplace were in a striped pattern of maroon, beige, and light blue. An arrangement of silk flowers in like colors perched on the mantle along with two crystal candlesticks with maroon candles. A print of one of Monet's water lilies painting hung on one wall. In front of the window, a Queen Anne end table held some knickknacks and a few family photographs.

Ethel tiptoed over to them and glanced long enough to recognize one of a much younger Edwin with his arm around Marjorie, who appeared to in her late twenties. A posed portrait of an elderly man and woman—her parents?—sat to the right while one depicting a young family propped to the left. A closer peek revealed the girl to be Marjorie at about age three in a back yard with the same couple, but a good thirty years younger.

At the sound of Marjorie's footfall, Ethel dashed to perch on the edge of one of the upholstered chairs. Her hostess entered with the posies in a lead crystal vase which she set on the table in the window. She picked up the framed picture of her and Edwin and brought it to Ethel. "This was taken about twelve years before he, well, became wrongly convicted. He came to celebrate my thirtieth birthday. Brought me this."

She fingered a heart shaped pendant on a delicate filigree chain around her neck. In the center sat an amethyst jewel. "My birthstone."

"How pretty. He must have cared deeply for you."

She nodded as her lips turned downward. "Yes, after we both grew up, I guess we sort of got close." She bent to sit on the couch, but then jumped up like a Jack-in-the-Box. "Oh, I haven't offered you any refreshments. I have iced tea and coffee cake. Hope that's okay."

Before Ethel responded, the woman zipped out of the room, leaving her guest still holding the photograph. She studied the picture in more detail. Edwin smiled, yet under his cheery expression, she detected a shadow of something else, like a secret. His eyes resembled dark sequins, as if he veiled another emotion. A roughness etched his demeanor like scratchy, light gray pencil marks eking outside the lines of a child's drawing. Could he have been as innocent as Marjorie supposed?

The hostess returned with a tray which she lowered to the coffee table. She handed Ethel a glass with a paper napkin cupping the bottom. "There. That's better."

The woman seemed so eager for company, her jittery movements made Ethel's stomach dance. "So, why did you decide to move to Alamoville?"

"Oh, when Edwin got out of prison, he wanted to settle in a retirement community so he wouldn't have to cook. He'd become used to regular schedules and a community environment. Being with people his own age appealed to him since he had been around seniors in the unit for so long." She smoothed her skirt over her knees. "I'd hoped he'd come live with me in Oklahoma where he grew up, but he turned me down. Said it would be too hard to come home."

"I can imagine so."

Her head made three rapid shakes. "Yes, so I decided to rent a house close enough to visit and perhaps go out to eat now and then. He'd hoped to get a driver license again and buy a car." She waved her arms around the room as her eyes glistened. "Now, here I am, and I don't know a soul."

Ethel swallowed the clump in her own throat along with a gulp of sweetened tea. An ice cube dislodged and clunked against her lip. Droplets of amber caffeine hit her white blouse.

Marjorie bounced to her rescue, paper napkin in hand. "Oh, I am so sorry."

"Not your fault. I put my big nose where it didn't belong." Ethel's face blushed at her Freudian slip. She cleared her throat as she dabbed her laced trimmed top. "Speaking of which, do you had any idea who might have wanted Edwin..."

The niece's eyes widened.

"Well, my best friend, Janie, is one of the ladies who discovered, um... your brother. Her son-in-law is the chief detective investigating the case and he has decided we can be of assistance by gleaning some background information. We decided it is the least we can do."

Marjorie's hand trembled as she slid a piece of coffee cake onto her plate. She took a bite and chewed.

Ethel waited.

"I guess it's all right to tell you. Edwin wrote to me quite often. I imagine I alone believed in his innocence. I mean, he wasn't a saint. Don't get me wrong. He'd had a few run-ins with the law in his time. Bar brawls, disorderly conduct. That sort of thing."

The woman's eyes darted around the room as if the boogey man hid behind the sheet rock. *What frightened her?*

Ethel gave her an encouraging smile. "Few of us have squeaky-clean pasts."

"True. But he had a bit of a reputation in our town. Never finished high school, you see? Expelled for fighting. The local judge gave him an option. Go to jail, or join the Army. Edwin signed up, and in three weeks, they shipped him off to Kuwait. When he came back, he'd changed."

"How?"

She shrugged and took a sip of tea. "It's hard to explain. I guess when you witness the atrocities of war each and every day these things have an effect on you. He seemed withdrawn, more than usual, and sullen. Almost as if life itself had been sucked out of him."

Marjorie paused for a moment, then continued. "He floated from odd job to odd job, never finding a career. Drank a lot. Probably did drugs." She ran her finger over the ribbing of the sofa cushion.

Ethel pinched her lips together but bent forward, hoping her body language would encourage Edwin's niece to continue.

Her hostess took a breath and rose to pace the floor. "Most people around town considered him a loser. So when the news hit the papers he'd been convicted of robbing banks, well..."

"I understand. Our country treats so many of the returning soldiers in such an unfair manner. Some never adjust back into society. We have a few at Sunset Acres who still have a disconnected look in their eyes."

"Yes. As if the civilian world never fully accepted them."

"But you said he'd written you about something from prison?"

She blinked. "Yes." Her voice lowered and she returned to sit on the edge of the sofa. "The inmates were being stirred up over the conditions. Horrid food, tight quarters. To make matters worse, in the middle of the heat wave, they had no air conditioning, though the prison provided huge fans. Edwin wrote to me about it. Said the vibrating noise put everyone on edge. Hard to sleep or even hear yourself think. Cooped up behind bars, tempers began to flare."

"I can only imagine."

"Well, Edwin voiced a complaint about how ill the guy who lived in the cell next to him became, which fell on disgruntled ears. The guards tightened down the screws, so to speak, to keep the men under control. Some of them blamed Edwin for the punishment."

"Are you serious?"

She nodded as she wrung her disposable napkin through her fingers. "Edwin rubbed three or four the wrong way, which stirred the cauldron further. Once word got around he'd be released, it became even worse. He feared for his life. One prisoner who worked in the laundry with Edwin threatened him. If Edwin didn't do what he said once he got out, he'd have his thugs hunt him down and..." Her finger slid across her throat.

Ethel sat back. "Did you tell the police?"

Marjorie shook her head. "I'm afraid to. What if he finds out I snitched and comes after me?"

"Do you know his name?"

"No. Edwin never revealed the name." Her eyes darted around the room. She made a hush gesture with her forefinger to her lip. Marjorie got her purse and dug out a pen. She scribbled something onto one of the paper napkins and handed it to Ethel. In a whisper, she added. "But he kept mentioning this." She proclaimed in a louder voice, "I'll get some more tea."

She glanced back as she left the room.

Ethel cocked her head to read what she'd scrawled. L.W.?

CHAPTER THIRTY-ONE

A rapid tap-tap-tap sounded on Janie's back door. "Yoo-hoo. Janie. You home?"

She pulled herself to a sitting position on the couch with a sigh. "Where else would I be?"

Betsy Ann's flats clippity-clapped across the floor into the living room. "Well, I think I found a lead, with the help of George's eagle eye."

"Who's George?"

Betsy Ann lowered herself onto a chair opposite the couch. She placed her purse on her lap and gripped the handle with both hands. "A man I met at the archives yesterday."

Janie's eyebrows disappeared into her forehead.

"He used to be a history professor at the university in Austin, and he likes to scrounge through old news clippings for fun."

"Sounds like a real party guy."

Betsy Ann squiggled forward. "Oh, he is very polite, gentlemanly, old-fashioned and quite intelligent."

"And charming?"

She blushed. "Well, he seems to be attentive to a woman's needs."

Janie sat up straighter. "Excuse me?"

Her friend's face turned three deeper shades of red. "Not in that way. We were in the library, for heaven's sake." She fanned her neck. "What I mean is, he listens, he understands when to respond and when a compliment is warranted. All quite above board."

The tension in Janie's temples relaxed. "Oh, okay. You worried me a little because you seem so—I don't know—glittery."

"Well, he invited me to lunch." She held up two fingers. "Twice. Today at the tea room of the gorgeous 1800s hotel downtown. You know, the one whose recipe book you gave me."

"Humph. Melody's favorite spot. Not many men will set foot in there, as if the testosterone will be sucked out of them if they even glance at a cucumber sandwich."

"Exactly. But he figured I'd like it so he suggested it. "

"Sounds like a peach to me."

"Uh huh. Though walking the two blocks in this heat wave almost wilted me. And George made note of it. Afterwards, he offered to walk back to his car and pick me up so I wouldn't get overheated."

Janie spurted out a laugh. "I think he's already got you overheated, and then some."

Betsy Ann's lower lip curled down. "If you are going to make fun of me..."

"No. Of course not. I am sorry. Being incapacitated has pushed my grumpy button."

"Well, I imagine it is hard to lie around all day. Are you in pain?"

Janie rubbed her hand over the splint. "No, not so much now that my foot is stabilized. And I have been able to put an itsy bit of weight on the heel."

Betsy Ann waggled her finger. "The doctor said..."

"I know. What info did you...and George...glean from the microfiche?"

Her eyes lit up, making Janie realize why they put light bulbs over cartoon character's heads. "Oh, yes. I tucked it away so I wouldn't forget." She pulled a folded piece of paper out of her purse and reached across the coffee table to hand it to Janie.

Janie opened the print-out and skimmed the article dated April, 2015. The report stated James Snow, Attorney at Law, had been instrumental in bringing forth new evidence to prove Edwin Newman's innocence. "So?"

"So George recalled him to often be the attorney for disgruntled prisoners. We researched further and he represented three inmates from 2008 through 2010 in heat-related illnesses. In 2011, he filed civil suits for five in one unit who claimed to have contracted food poisoning from bad beef."

"Ah. An ambulance chaser, except he's more of a handcuff chaser, I guess."

Betsy Ann nodded. "Other attorneys call him the jailhouse dog, according to what George discovered. But here is the interesting thing. Marjorie Spellman had hired an attorney in Oklahoma, where she lived, to handle Edwin's case."

"Where Edwin grew up."

"Right. But this guy convinced her to fire the other one and go with him since he had a license to practice in Texas."

Janie titled her head to one side. "How did you find that out?"

Betsy Ann dug in her purse again and pulled out a small tablet. She licked her forefinger and flipped through a few pages. "Ah, here we go. An article in the Houston paper dated February 10th, which George located for me. But, of course, the reporter worded things more carefully."

"So? It makes sense, right? He was imprisoned here in this state."

"Yes, but the other attorney in Oklahoma could have been retained as a consultant. But this way, he didn't receive any compensation from the settlement."

"Ah." Janie twisted her torso to reach her glass of tea. After taking a long sip, she commented. "Am I guessing you think this might be a motive? I mean why kill Edwin? Why not snuff out the—what did you call him? The jailhouse dog?"

"Because Edwin instigated the change. According to the article, he wanted to hire Snow because he often proved to be the prisoner's advocate for several men in his unit."

"Still, an attorney chopping up a client? Doesn't fit the M.O."

Betsy Ann wrinkled her brow. "M.O.?"

"Modus operandi. His preferred method."

She nodded. "True. But hiring someone to do the dirty work might, yes?"

The doorbell dinged.

"I'll get it for you." Betsy Ann lifted herself from the chair and padded to the front door. Ethel burst in.

"I just had a nice long talk with Marjorie Spellman." Her eyes glowed with accomplishment.

Janie waved her into the room. "Do tell. Betsy Ann has information as well. Why don't y'all get yourselves something to drink from the fridge? Grab the tub of humus as well. The whole-wheat crackers are in the pantry."

A few minutes later, the three amateur sleuths gathered around the living room coffee table. Janie and Betsy Ann caught Ethel up on the conversation before listening to her report.

"She seemed jittery, as if she suspected the place to be bugged."

"So you think this L.W. may have had a grudge against Edwin?"

"Marjorie suspects something or she'd have told me his name out loud. Do you think he is out on parole?"

Betsy Ann waved her hand. "I bet he's still in jail and has people on the outside. You said it's easy to look them up on the computer, right?"

"Yes. Texas Public Information Act and all."

Ethel patted her hand. "I'll go get your laptop."

"Got it right here on the floor."

Janie placed it on her lap, clicked the keyboard and squiggled the shiny blue mouse with her right hand. "I am so glad Melody bought me this wireless contraption for my birthday. I never could figure out how to use the square in the center of the laptop. Hurt my finger after a while, and the cursor never ended up where I wanted." Her eyes dashed back and forth over the screen.

"Well, with such a bright, metallic color, you won't lose the thing often." Betsy Ann grinned.

"Unless Mrs. Fluffy bats at it and scoots it under the couch." Ethel scoffed as she leaned in to view the monitor. "Well?"

"Looking...looking. Ah, here. Weber, Lenny. Watson Pack Unit. Age 64. In for armed robbery, assault with a deadly weapon and attempted murder. Incarcerated 1982, transferred in 2009. Wow, a lifer."

The three women all turned to each other as sly grins etched their lips. Ethel rubbed her arthritic hands together. "At last. Now we are getting somewhere, ladies."

CHAPTER THIRTY-TWO

Janie phoned Blake to relay what her team had unearthed. He whistled over the fiber optic wires. "Well, I must say. You ladies are taking this seriously. Good job. We can take it from here."

She pressed her molars together. *Why do I feel as if I'm being dismissed?* She envisioned him patting her on the head, handing her a quarter for her efforts and telling her to return to the playground. "Blake, we can do more if you allow us to help."

"Such as?"

"Try to contact the Oklahoma attorney and get his spin. Talk to some of the released inmates and their families suing over the conditions, maybe even..."

"Whoa. If you are thinking of a road trip to Oklahoma or Navasota, think again. Beside, you're not supposed to leave the house, much less drive."

Janie exhaled a long breath. "Heard of an invention called email? And this thing called a phone can be used to speak with other people, too, Blake."

"Don't get sassy."

"My foot hurts and I'm sick and tired of this couch. My rear end keeps going to sleep."

He chuckled. "I know it's tough to have your wings clipped, old bird. You thrive on your independence, as I always suspected you would. I remember how worried Mel got after Jack died. I told her you'd be fine."

"She figured I shrivel up and suck my thumb, waiting for the grim reaper to find me and leave her an orphan. Matthew had his concerns as well, but my children should have known me better than that."

"How are he and Tiffany, and the kids?"

"A lot cooler in New Jersey than we are here. But, Blake, back to the subject at hand."

The sound of him shifting in his home office chair filtered into her ear, followed by the telltale squeak of the hinges as he sat back. She envisioned him with his boots propped on the desk. And her daughter's deep wrinkled frown if she caught him. The image made her giggle inside as he responded.

"Okay. Thursday, I'm interviewing Edwin's old roommate. I'll see if he'll tell me about Lenny Weber. I'll talk to the guards and the warden as well."

"And what do you want us to do, Blake?"

"Since I can't stop you, why don't you keep shaking the bushes for information? Someone hated Edwin Newman enough to kill him in such a heinous manner. Which took planning. What we call premeditation. I suspect you're correct. The perp had to have been hired for the job."

"A paid executioner."

He grunted. "Afraid so. The coroner's report confirmed the weapon to be a power saw of some sort. Like they use in a meat packing plant. I have a surveillance team monitoring the one about fifteen minutes west of Sunset Acres."

Janie's brain flashed. The man who had broken in her apartment had hands with a lingering odor of hamburger meat. Had she crossed paths with the murderer? "Blake?"

"Yes, Janie. I recall your statement about what your intruder's hands. Don't worry. Extra patrols are cruising your village. He won't get into your place again. Not on my watch."

Her throat muscles eased. "Thanks, Blake."

"That's what I'm here for, Janie. Just promise me one thing, okay?"

"Sure. What?"

"Let's not talk about this in front of Mel and the kids. You know how she worries about you."

Janie grinned. "I do. As if her daughterly duty demanded she get an ulcer because I'm looking seventy-five in the face in a few years."

Blake's chair squeaked again. "I hope I am half as active when I get to be your age and still have a sharp-as-a-tack brain like yours. You're destined to outlive us all, Janie. I plan to do everything I can to ensure it happens."

Janie's face warmed. She heard his unspoken message loud and clear. Blake Johnson now respected her as much as she did him. Who knew? "Goodnight, Blake."

"Night."

She sighed and stared at the black screen on her cell phone as a sliver of a smile etched across her lips. Sleuthing for the Alamoville police detectives might turn out to be a permanent thing. Wouldn't Jack have gotten a kick out of that?

"Here's to you, my love." She toasted the ceiling with her iced tea glass and nestled back into her pillow for some more internet surfing.

CHAPTER THIRTY-THREE

Thursday morning arrived with a mockingbird singing outside her window. Janie smiled for the first time in days. This evening, the girls would come to play Bunco. A break in the boring routine of slouching on the sofa as the world turned without her. As she scooted and hobbled to the kitchen to brew a cup of coffee, a ring tone on her cell phone played "Unchained Melody."

"Good morning, sweet daughter. How are you today?"

"My, don't you sound chipper? I have a surprise for you, Mom. I am sending the lady I have used for years from the Maid to Order service to come clean your condo this morning. That way, the place will be sparkling and shiny for the Bunco Biddies."

Janie squeaked a response as she tried to keep her heart from melting into her tear ducts. "Oh my, Mel. Are you sure? How thoughtful."

"Well, she is good. I trust her, and to be frank, I don't have the time. If you need help with laundry, she can do some as well. Her name is Miranda."

"What time?"

"Oh, in about an hour."

Janie rested her hip on the kitchen counter as the aroma of brewed coffee filled the room. "You get the best daughter of the year award."

Melody snickered. "Talk later, Mom. Gotta dash."

Janie shot a glance to the ceiling and mouthed the words, "Thank you, Lord."

The phone chimed again. Janie recognized Betsy Ann's number.

"Hi."

"Janie? Guess what? Last night, George located the ex-prisoner who filed the first civil action against the Texas prisons. And guess who his attorney is."

"No."

"Uh huh. The man lives near Dallas. George is picking me up in thirty minutes and we are going to go speak with him."

A splash of caution chilled Janie's face. "Whoa. Wait. You just met this guy. Are you sure you want to travel two to three hours and back with him?"

A nervous giggle came through the receiver. "Oh, Janie. If you'd met him, you wouldn't need to ask. Besides, Ethel is coming as well, so see? We'll have a proper chaperone. Since we aren't meeting the gentleman until twelve-thirty, we'll grab lunch on the way. We'll be back in plenty of time to meet so we can catch you up before the Bunco Biddies arrive at six."

"Oh, very well. I worry about you at times."

Betsy Ann sniffed. "Which is why you're a good friend, even if you do try to run everyone's lives."

"I do not!"

They both chuckled and hung up.

An hour later, Blake called. "Janie, I spoke with the warden on the phone. I have an appointment at two to speak with Edwin's old inmate. Lenny Weber transferred two weeks ago to the facility near San Antonio. Seems he caused quite a ruckus in Navasota and they decided to nip things in the bud. He's a pretty bad dude, with many connections on the outside."

"He did? That didn't come up on the computer."

"Perhaps the state data entry clerks are running behind. They have a lot of prisoners to keep up with, much less arrest records, transfers, paroles...."

"Hmmm, so you think he made have ordered the hit?"

"Too early to tell, but sure is a possibility. On the way to Navasota from the unit in Abilene in '09, his gang tried to hijack the transport van. The warden caught wind of several other attempts and the man is known for making demands of the prisoners who are being released. If they do jobs for him, he provides protection and income once they get out."

Janie thumped her fingernails on the back of the couch. "Sounds as if you may be on the right trail."

Blake laughed. "We'll see. Half of my job is tracking leads only to run into brick walls and dead ends."

"Thanks for the update. So we proceed as planned?"

"Yep. Keep researching at your end and trying to piece together Edwin's movements in the village from Friday until you two found him on Tuesday."

Janie snapped her fingers. "Which reminds me. Dark van with a dent in the door."

"What?"

Janie huffed a breath over her bangs. "My fault. I forgot to tell you. Ethel went to visit a friend of ours in the assisted section. Peggy Williams. She had a turn for the worst and her kids worried about her ability to live independently."

Blake's voice became rushed. "And...?"

"And, as she sat in her wheelchair in the observation lounge, she spotted a dark delivery truck with a huge dent on the passenger side drive through the security gates to the dumpster."

"When was this?"

"Two Mondays ago at a little after two in the morning."

"Indeed?"

"Yep. And she thought it strange not only because of the hour, but the fact she had seen the exact same one leaving Sunset Acres earlier in the evening. So whoever drove had fairly extensive knowledge of our community."

"Such as?"

"The gate code and the fact our trash pick-up is around seven on Tuesdays."

"Ahhh. So do you believe Edwin told his assaulter the code?"

"It is possible. "

"Which means he knew the perp."

"That's one theory. Here's another. My guess is the murderer either did his homework in hurry or has a relative who lives here. I can ask Mrs. Jacobs when she last had the code changed. I have six months ago in mind, but time flies at my age."

"Yes, do that. In the meantime, I'll send one of the men to go talk with Mrs. Williams."

"Oh, she'd love that. I don't think her kids visit her often. I will try to determine if Edwin had any visitors other than a woman who drank beer and had ruby lips."

"Janie, promise me you won't..."

"Oh, and another thing. The Red Oak police department reported a small moving van with a huge dent in the door stolen from a nearby body shop three weeks ago."

"Now, how in the world did you…?"

She cut him off. "Bye, dear. Your sweet wife has hired a maid to come clean the place and I must get dressed before she rings the doorbell."

CHAPTER THIRTY-FOUR

Blake stared at the phone for a minute. At times, his mother-in-law seemed so sharp and at others, a bit loony. Yet all the time, she could be charmingly aggravating. Well, he imagined older people might have different perspectives on things. He'd never been around anyone her age before. His grandparents died before he hit high school and his parents were killed in a car accident right after Jamie was born. As horrific as it was at the time, he considered it a blessing in disguise. He'd never witness them wither into feebleness or dementia.

Shuddering off the morbid segue, he jotted down the info on the stolen van and Peggy William's name and walked down the hall to the common area where three investigative detectives shared an office. Connor Hemphill sat hunched over his computer, his eyes darting back and forth at the screen.

Blake sauntered over and sat on the edge of the desk, unnoticed.

"Your wife better not catch you looking at that stuff."

Hemphill jolted. "Huh? No, sir. I'm checking inmate records of who has been released from Watkins Pack over the past year and who their parole officers are."

"Only kidding." He slapped him on the back. "I got another lead for you to follow."

The twenty-eight-year-old man pressed his spine into the back of his office chair, arms crossed over his chest. "Shoot."

Blake handed him the piece of paper. "Head over to Sunset Acres. Talk to this lady. She may have witnessed something. She's in the assisted living section. Oh, and be prepared to have your ear chewed off. Understand her family doesn't visit her much and she gets lonely."

The underling's mouth scrunched to one side. "Seriously?"

Blake snickered. "You'll make her day, if not her week, you ol' charmer."

"Right." Hemphill pushed his desk chair away and clicked off his monitor. "Want me to check in on your laid-up mother-in-law while I'm there?"

"I don't want to torture you. Besides, she's occupied this morning with other things. My cunning wife has seen to it."

Blake couldn't help but notice his officer's shoulders relax a touch. Hemphill nodded and turned to leave. He handed the other info to Phil Edwards, another one of his investigative team.

"Call Red Oak. Get the scoop on this robbery for me, will you? Thanks."

Having someone bustle around her as she perched on the couch like Queen Elizabeth on her throne unnerved the independent spirit in Janie. Miranda must have sensed this because her smile became extra sugary and she asked a myriad of questions to ensure she did what Janie wanted. After an hour, the cleaning woman brought in a basket of laundry, warmed from the dryer.

"You watch as I fold so I make sure everything is the way you like it."

Janie motioned her to sit. "Why don't you give me half? I can at least do that much."

Miranda smiled. "As you wish. I will put the second load in the machine."

In a few minutes, the sound of water rushing and a lid thumping closed echoed from the hallway. The maid came and plopped in one of the side chairs. "You have a wonderful condo, Mrs. Manson. Very spacious. Almost as big as Mildred Fletcher's."

"Oh?" Janie's eyebrows arched into her curls. "You know her?"

"Uh, huh." Miranda shook out a pair of slacks and folded them on the seam. "I cleaned on Saturdays for her when her nephew, Bobby, lived with her for a while."

"I remember. He moved in with her for about six months after he fell on hard times. He landed a job nearby about a month ago, right?"

"Yes. He works at the supermarket where my son, Juan, works. They are about the same age." Her lower lip pouted. "My Juan got in with the wrong gang, just like her Bobby. Sons, you try to raise them right, but..." She sighed.

"Well, you know what they say? Boys will be boys."

"Yes." She stopped for a moment, a towel draped over her lap. "But this store is run by a nice Christian man who believes in giving people a second chance."

"Hmmm." Janie dug deep into her memory to recall what petty crime Bobby had been convicted of doing. He'd been given probation and community service, but did he serve any jail time?

She recalled Mildred being heartbroken because he lost his football scholarship to the university and dropped out. His coach had banked on him making it to the pros. He definitely had the build for it, according to Mildred.

Miranda stood up, basket on her hip. "Well, I'll go put this on your bed. Is there anything else you need before I leave?"

Janie scanned the room, which glittered in the midday sunlight. An aroma of pine permeated the condo, and if she did say so herself, the cleanliness met a higher plane than her normal standards. When the maid returned to the living room to get her purse, Janie grinned. "I understand why Melody sings your praises, Miranda. Everything looks lovely."

The lady waved away the compliment and lowered her eyelashes. "Pfft. Not at all. Take care, Mrs. Manson. I hope your foot heals fast." She closed the door behind her.

Janie ate her lunch as she tuned into the Austin noonday news. Two more convenience store robberies and a group of kids keying cars with gang language in the outlet mall parking lot topped the headlines. Why did she turn the darn thing on? Noise, perhaps. After a while, the mantle clock's ticking in the silence got annoying. So did Mrs. Fluffy's snoring as she took her long overdue nap after cowering under the coffee table while Miranda shuffled about.

Four commercials later, the weather portion came on. The meteorologist predicted another four or five days of the heat wave before a twenty percent chance of showers might cool things off early next week.

The jingle for a news-breaking item hit. The anchor man picked up a piece of paper.

"This just in. State police officials have confirmed the botched breakout attempt to free Lenny Weber from his transport to a new prison unit near San Antonio two weeks ago has led to the arrest of a man named Emilio Lopez, believed to have befriended Edwin Newman while in the Watson Pack Unit. You may recall, Newman was falsely accused of three bank heists and had been released last month, only to be found dead in a dumpster at a local retirement community. Lopez, age thirty-two, is the son of one of the bank robbers with whom Edwin had been identified. He was placed on parole after serving a three-year term for petty theft. He and Edwin worked in the laundry facility at Watson Pack, though Edwin resided in the over fifty-five unit."

Janie speed dialed Blake's number.

He answered. "Yes, we know. I'm at the prison now. They processed Lopez fifteen minutes ago. I'm making arrangements to interview him now."

A tingly giddiness spread over her. Somehow, Weber, Lopez, and Newman all intertwined. Perhaps Edwin had not been as innocent as everyone thought? Hardly a coincidence he met Lopez's son while incarcerated. Possibly, Emilio Lopez sought him out, thinking he was Edward Norman.

She looked down at the tangle of crochet string Mrs. Fluffy played with on the rug. Yes, this case resembled the mess the cat made. Which way should she pull to unravel the jumble of threads?

CHAPTER THIRTY-FIVE

George's late model sedan sailed along I-35 as if gliding on butter, even over the construction zone's uneven lanes. "Will they ever finish this stretch of real estate? It seems as if this highway has been torn up for decades."

Ethel leaned forward, her head between the bucket seats in front. "Yep. Has been. As soon as they finish one section, they start on another. I remember driving from Austin to Waco for the college football games and snail-pacing through construction zones." She scoffed. "I'm not saying how long that's been."

Betsy Ann giggled.

They decided to eat brunch at Czech restaurant on the way to Hillsboro before the highway split into east towards Dallas and west towards Fort Worth. At twelve-thirty on the dot, they arrived, with the help of George's global positioning system, to Albert Washington's home in Grand Prairie. The clapboard house boasted a wide front porch. Washington sat in a rocker sipping lemonade as the threesome traipsed over the cracked concrete sidewalk flanked by threadbare, browning patches of grass.

The tall, lean man assisted the ladies up the rickety steps. "Howdy, you must be Mrs. Hunt and Mrs. Mitchell." He turned to George and narrowed his gaze. "And, you are who, sir?"

George's eyes twinkled. "Merely the chauffeur delighting in these lovely ladies' company for the day."

Washington gave him the-once-over look.

He extended a hand. "Name's George McGuffy, retired university professor in Texas government and history. So you see, I'm quite interested in hearing your story."

"Well, okay."

The man nodded and led them into his dim-lit living room. The space resembled its occupant. A touch disheveled and rough, yet a homey charm oozed through the walls. Albert Washington possessed the coarse edge many retain after experiencing prison life. However, humbleness exuded from his demeanor which gave Betsy Ann an immediate sense of trust. She and Ethel sat on the couch's edge as George pulled over a dining room chair. Albert nestled his six-foot bones into an easy chair with darker stains near the head rest and a few frayed edges around the arms. On the scuffed coffee table in front of them sat a tray with two glasses and a pitcher of ice-cold lemonade. A fly buzzed over store-bought sandwich cookies on a plate.

"Oh, let me get ya a glass, too, sir."

"Thank you, and please. Call me George."

He gave a short half-bow. "Mighty fine, George." He thumped across the pine floors into a green linoleum kitchen with metal cabinets.

Betsy swiveled to take in the decor as Ethel shooed the buzzing insect from tasting the cookies again.

Albert brought a glass and polished the rim on his shirttail. "Here ya go."

George gave him a grin, but Betsy Ann detected his jaw twitch at the idea of drinking out of the glass now. From the small amount of time she'd spent in his presence, she surmised fastidiousness had to be George's middle name. She brought her fist to her mouth to stifle a giggle.

Albert played mother and poured the drinks before settling back into his designated chair. After a long sip from his own glass, he pointed the beverage in their direction. "Now, tell me why you drove all the way up here to pay me a visit."

Betsy Ann wiggled on her cushion and pushed back a lock of hair. "We are interested in your civil suit against the prison system for the heat related illnesses..."

He shot forward, his voice louder and more brisk. "Lady, men died in there. I's seen it."

She dropped her gaze to her hands.

Ethel spoke. "We mean no disrespect, Mr. Washington. We simply want to learn what your attorney did. An inmate at the Watson Pack unit, who is now deceased, may have suffered from similar conditions, and we told his niece we'd find out what we could. We suspect he was killed because he complained too much."

The roughness disappeared from Albert's face. He lowered his chin. "Which is why I waited until I's out of the blasted hothouse before I blew the whistle. Feared for my life, I did. But my conscience wouldn't let me keep silent. People need to know."

George took a turn. "And you believe your attorney, as your spokesman and advocate, has made progress in letting the public become aware of these inhumane atrocities?"

Albert chuckled. "Yo sho' do speak like a professor. If you mean does anyone on the outside give a flip now, heck no. In fact, some folk say it serves the prisoners right to swelter after the crimes they've done. Why spend tax dollars on air conditioning for us in jail when law-abidin' citizens go without in our inner-cities?"

Betsy Ann raised her hand. "Mr. Washington. Are you telling us you were afraid someone would do you bodily harm if you reported these things while you were in prison?"

"Lady, you ain't ever been in jail, have you? You never make friends, you only size up your allies and your enemies and try to keep some space between them. If you complain about the conditions, the guards may punish the inmates you don't get along with so they'll come after you for being a stool pigeon. Whine, and a shiv ends up in your gullet." He zeroed in his gaze at her. "Clear 'nough?"

"Yes." She took a long drink of lemonade.

"Good."

The only sounds for a few seconds were the fly hovering over the food and the old, wooden ceiling fan blades wobbling above their heads.

Albert eased into the cushions of his favorite chair and crossed his leg. "Sounds like your friend, if he blew the whistle like me, didn't guard his back good."

"No, he didn't. Ended up chopped up in our community dumpster." Betsy Ann swished her hand over the cookies before taking one.

To their surprise, Albert burst out into a deep laugh. He wiped his eyes and nodded. "I done heard about that. He and I had the same attorney. They put him in the clink thinkin' he was another guy, right?"

"Yes." George volunteered. "These sweet ladies live there and they are trying to help bring justice to his senseless killing."

"Justice? Ain't no such thing. All about who has the best attorney and who rubs elbows with who. Even when you get out, you gotta be wary of the shadows, get my drift? Mind your p's and q's as my momma always said. Those still running things on the inside want to make sure you ain't snitching on them to your P.O. or the cops in order to keep them off yo' back."

Betsy Ann mouthed the letters to Ethel. "P.O.?"

She leaned in and whispered in her ear. "Parole Officer."

"Ah."

George spoke up again. "So, it would be feasible to believe Edwin Newman's death might have been due to the fact he made enemies in prison and they put a hit out on him?"

Albert rubbed his chin. "Possibly. They may have given him an errand to do to secure his safety on the outside and he didn't come through because he got that huge settlement from the State."

Ethel slapped her knee. "Never thought of that."

"Yes'm. 'Taint easy being an ex con. Hard to find steady work. No one wants to hire ya. You end up relying on the cartel to land you odd jobs. Mostly deliveries, get it? Make connections. Me, I was tempted but never sunk that low. I had family who helped out."

"I can tell you are an honest man, Albert Washington." Betsy Ann gave him a huge smile.

He chuckled. "Not too honest, ma'am. I did do fifteen years fo' robbing a 7-11. But I's learned my lesson. Wished I'd not been so cocky and stupid back then, but there you go."

A moment of uneasiness again clouded the small parlor. Ethel and Betsy Ann eyed each other.

Albert titled his head. "Course, the system probably ain't all that pleased about his circumstances. If I was them, I wouldn't want him blabbing stuff to the reporters about how they got him on trumped up charges. Ain't saying all law officials are corrupt, but he did embarrass a few of them. Maybe they feared he might get on some of them talk shows and too much attention might turn towards their boo-boo unless they shut him up. Just like roaches when you flick on the kitchen light, they'll scurry back to the cracks where they can hide."

The three guests exchanged gawks.

Ethel set her glass down. "Thank you, Mr. Washington. You have been a big help. With summer approaching fast, I hate to think about all those men existing without proper ventilation. Do you have a number for your attorney? We'd like to speak with him about helping any way we can."

He nodded and rose with effort from the sagged cushion. "Got his business card in the back. Take me a minute to locate the thing, okay?"

He returned with a yellow, lined piece of paper ripped from a tablet, on which he'd scrawled the attorney's name and two phone numbers. After handshakes and well wishes, the trio headed back to Sunset Acres.

Ethel buckled her seat belt in the back as George started the car. "Do you think some corrupt law officer would do such a thing?"

George shrugged. "They do on TV all the time, and doesn't art imitate life?"

Betsy Ann clucked her tongue. "I prefer living under a rock, assuming everyone is honest and trustworthy. Oh, why did I ever spot Edwin Newman's leg?"

CHAPTER THIRTY-SIX

Janie recognized the tell-tale sound of the postal truck's engine. The mantle clock bonged the half-hour. 12:30. *Right on time.*

She retrieved her metal peg-leg contraption. Despite the heat, a little fresh air could do her nothing but good. Bent knee strapped to the device, she edged through the front door and down the ramp to the sidewalk, thankful handicapped accessibility came with each condo and garden home in Sunset Acres.

As she hobbled to the mailbox, the steam from the concrete waved up to meet her. Beads of perspiration formed on her temples by the time she'd navigated the short trek to the shadier section near the curb. Then she gazed downward and let out a frustrated sigh.

The distance from the cement hump peeking past the grass edge to the asphalt pavement might as well be the Grand Canyon. How on earth would she get down to the street level to get out her mail? *Oh blast it all. I can't wait until the doctor allows me put weight on this foot.*

Janie peered up and down the block. Not a soul to help her navigate the curb. A saying flitted through her mind. She clucked her tongue and repeated it out loud. "Only mad dogs and Englishmen go out in the noonday sun."

Some famous comedian had sung it. Red Skelton? No. Ah yes, Noel Coward. Now what had made her think of that?

She grasped the top of the mailer and put all of her weight on her good leg in order to maneuver the bent knee metal thingy down to the road. Pfft. She felt like Long John Silver with a peg leg. She should get an eye patch and rent a parrot. Mrs. Fluffy would like that.

Somehow, in the process, she twisted and whacked her bad foot on the post. Janie clamped her jaw to keep from verbalizing what flashed through her brain. With her arms draped over the mailbox, she squinted her eyes shut and took three deep breaths to calm her nerves.

"You should be inside, lady."

She jerked and almost lost her balance. A hooded, husky man hovered over her. The same one who had been in her living room. "Who are you?"

He clamped a meaty hand over her mouth. "Shut up and listen. I thought I made things clear. Drop the snooping. Now."

He thrust something under her neck. A sharp edge pierced her skin as a stinging pain told her he meant business.

Spunk pumped though her veins. "You better not hurt me, young man. My son-in-law..."

The gruff voice growled. "Yeah, I know. But he ain't here, is he?"

Before she spoke again, he pushed her against the post and sprinted down the block to the alleyway.

Where is a cop when you need one?

With a shaky hand, Janie righted herself and scaled the curb back to the sidewalk. As fast as she could hobble, she inched toward the door. Beads of sweat cascaded down her face. Seconds may well have been minutes.

Everything seemed in slow-mo.

Her heartbeat thumped against her chest.

The click of her metal stump echoed like a base drum.

Hurry, hurry.

Somewhere off to her left, a dog barked a frantic warning. She recalled that yipping from her morning jogs. The mutt lived one block east near on Rosy Skies Trail near the golf course. That must be the direction he went. Beyond the fourth and fifth holes lay a shady creek, then mesquite and cedar dotted fields past the barbed wire fence. From there, the highway lay only a hundred yards away. Drat it all. Her assaulter would be long gone by the time she got inside. Oh, why didn't she pocket her cell phone before venturing out?

At last she reached the door and turned the knob. She slumped inside, slammed it, and flipped both dead bolts before leaning against the jamb to allow the tears to flow—part out of fear, the rest out of pure frustration. Janie hated being anything less than independent and self-efficient.

Hand to her bosom, she exhaled in short, uneven breaths. She willed her breathing to slow and become steadier. The cotton feeling in her ears lessened and the tingly sensation in her scalp begin to ebb.

Mustering renewed strength, she hopped to the couch and swung herself into the cushions as she grabbed her cell phone and punched in 9-1-1.

Within minutes, the sirens wailed outside her home once again. My neighbors are going to petition to evict me now, for sure.

Through the sheer curtains, she spotted a police cruiser pull in front of her condo. Two patrolmen got out and walked to the door. Janie eased herself up one more time and limped across the room to thrust it open just as a policeman's hand rang the bell. Seeing her incapacitated state, he flung open the screen and caught her as she tumbled towards him.

He held on as she sniffled and clung to his arms. His assistant scooted behind to press a hand on her back. "Mrs. Manson? Let's get you inside where it is cool."

She nodded, unable to make the words roll over her tongue.

The officers helped her back to the couch and settled her onto the cushions. One swung her leg onto the stack of pillows. The other handed her the now diluted tumbler of iced tea. "Take a few sips of this, catch your breath, and then tell us what happened."

Her hand shook as she brought the straw to her lips. The cool liquid tumbled over her tonsils along with half the angst of the moment. She closed her eyes, leaned her head back and sighed. "Thank you. I'm better now."

The one named Gonzalez, according to his badge, gave her a soft smile. "Take your time."

"No. No, you have to go find him. Young, husky, like a football player, wearing black sweats and jacket with a hood. He went that way into the alley and back by the golf course." She pointed over the sofa towards the southwest.

"He was on foot?"

"Yes. And he threatened me. Put a knife to my neck. Here." She showed him the right side of her throat.

The younger of the two officers moved his head closer to her. His badge read Branson. She recognized him from the last time. "Sir, a puncture is visible, and a small amount of blood has oozed."

Janie felt the rest leave her face.

"Now, Mrs. Manson, all is fine. Only needs an adhesive bandage and you'll be right as rain. I'll get my first aid kit."

Gonzalez spoke into the microphone attached to his shoulder. As he gave her description to the dispatcher, she nodded and answered his questions. His partner scribbled into a notebook, and each time her gaze shot in his direction, gave her a warm, encouraging smile.

Then whole thing replayed in her head. "Oh, my."

"What is it, ma'am?"

"He must have been waiting for me. He knew the mail always comes at this time. He plotted the route of how to exit the fastest." Her fingers grasped the policeman's arm. "He's been stalking me!"

The two exchanged a nod. "It's okay. You're safe, now. We're here."

"Thank you." Janie sipped some more lukewarm tea and leaned back to still her racing heart.

After a few more minutes of one interviewing her while the other one shooed away curious onlookers off her miniscule lawn, Janie calmed down enough to offer them some brownies. Anne Schmidt had brought them over the day before, along with a get well card showing a cat with its paw in a sling.

"So he wore no gloves? And you're sure it's the same guy as before?

"Yes. Positive."

"Branson, get the fingerprint kit. Check if any show up on the mailbox. We have Mrs. Manson's on file from the last time. The only other ones should be identifiable through the postal service." He turned to Janie. "All federal employees must agree to undergo fingerprinting as part of the job screening process."

"I see."

His cell phone jingled. "Yeah?" He nodded and replied, "Uh huh" several times.

Janie pressed her lips together and listened.

"Well, keep patrolling. He may be hiding until the coast is clear."

The door flew open and whammed into the wall.

In the entry way straddled a red-faced Blake Johnson. "I want all four units crisscrossing the entire village. Also men on foot checking alleyways, the creek area, and under bushes in the neighborhood. Oh, and check for any breech in the barbed wire."

Janie's lips quivered. He might as well have worn a red cape and a T-shirt with an "s" on it.

CHAPTER THIRTY-SEVEN

From behind him, Melody rushed forward and crouched near the couch. She pulled Janie into an embrace. "Mom, are you all right?"

Janie pulled away and motioned "yes" with her head. Their glistening eyes scoured each other's faces for a minute before the two women drew themselves into another hug. She picked up on Blake's voice off the right.

"I'm half-way to Navasota on Highway 79 when the call comes through the radio. Flipped on my lights and siren. Didn't realize my car did one-twenty."

The Officer Gonzalez chuckled. "She's okay. We interviewed her. A touch shaken up. He drew a weapon, though. She thinks a knife. Has a small slash on her neck."

Melody gasped. "Blake. Do something."

He gave his wife the same reassuring smile he'd given Janie.

"I have all four units scanning the area in a net pattern. We'll get him."

Jane rubbed her daughter's arm. "How did you get here?"

Pushing some of her curls off Janie's forehead, she sighed. "Blake phoned me as soon as he got word. I've been in Lampasas at an Optimist's soccer council meeting. They are hosting the regional finals next year on their fields and being on the team's council here, well several of us..." She stopped and took a breath. "Never mind. I'm here now. That's what counts."

Janie took her daughter's hands in hers. "Miranda came this morning. She did a wonderful job."

"Oh, I am so glad. Would you like her to return next week? I'm sure..."

"Ladies?" Blake's baritone echoed through the living room. "I think Officer Gonzalez would like to wrap things up."

Chins dropped in penitence. Both women turned their attention to the policeman chomping a brownie. He shoved the rest in his mouth, wiped his lips with his hand, and swallowed as he gazed up at his boss. "She offered, sir."

Blake cocked an eyebrow and took one for himself. "Continue."

He paced the room as Gonzalez stammered through the information, glancing at him every few seconds. His previous confidence must have disappeared down his gullet along with the tasty treat.

Janie shoved her hands to her hips. "Blake, sit down. You look like a caged lion weaving back and forth. You're making everyone nervous."

Gonzalez widened his eyes at Branson, who had returned with the fingerprint kit, his upper lipped curled to the left in a semi-smile. "Got three complete and two partials off the mailbox."

"Good. Run them." Blake exhaled through his nose and perched on the arm of the sofa, next to his wife who fluffed Janie's leg pillow.

"Thank you. Melody, dear, would you bring in some glasses and the pitcher of sun tea?"

Calm, collected, and in control once more, Janie's hostess genes kicked in. She ran through her statement again as the policeman polished off the plate of brownies.

After Officers Gonzalez and Branson exited, Melody collected the paper napkins and platter of crumbs. "Mom, were these for Bunco?"

"Oh well, I'm sure the Biddies will bring plenty of goodies this evening. Remind me to call Eleanor and ask her to bring some more iced tea. She sun brews her with fresh peaches."

Blake gave his wife a peck on the temple. "Gotta git, honey. You'll stay here for a while longer?"

"Yes, until three-fifteen, then I must dash to meet Erin's school bus. Jamie is staying late for practice. He's getting a ride home with Jeremy."

"Okay."

She placed a hand on her husband's arm. "We shouldn't expect you for dinner, then?"

"I'll let you know."

Janie spotted disappointment edge Melody's eyes, which she tried to hide with a sweet grin. She reached up to her husband and stroked his hair. "Go do your job, sweetheart. The kids will understand."

He gave her and Janie a quick head bob and left.

"I'm sorry, Mel. He has enough to do without all this." She waved her arms around the room.

"Mom, why is this horrible thug threatening you?"

Janie glanced away, recalling Blake's admonition. "I found the body, dear. I guess he wants to make sure I keep my mouth shut. Or perhaps he is trying to send a threat to Blake through me. He knew Blake's my son-in-law."

"How?"

"Edwin's murder has been on the news, Mel."

Melody worried a piece of fringe on Janie's afghan throw. "Oh, why did you let me marry a cop?"

"The first time someone chunked a brick through our sitting room window with threats tied to it, I asked my mother the same thing. You were only two at the time, playing with your dolly. We were having a tea party. I'd gotten up to get us cookies. The thing missed your head by inches."

"Oh, Mom. I never knew."

"Being a cop's wife isn't for the fainthearted, but Blake's a good man. So was Jack. You have to weigh the good with the bad."

Melody's lower lip vibrated.

Janie pulled her daughter's head to her shoulder as Melody let her emotions spill out in soft sobs.

CHAPTER THIRTY-EIGHT

At last, Janie sat alone in her living room, the mantle clock ticking away her life. She scanned the myriad of footprints on her rug. Melody's, Blake's, three police officers, and the sketch artist. None of Mrs. Fluffy's. *Now where did that cat run off to?*

Probably deep under her four poster bed. She moved her shoulders in a slow circle to ease the tension so she could objectively ponder what happened. From the panoramic perspective of a bird hovering over the yard, she tried to envision the ordeal.

Who had stalked her and been bold enough to threaten her in broad daylight? A flash went off in her mind. *Only mad dogs and Englishmen...* Someone who surmised the pattern of the elderly. At noon, everyone is either in the dining hall, eating, or taking a nap or watching the news. No one had been out and about except her. And her assailant knew that to be a fact.

The thought gave her the shivers. Who could he be? Anybody. Perhaps a goon for Lenny Weber? A hired thug of Edward Norman? Wherever he had escaped to, he might still have connections in the states, unless he died eight years ago as Blake said.

She shook her head. Who else? One of the other two robbers with slithery tentacles reaching beyond their jail bars? They no doubt wouldn't want people nosing into their affairs. Perhaps they hid the stolen money and had silenced Edwin so he couldn't get to their share. In fact...

Janie scribbled a new revelation on her trusty notepad before it dissipated back into her brain. What if Edwin had been paid to take the fall for Edward Norman? She tapped the eraser end to her chin. He only drove the get-away vehicle. They figured he'd get a lesser sentence. In the meantime, Edwards slithers off under a rock with the loot.

Nah, it didn't make any sense. Criminals never think they will get caught. She crossed the thought out, scratching her pencil over the entry several times. But the idea continued to niggle her. Why?

She hobbled into the kitchen to get a cold glass of water. Mid-gulp, it hit her. She slammed the plastic tumbler onto the counter top and limped to her bedroom as fast as she could on the new-fangled peg leg. She opened the file folder containing the court transcripts onto her bed and began to flip through the pages. Her eyes scanned the testimonies.

Ah. She drummed her fingernail on the printed line. The three were not arrested at the scene. They were apprehended days later. Edwin first, outside a bar, then Lopez and Smithers in an abandoned house on a ranch called the Lazy West. Had Edwin been hired as a red herring to resemble Edwards while the others planned their escape with the estimated five million dollars? What if he snitched on them as part of a plea bargain and his action backfired? No, no, no. He'd have been stabbed in prison if that were the case. Argh. She rubbed her eyes.

Mrs. Fluffy hopped up in the middle of the report and proceeded to raise a leg to the ceiling in preparation for her afternoon bath. Janie stroked her fur. "He wouldn't have been that stupid, would he, girl? He'd be afraid they'd come after him. Unless he had gotten wind Edwards died in South America. But how would he learn that? No, something else happened after Edwin got out of the pokey to get him butchered."

She slammed her hand onto the mattress, causing her cat to jostle mid-lick. "Of course. Emilio Lopez relayed a message to Edwin from his father. Which is why Edwin hired the jailhouse dog attorney. Maybe they offered him a piece of the pie if he got out, retrieved the stolen money, and banked their share in some foreign account. But would they trust him to do it, kitty? What do you think?"

The animal rolled over to lick her paw.

Janie scoffed at the lack of concern in her feline.

"Speaking of being butchered. Who is my assailant who works with raw meat?" She leaned back onto her duvet and worked the theory out in her brain. All of her speculations didn't account for the reason Edwin had reacted to the scar-faced man in the Get 'em and Go. Emilio didn't have a slash down his cheek like his dad. So it had to be someone else. But who? If Edwin recognized the hit man from prison and figured he came after him, wouldn't he take precautions?

She bopped the palm of her hand against her forehead. "Unless he'd found the cash and thought he'd bribe the killer."

Janie made record time back into the living room to where her cell phone lay. She punched in Blake's number.

"Yes, Janie."

"Are you on the road?"

"Yes, back to Navasota. Something you need?" His voice sounded as if he tried not to be as terse this time.

"No, but a thought occurred to me. What if Lopez, Smithers, and Edwards paid Edwin to take the fall but, through Emilio Lopez, arranged for that shyster attorney to get him out?"

The whoosh of the car traveling along the highway hummed in her ear. Then Blake's voice came through the receiver. "You can't call him a shyster, Janie. It's only jealous attorney talk because the guy found a niche for his practice and often ends up the hero in the headlines. Edwin didn't deserve the sentencing, and the charges brought against the Texas Prison System are not trumped up..."

"Yes, yes. Whatever. But what if Edwin isn't...er, wasn't as innocent in all this as we assumed?"

"Okay? There's an interesting twist."

She nodded but realized he couldn't see her gesture over the phone. "Maybe the deal was to get him out and have him hunt down the stolen bank money. If Edwin double-crossed Lopez and Smithers, they might have hired a hit man, perhaps an ex-con Edwin knew, to do away with him. Thus the thug with the scar who freaked Edwin out."

"Hmmm. Good reasoning, Janie. Jack's detective instincts must have rubbed off on you. We'll check out that angle while we are at Watson Pack. Check for any men with scars who were recently released."

"Thanks. Perhaps you'll discover a connection. Still, the business of a woman with black hair and ruby lips visiting him only a day or so after he moves in still haunts me."

Blake laughed. "Come on. He'd been in prison for years. Don't tell me you're that naive."

She cleared her throat and felt a warm sensation inch into her face. "Oh, well, of course. Guess he might want companionship. I mean..."

His tone became stern. "Stay put, Janie. Don't get any ideas now. You ladies are supposed to poll your neighbors, not ex-cons or their kin. And definitely no ladies of the evening, okay?"

"Drive safely, Blake." She punched off to end the conversation. A tingling behind her ears spread across into her smile. As Ethel loved to quote, the game once again was afoot.

CHAPTER THIRTY-NINE

Blake tapped his knuckles on the steering wheel after he switched off his Bluetooth. His partner turned to him. "What she say?"

"Sometimes, I have to put up with my mother-in-law's quirkiness. But on days like today, I realize she's made of pretty stern stuff and still has it up here, ya know?" He pressed his finger to his temple.

"Yes, sir."

He glanced over before returning his attention to the road. "So instead of whimpering over a man who threatened her at knife point, she starts churning out a new theory."

"And what would that be?"

"Well, Connor, she asked what if Edwin had been paid to take the fall for Edward Norman all along, allowing Norman to hide the loot and skip the country. After all, they arrested Edwin outside a bar several days later, as I recall."

Connor Hemphill protruded his lower lip. "So he assumed Norman's identity, went to trial knowing he'd be able to plea bargain for a lighter sentence as an accomplice since he drove the getaway car?"

"That's her theory. Then Lopez and Smithers get caught anyway, and they surmise it's because Edwin squealed."

"Sorry, sir. Doesn't jive. They'd have someone shiv him in the county jail. Man never would have made it to the unit."

Blake wobbled his head back and forth. "Unless something else happened during those years he lay in prison. Janie hinted that maybe the plan was for him to get out on a technicality and hunt down Edwards and the dough. How long did his niece fight for his release?"

Connor thumbed through his notes. "A little over a year."

"Hmmm. He had been incarcerated for quite a while before that. So what, all of a sudden, made him a target when he got out? His face in the press? His settling in this area instead of Oklahoma? The money the State of Texas awarded him?" He motioned to his underling with his chin. "Motive, Connor. Until we nail that, none of these puzzle pieces will begin to fit."

Janie eyed the digital clock on her bed stand. 3:15. Betsy Ann and Ethel, along with George, should be driving back from Dallas by now. They were due over at five to pow-wow and help set up the card tables. The Bunco Biddies would start to arrive at six-ish. And what to do until then? Her body screamed for a nap, but her brain swirled too fast.

Oh, if only the doctor would let her drive. "Well, then what, Janie? Where would you go?" She chided herself for whining and tottered back to the sofa. The players were in motion, so she'd done all she could. She clicked through the TV channels and landed on a game show. A switch in thought power might ease her mind into a more restful state.

Sure enough, within a few minutes, her head tilted back onto the pillow.

Connor Hemphill and Blake entered the first gate of the prison. "Sorry sirs. Visiting hours are over at four."

He flashed his badge, again. "We aren't here to visit. We are here to interview Edwin Newman's cellmate, Joseph Sanders. Need to chat with the warden as well."

The guard shuffled through his papers. "He's left for the day. You were to be here at one."

Blake sucked in a lung of air to keep his cool. "I called. We had an emergency situation." His voice pitch heightened as he spouted each word. "Now, do we get to talk with Sanders or not?"

The guard's face reddened. He led them into a small, windowless room away from the public. "Wait here, sirs." He motioned to a row of four institutional-styled, plastic chairs.

Another guard sat behind a teller-like window. "I need you to surrender your guns, communication equipment, loose change...you know the drill. Shoes off as well, please."

After ten minutes the first officer returned. "You're cleared, but only for fifteen minutes. This way, please."

The detectives were buzzed through a steel door with chicken wire layered between green coated glass panels in the upper half. They walked down a long corridor, out another door and through a breezeway into a second building. A security officer stood on the other side of a similar window as if ready to take their movie tickets. "Detectives Johnson and Hemphill to see Joseph Sanders, number D158239."

"Badges, please?"

Blake and his partner slid them through the slit in the glass. The guard took his sweet time eyeing the IDs and writing down their numbers. Raising his glance to their faces, he shoved the identifications back towards them. "Okay."

He relayed to have the prisoner brought down to the interrogation room.

Hemphill rocked back and forth on his heels.

"First time?"

"Yes, sir. Shows, huh?"

Blake scoffed. "Never fun. But gives you a good feeling knowing the scum you help put in here are likely to stay put."

Hemphill humphed. "We wish."

A buzzer vibrated and the lock on the door released. The two were led down a short hall to the right and into an eight-foot by six-foot room with only a table and four chairs. Blake sat down. Hemphill dug out a pocket recorder and placed the device on the Formica top.

Within a few minutes, the door on the opposite side opened and a small man dressed in prison garb entered. He looked more like a tax clerk than a criminal. Bald, with wispy gray hair on either side of his ears, his wrinkled skin appeared to be weathered by age and sun. His hands were clamped together. The guard pushed the inmate's shoulders, indicating he should sit. Next, the inmate's handcuff chains were attached to two metal rings at the edge of the table. With a scoff, the prison official put his thumb and forefinger to his temple in a mock salute. "Gentlemen, he's all yours for fifteen minutes."

After the door closed, Sanders stared at them, his jaw working a piece of chewing gum.

Blake introduced himself and his partner. "We understand you were Edwin Newman's cellmate."

He slid down into the chair as far as his chains would allow. "If that's what you want to call him. Didn't change his name until he got a squeaky-clean attorney. Up until then, everyone called him Norm."

Hemphill scribbled in his notebook and cocked an eyebrow. "You know he's dead, right?"

"If you mean the man who occupied the other bunk, yeah. So?"

Blake and Hemphill exchanged glances. 'Did anyone put a contract on him?"

"Pfft. Think I'd tell ya?"

"What you say won't go past these walls." Blake set his jaw and clicked off the recorder.

Hemphill sputtered. "But, sir—"

Blake raised one eyebrow. "This is my investigation, Sergeant."

Sanders chuckled. "You two can play good-cop-bad-cop all you want, but time's running out and I ain't talking. I'll be in enough hot water when they learn I'm in here with ya."

Blake stared into the man's eyes. "Okay, you don't have to answer. But we have to ask. Your choice if you wish to say yes." He held up one finger. "Or no." He lifted two fingers off the table.

Sanders noted his hand signals, stone-faced. He shifted his gaze to Blake's face. "Do what ya gotta do, man."

"Do you have reason to believe Edwin's life was in danger while incarcerated here?"

Sanders fixated on the wall behind them and chomped on his chewing gum.

"Did you catch wind of anyone wanting to oust him once he was released?"

He shifted in his chair as he continued to concentrate on some spot a tad above Blake's head.

"Sanders, did Edwin ever confide in you about any deal he made with two prisoners named Lopez and Smithers to assume the identity of Edward Norman?"

The prisoner dashed his eyes for a second to Blake, but went back to staring at same imaginary spot as before.

Blake eyeballed the wad of green as it swirled over the inmate's tongue. *If he smacks his gum many more times, I'm gonna lose my cool.*

The door opened. "Time's up." The guard unhooked Sanders's chains from the table and led him out of the room. The guy never looked either detective in the eye.

Hemphill heaved a long sigh. "Talk about a waste of time."

A smirk curled across Blake's lips. "Not necessarily. By not answering any of my questions, he said a great deal."

He got up to exit and snickered at the crinkled brow of his underling.

"Body language, Connor. He spoke volumes with his subtle gestures. Did you expect him to do otherwise?"

"Guess there's a lot I still need to learn."

The two chuckled as they exited the building and shuffled to the institutional chairs room to collect their department-issued paraphernalia and shoes.

CHAPTER FORTY

George dropped Ethel off and drove the short distance to Betsy Ann's. He parked at the curb and turned to face her. "Thank you for allowing me to come along. Quite an adventurous day, I must say."

He stroked her forearm, which sent tiny little prickles up her veins to her heart. George walked around and opened her passenger side. He extended his hand, and when she placed hers inside his grip, she took a sharp breath as her cheeks rose in body temperature.

His left eyebrow cocked and a smirk cupped his mouth. "Here you are, m'lady."

"Thank you, George. For everything. But buying my and Ethel's lunch seemed a touch much."

"Not to me." He tucked her hand in his arm and escorted her to the stoop. When they reached her door, he took her fingers and squeezed them. "I have a confession to make. I volunteered for this mission for the sole reason I wanted to spend time with you. Besides, now I know where you live." He winked and bent to brush her cheek with his lips. "And I have your phone number, which I hope to use to call you again soon—with your permission."

She fluttered her eyelashes. "Of course, George. I'd like that."

He back-stepped. "Good. Until we speak again."

Betsy Ann held her breath as he bowed and pivoted to walk to his car. Halfway down the sidewalk, he stopped and turned in her direction. "I will wait here until I am confident you are safe inside your abode."

She gazed at him. "Oh, yes. Thank you." She jostled her keys from her handbag, unlocked the front door and slipped inside. Before she shut it, she gave him a wave.

He returned the gesture with another wink and drove off.

Betsy Ann leaned against the jamb, her hand to her chest. Her feet seemed to float above the floor. She hummed as she hung up her purse and scarf and glided into the kitchen to fix a cup of tea before changing for Bunco.

She never expected to feel this way again.

At five after five, Ethel and Betsy Ann turned up the alleyway to Janie's house at the same time. "So, we meet again."

Betsy Ann brushed the comment away with one hand as a gelatin mold jiggled in her other. Ethel carried a casserole papoosed in a quilted cover.

"I'm contributing Bing cherry and walnut Jell-O salad. What did you bring?"

"My famous chicken enchiladas with mozzarella topped with sour cream jalapeno sauce."

"Oooh, yummy."

The two entered Janie's back door. "Yoo, hoo. We're here."

In the distance Janie's more chipper than normal voice sung out. "Come in, come in. Boy, do I have things to share with you."

The ladies set their dishes in the kitchen and shuffled into the living room.

"How did the road trip go?"

Ethel and Betsy Ann eyed each other and shrugged. "Okay. Albert Washington turned out be an interesting man."

The two took turns recapping their conversation and adventure, except Betsy Ann left out the part of George walking her to her door.

"So, tell us what you did all day. Lie around eating chocolate truffles?" Ethel grinned.

Janie swiveled her leg to rest on the coffee table. "Melody hired a cleaning lady to come give the place the once over."

"I did whiff a pine-like aroma when we came in."

Betsy Ann agreed. "And the room is so sparkly and clean." She paused, hand to mouth. "Not that your place ever is disheveled. You're a meticulous housekeeper. It's only with your foot and all..."

Janie chuckled. "I understand. To continue. Next, I ate lunch, watched the noonday news, and learned Lopez's son Emilio was in the same unit as Edwin."

Betsy Ann shook her head. "I thought only senior citizen prisoners were sent to Wallace Pack."

"Evidently one section is, but not the whole facility. Back to the point, the police arrested him for a botched attempt to hijack the transport vehicle carrying Lenny Weber from Navasota to San Antonio."

Ethel leaned back. "Wow. That is interesting. Did you tell Blake?"

"Yes. He already knew. But then I went to get the mail..." She paused for effect. "The man who broke into my home before lurked nearby. He pinned me against the post and put a knife to my neck."

Betsy Ann shot to her feet, spilling the contents of the purse she'd laid on her lap. "What?"

Ethel's face paled. "Are you serious?"

Janie smiled. "Yep." She pointed to the flesh colored bandage near her jugular vein. "Ask anyone. Police, sirens, fingerprinting team, sketch artists. They all crowded into my condo, again. I think Mrs. Fluffy may disown me if this keeps up."

"Did they catch the guy?"

Janie shook her head. "Not that I know of. Which means he plotted this community and its grounds quite well."

Ethel gulped. "My, what a comforting thought."

"Are you going to tell the ladies?" Betsy Ann asked as she gathered her items from the rug and shoved them back into her bag.

Janie waved her wrist. "I gather most of them have found out by now, as would you two if you hadn't gone traipsing all over North Texas."

Betsy Ann pouted to Ethel. "We did kinda miss the excitement."

"Yes, but lunch was superb, and I think George likes you." She waggled a finger at her friend, whose rouge darkened by three shades.

Janie laughed. "I'll relay all when everyone gets here. But the clock says twenty 'til, so would you mind getting the card table and chairs from the guest closet and setting them up?"

Her friends jumped to follow her command.

One by one, the Bunco Biddies entered, chatting and sampling what each had brought. A folding table had been set near the sofa, making it easier for Janie to play. Betsy Ann patted her shoulder. "You are exempt from moving, even if you don't score the highest."

After everyone had stuffed themselves with the latest recipes gleaned from postings on the social media, they settled into three groups of fours and rolled to determine who'd go first at each of the tables. The bell dinged and the fast-pace attempts to roll as many ones as possible began. When someone at the head table rolled three dice all landing on one, the round ended, scores were tallied, and the ladies with the higher points switched seats. The whole process started over with twos. Afterwards, they rolled for threes, then fours, fives, and sixes.

Janie received the prize for the most Buncos, or rolling the same number on all three dice. Mildred won the highest score, which under normal circumstances would have her grinning like a cat who just dined on grain-fed mice. Tonight, however, her mood remained subdued. Before Janie got the chance to question her, she dashed out the front door with the remnants of her caramel fudge torte in hand.

"What's up with Mildred?"

"Dunno." Ethel wiped the water rings from the card table. "Ever since the funeral, she has been quiet. Maybe the gruesomeness of what happened next door is sinking in."

Janie handed her the tally pads. "I guess that make sense."

Betsy Ann spoke up as she gathered the other tablets and dice. "I recall her nephew visiting her last week. You know? The one who is the butcher and gets her those great cuts of stew beef for her famous goulash?"

"Oh, yes. He gave her the biggest lamb roast for Easter. So tender, the meat fell off the fork." Ethel licked her lips at the memory. "Oh, you didn't come, did you Janie? You were at Mel's."

Janie smiled. "Hmm, a great day. Sunny, cool. Jamie hid the golden egg with a dollar bill tucked inside and Blake's great niece found it. She's only three. You've never seen such a grin on a child's face."

"Well, I thought he'd cheer her up, but she's seems even more moody."

"They may have had words." Janie stopped. "Wait? Did you say he's a butcher?"

"That's right. At Fred's Foods down the road."

Janie plopped on the couch, rubbing her forehead. She recalled her conversation with Miranda about her son Juan who worked there as well.

"What is wrong, Janie? Are you too tired to meet?"

She re-positioned her elevated foot and grimaced. "No, racking my brain. Tell me. What does Bobby look like?"

Ethel titled her head up to the ceiling. "Let's see now. He is tall, rather brawny. Broad shoulders and stocky. Played linebacker. I'd say early twenties by now. Single."

A chill tickled Janie's earlobes. "Does he have a gruff voice?"

Ethel nodded. "You could say so. I recall the first time I met him. I thought to myself, I sure wouldn't want to make him angry."

Betsy Ann shook her head. "He is a giant, but he is as gentle as a kitten. In fact, he loves Poopsy so much. That dog became quite attached to him while he lived there and vice versa. I remember Mildred being a tad jealous."

The blood rushed from Janie's face. Now she knew who had broken into her home smelling like raw meat and slapped her and today, shoved a knife to her neck.

Moreover, she discerned without a doubt he'd been involved in Edwin's death. But why? Over his love for his aunt's dog?

CHAPTER FORTY-ONE

Janie wanted to pace, which is how she thought things through. Of course, her foot wouldn't allow her that privilege. Nor could she walk or drive yet, so the idea of having to totter over to Mildred's garden home one block over and two more down lasted about thirty-seconds. It would take her at least a half-hour to hobble in that direction, and the temperature, which had yet to drop below eighty even at nine at night, might wilt her. Having the Bunco Biddies over did relieve the doldrums, but all the chattering and dice rolling drained her energy tonight. No way would she make it to Mildred's front door.

Mrs. Fluffy sat under the coffee table and peered up at her mistress. A small questioning mew let Janie know the animal sympathized, worried, or wanted some of the chicken spread Betty-Lou brought. Janie bent down to face her. "What? You should know by now I don't speak cat."

She thrust her back into the cushions. How could she suspect Mildred's nephew? She'd never met the kid. Well, yes, unless...

Should she call Blake? Not until she had reasoned this through without a shadow of a doubt. Only then would she muster up the confidence to accuse Bobby of being the one who threatened her. Mildred would never forgive her otherwise.

The gals did convey Bobby had landed on the wrong side of the law before. However, the idea he'd kill someone because he threw a mug at a dog seemed over-the-top weird. Something else triggered his actions. But what?

He did match the description, even down to the reason his hands smelled like hamburger. Plus, having bunked in with his aunt for a few weeks, he must have learned about the community's schedules and layout. It would be easy for him to find a cubbyhole in which to hide until the police search thinned. A bush, under someone's deck, even in the maintenance shed off the first tee. He could become invisible in the nursing or assisted living sections if he figured out a way to get in without being detected. Oh, yes. Dozens of places to lay low. She'd have to remember to speak to the neighborhood watch committee about how unsecure their community really was.

Janie's brain bounced these ideas around like a tennis ball volleying between two professional Wimbledon players. One thing for sure, she and Mildred needed to have a heart to heart. The possibility was that Mildred knew nothing about her nephew's shenanigans, though something told Janie it wouldn't be the case. Her unusual moodiness would make sense if her conscience tickled her.

Janie slapped her cell phone against her thigh. She hated to call Ethel so soon after she'd left. Even more, Janie loathed being dependent on anyone. But she needed a ride and having a witness might be a good idea. Besides, Mildred and Ethel had a history of confiding in each other. And Ethel looked after Poopsy from time to time when Mildred had to go out of town or into the hospital for her diverticulitis. If anything, Ethel would be honest enough to tell Janie if she barked up the wrong tree, no pun intended.

Ethel answered after the third ring. "Janie?"

"I hate to ask you this, dear. But, could you swing back by?"

"Sure. Are you okay?"

Janie scoffed. "Yes. I think I have worked something out about Edwin Newman and I need to bounce my theory off you before I pursue it."

Her friend's voice became more high-pitched and rapid. "Oh, of course. Be right over. Happy to help. Hang tight."

Six minutes later, Ethel's tell-tale rap-rappity-rap hit the back door. Janie yelled out, "Come on in."

She did and zipped into the living room, giving Mrs. Fluffy a quick pat before settling into one of the side chairs. "So, whatcha got?"

Janie squiggled to face her. "All right. Hear me out. I understand this will seem absurd, but..."

After she laid out all the evidence including the build, approximate age, hand odor, and knowledge of Sunset Acres, Janie peered into her fellow sleuth's eyes. "Well? Am I nuts?"

Ethel's stone-faced reaction made Janie ponder if she thought so. But, after a minute, her friend's eyebrows moved closer together and the wrinkles on her forehead deepened. "Hmmm. I'm not sure. It does add up. But I am not certain about the motive."

"That's my quandry. I can imagine him stomping over and belting Edwin in the nose, but to murder him and systematically haul him off to be chopped up, much less deposited in our dumpster? Too bizarre. Unless he's, you know..." She made a circling motion with her finger near her temple.

"Oh, Bobby's a weird duck, I'll grant you that. Didn't get Mildred's social genes. But I agree, it doesn't jive."

"So why would he threaten me—twice?"

Ethel rose to pace. Janie wished like all get-out she could join her. Instead, she closed her eyes and listened until her friend's footfall stopped.

"He does possess a somewhat shady past. Someone could have hired him to threaten you."

"Yes, it has to be the answer." Janie swung her foot around and whacked the outer edge on the coffee table. White, hot pain dashed up her calf. "Ow."

"Careful. Let me get you some ice."

Janie massaged the splint, as if it did any good. "No, I'm fine. Stupid foot." She inhaled and relaxed her shoulders. "Do you think we should speak with Mildred? After all, she hasn't seemed her cheery self."

Ethel lifted her shoulders to her ears. "Wouldn't hurt. Wanna go now?"

"Yes. If she's home."

"At nine o'clock at night? Where else would she be?"

"Even so, let's call first." Janie bent to grab her cell phone.

"Uh-uh." Ethel's hand came down on top of hers. "That'll give her a reason to back out. Come up with some sort of excuse why now is inconvenient. Element of surprise is best."

"Oooh, my mother is rolling in her grave right now." Janie winked.

Ethel returned the gesture. "Emily Post would slap our hands with a ruler." She snatched her handbag. "Let's go."

CHAPTER FORTY-TWO

Rap-rappity-rap. They listened as Mildred's footsteps came to the front door. "Who is it?"

"Ethel, and Janie is with me. Mildred, sorry for popping in, but can we speak with you?"

A worried seventy-year-old face peeked through the beveled glass panel flanking the door. It creaked open. "I guess. Though I am in my duster."

Ethel pushed her way in. "No need for formalities with friends." She held the passage way wide for Janie to wobble in.

Mildred waved her hand. "Janie, you sit in this chair by the bay window so you don't have to hobble far. I'll get us some iced water." Her smile dissipated as she pivoted with hands clasped and scurried towards her kitchen.

Ethel smirked and sat in the other chair. She leaned in and mouthed the word "nervous" to Janie then titled her head in the direction Mildred had disappeared.

Janie nodded as she smoothed her pant leg over her cast.

In a few minutes, their reluctant hostess entered with three glasses clinking on a tray. "Here we are, ladies." She handed them each a glass wrapped in a flower-patterned paper napkin.

Janie took a long sip as she waited for Mildred to be seated. She patted the metal peg-leg propped against the upholstered arm her chair. "Thanks. This contraption takes the stuffing out of you after a while."

"Good exercise I imagine." Mildred gave her a taut smile. "Though it takes a bit of getting used to, I'm sure."

"Umm, but saves the arm pits."

The three shared an anxious chuckle.

Janie set her glass on the coaster. "Mildred, I have been threatened twice now by a hooded man whose hands held the distinct odor of raw hamburger meat."

Mildred's eyes darted between them. "Oh?"

"Yes, and he fits Bobby's general description, according to Ethel."

Ethel nodded. "Mildred, you have been acting strange since the funeral, and we are worried about you. Is there something pressing on your mind? Do you believe Bobby may have something to do with Edwin's…er, demise?"

Janie bit her lip. Ethel could be blunt at times. She expected Mildred to explode, defend her nephew, and ask them to kindly vacate her home. Instead, she whimpered and snatched a facial tissue.

"Oh, my word. I don't know. I just don't know." Soft sobbing commenced. Her two friends sat in silence until she composed herself.

Janie sugared her tone. "Take your time, dear. We're here to help."

Poopsy waddled in, the nose scab visible from a distance. She plopped at her mistress's feet and lifted her mournful eyes.

Janie's heart tugged.

Mildred dabbed her cheeks and in a wobbly voice, apologized for her breakdown. "I figured something gnawed at him. When he saw Poopsy here"—she reached down and stroked her pet's fur with tenderness—"his face turned the color of a tomato stewing in a pot."

"Do you think...?"

"Oh, good heavens, no. He'd never go that far. But I feared he'd do something. When you told me about Edwin Newman my heart nearly jumped out of my body. I had an inkling Bobby might be in the middle of this mess somehow."

Ethel scooted forward. "Did you confront him?"

She wrapped the tissue through her fingers. "Not in so many words. But when I told him the news, his face changed. His jaw tightened, the same way Joe's used to when Mom caught him doing something he shouldn't."

"Joe is your brother?"

"Yes, Bobby's dad. He never did hold a job for long. Always hung out with shady men and went to bars instead of coming home. He skipped out on Bobby and his mom years ago. I always feared Bobby would follow in his footsteps. Apple doesn't drop too far from the tree, does it?"

Janie shook her head. "Often times not."

Ethel cleared her throat. "Did he say anything to you at all?"

"Told me to mind my own business when I asked him what he..." She pushed her scrunched hankie to her mouth.

"I see."

The tears began to trickle down once more. "I'm all he has now. His mom committed suicide right after he turned eighteen. Such a troubled youth. He'd mope in his room all the time. Then burst out the door and never tell me where he went. Oh, I've worn my knees out praying for that boy."

Janie patted the air with her hand as far as it could reach toward Mildred's knee. "I'm sure God heard each one, dear."

Mildred sniffled. "He got into a rough crowd and they robbed a convenience store. Bobby only did three years since he didn't have a weapon."

"Where was he incarcerated?"

"Oh, up the road about an hour near College Station. Navasota, I think?"

Ethel and Janie exchanged glances.

"When he got out, I'd moved to Sunset Acres, so he stayed with me until he found a job." She took a sip of her water. "I thought he'd been doing okay. Has a small garage apartment and a used truck."

"Not a dark van?"

"Huh? No. One of those small pick-ups. Green. Why?"

Janie brushed the thought away. "Go on. You were saying?"

"I'm sure you can understand. I didn't want to slam the door on our friendship. So I didn't pursue it." Her lower lip began to shake again and her eyes shimmered.

Janie wanted to get up, hop over, and hug her friend. She told her so.

Mildred smiled for a brief moment and dabbed the tissue to her eyelids. "I should show you what I found in my trash can. I took the bag from kitchen bin outside before I left for Bunco because it had a tuna can in it from lunch and I didn't want it to stink up my house. Anyway, I opened the garbage lid and there it lay."

"What?"

"I'll go get it." She walked toward the bedrooms. After a couple of minutes, she came back clutching some dark cloth. She held the piece up.

A black, hooded fleece jacket.

Ethel gasped.

"Bobby wore one just like this when he visited me."

Janie sat straight. "Today?"

She bobbed her head. "Yes, he came for lunch on his break from the grocer's but had to leave at 12:20 for some reason. Appeared to be in a hurry."

Ethel took the clothing into her hands. "And you are sure it's his?"

Mildred motioned for Ethel to take a whiff.

Ethel's eyes widened. "Oh, my word. Janie, it smells like hamburger juice."

CHAPTER FORTY-THREE

First they prayed with Mildred as she wept. Then Janie called Blake.

"This doesn't make sense." His frustration blared through his gruff tone.

"I understand. But..."

Blake's sigh through the receiver resembled a rush of wind signaling a storm approaching. "Be right over. Tell Mildred to hang tight."

Fifteen minutes later, he appeared on her stoop.

She hung her head and stared at a spot on the carpet as she spoke. "Bobby's been in trouble before."

"Yes, we pulled up his info. But he seems to be clean, now." Blake's tone softened as soon as he glimpsed her red-rimmed eyes and runny nose.

Her damp eyelids lifted. "But is he? Maybe he hooked up with the wrong type again."

Blake crossed one leg over the other. "Hate to say it. but more likely than not, it's true. Prison does very little to reform nowadays.

A few turn their lives around, or have good intentions, but they are tossed back into society with little or no assistance and flounder like a fish flopping on a river bank. Gangs snatch them up and help them back into the swim. It's like a community."

Janie shook her head. "Even if he's the one who has been threatening me, which appears to be the case, I can't fathom him murdering anyone. Can you?"

Blake scratched his eyebrow. "He's probably a messenger. My guess is he mouthed off at work about Edwin bonking Mildred's pup in the nose and his ranting fell on some hard ears. They either paid him to be their delivery boy or pressured him into the job."

Ethel nodded several times in sequence. "Yes, I recall an episode on TV where..."

"Not now, Ethel." Janie shot her a stern, teacher-says-to-be-quiet expression.

Blake's mouth smirked for a spilt second before returning his attention to Mildred. "Do you think he'd speak with me?"

Her chest rose and fell. "I'm not sure."

"What time does he get off tomorrow?"

"Four, I think."

"Why don't you have him drop by after work? Tell him you are in desperate need of his help. I'll swing by in an unmarked vehicle. Perhaps if he is out of his element, he'll be more willing to be forthcoming as to his recent activities."

Janie sat in Blake's car for a good fifteen minutes as they discussed the case, out of the earshot of well-meaning Ethel. "You are a kind man, Blake. You have every reason to storm in and arrest him now."

"Not really. We need to be sure."

"Hmm, yes. And nothing about this case is sure so far, right?"

"Nope. Well, better get you inside."

Janie frowned as she waved good-bye and then double-bolted her front door. Hobbling back to the couch, she perched on the edge and drummed her fingers on the arm rest. The pieces of the puzzle were not fitting. A jagged edge of one piece of evidence protruded too much and a curve in another didn't seem to fit.

First piece. If Bobby had been solicited to help, how much? Did he drive the dark, beat-up van? Did he steal it? Or had they only coerced him into bullying Janie because his aunt played Bunco with her?

She shook her head. No, He had to be more involved. Someone told Edwin's killers—and yes, there had to be at least two to drag a body, chop it up and bring it back—about the layout of Sunset Acres and the timetable for the trash pickup. That someone had to be Bobby.

And what of the Eduardo Lopez connection? He most likely resembled his dad. Is that what freaked Edwin? No, he didn't have a scar on his face. Still, it's no coincidence the ex-con ended up in this area. Then again, the attorney might be the common denominator. Perhaps not. That didn't quite jive either.

What about the initials L.W. Marjorie scrawled on the paper napkin? They had to stand for Lenny Weber, who had threatened Edwin in prison. How did he fit into the picture?

Finally, did the fact Edwin had been mistaken for Edward Norman have anything to do with his demise? Had Lenny thought he put the screws to Norman instead? When the truth came out, had that misidentification been the catalyst which led to Edwin's gruesome demise?

Her head hurt.

Janie wobbled down the hall and took a long, steaming shower to ease the tension as she perched on her bath chair. Then, wrapped in her favorite cozy robe, she fixed herself a cup of chamomile tea and settled in to watch one of the old black and white TV sitcoms on cable. After a while, the combination eased her into sleepiness. With a deep yawn, she eased her way to her bed and slipped between the covers.

She dreamed she ran down a dark alley to the assisted living center, chased by Bobby hanging from the van as he grabbed her hair with one of Edwin's severed hands. Following in pursuit, Blake kept making wrong turns as the Bunco Biddies, all wearing black hoodies, hid in the carports and screamed.

With a gasp, Janie jolted from her bed before her conscious brain reminded her about the bum foot. Down she tumbled in pain. She sat on her behind on the floor and sniveled. Mrs. Fluffy bent forward from the twisted bedspread and licked her mistress' ear.

She batted the cat away and pouted. Arggh. Janie slammed her fist against the bed. Maybe she wasn't cut out for this sleuthing stuff after all. What had she been thinking?

Remorse set in as Mrs. Fluffy gave her a questioning mew. Janie twisted around to gather her whiskered companion into her arms. The sympathetic purrs lulled her into a calmer state.

"I'm sorry, sweetie pie." She snuggled her face into the kitty's fur. "Oh. Mrs. Fluffy. What am I doing? Trying to keep Jack's memory alive? Or make myself seem important?"

Mrs. Fluffy gave her a chortle.

Janie set the animal down and rolled to the side to rub her sore backside. "And look where it's landed me. Literally. I feel as if God has just spanked me."

She stretched for her metal contraption and used the handle-like a cane to ease herself up. With several groans, humphs, and a few hops, she righted herself and scooted back into bed.

As if lightening had struck, a thought entered her head. Bobby and Edwin, both newly out of prison, had to do that as well. There lay the connection.

She sat straight up and grinned.

Of course. Now she understood. The pieces snapped together.

She texted Blake. Breakthrough in case. Pick me up before you head to Mildred's tomorrow. Will explain then.

CHAPTER FORTY-FOUR

With Blake's hand hovering to catch her, Janie limped to the car idling in the alley. "Are you sure this is wise for you to come? If he catches a glimpse of you, he may bolt."

"That's a chance we'll have to take now, right?" She brought her leg around and placed her splinted heel on the floorboard.

Blake closed the door and dashed around to the driver's side. He got in, clicked his seat belt, and glimpsed in her direction. "So, tell me."

"Not until I see Bobby's reaction to me when we walk in."

"Jannniiie?"

His questioning tone reminded her of her second-grade teacher when she'd eaten half of the paper paste. She clamped her lips together and stared out the passenger side window.

He huffed into his collar and put the car in gear. "I have a bad feeling about this." He reached for his phone. "I'm calling the station for a patrol officer to stand by, just in case."

"I doubt we'll need that. I think Bobby will cave. He's a tadpole treading in an ocean of sharks."

Blake exhaled through his nostrils. "This is against my better judgment, not to mention protocol."

She extended her hands out to her sides, elbows tucked to her waist. "We're only going to have a friendly chat with a wayward young man. Nothing official."

"Right."

As they circled the block, a green truck sitting front of Mildred's garden home came into view. Blake turned to the left and entered through the alley. He let Janie out and parked in one of the empty carport slots. She waited, patting the perspiration from her brow with a hankie.

With a jerk of his chin, he mouthed in her direction. "Ready?"

She raised and lowered her head quickly several times.

Blake swung open the kitchen door and traipsed in with Janie teetering behind him.

Bobby shot to his feet, spilling his lemonade. He narrowed his eyes as he pivoted, and yelled through clenched teeth. "Aunt Mildred?"

"I'm sorry, but..."

Bobby didn't wait for an explanation. He dashed for the front door.

Blake dodged and slammed himself against the wood before Bobby reached the entryway. "Sit down, son. We need to talk."

"No way, man." The two men wove back and forth like animals about to pounce. Bobby jolted and ran towards Janie. She stuck out her purse and whacked him in the gut.

"Ohhh." He bent over but swirled behind her. He grabbed her, wrapping an arm over her shoulders, and clenched Janie to his chest. In his other hand, he clicked open a switch blade and pressed the edge against her neck. "Don't come any nearer or the old broad gets sliced."

Janie wobbled to keep balanced, wishing her bent-behind leg could catch his groin, but he'd thought of that and moved to the side. He began to back them both into the kitchen.

Mildred brought both hands to her open mouth and whimpered.

Blake extended his in front of him, fingers widespread. "Come on, son. Let's not get stupid. All we want to do is talk to you. You aren't under arrest. Not yet."

The young man's eyes darted about the room as he inched backwards a few more steps with Janie in tow. "I mean it, man. One sweep and she'll bleed out before you can get help."

The detective lowered his arms. "You wouldn't do that, Bobby. Not to your aunt's best friend."

"I might." His jawline tightened against Janie's temple, as did his grip around her.

"Blake. Let me speak with him alone. I can get to the bottom of this." Janie widened her eyes in a plea for her son-in-law to relax.

Blake took a military at-ease stance. "Son, release her. I promise I won't cuff you, okay?"

She felt Bobby's muscles twitch.

Even though Blake had lowered his arms to his sides, his voice oozed authority. "Drop the knife and kick it towards me. Don't get yourself deeper than you already are."

At once, the twenty-two-year-old tensed. The blade sliced across Janie's face as he pushed her to the linoleum.

Mildred screamed.

Bobby straddled his legs, bouncing his weight on one foot and then the other. With a jut of his chin, he egged Blake to jump him. "Come on, copper. Let's dance."

Blake's face reddened. The veins in his neck popped. He charged head on into Bobby and butted him in the stomach. Janie rolled to the side as the two hit the ground in a loud thud which rattled Mildred's china cabinet in the next room.

Blake flopped the kid over and sat on his buttocks as he twisted the knife from his grasp and tossed the weapon across the floor. Janie wiggled for the handle.

"No, don't touch it. Push it further away with your elbow."

She did as he told her. As fast as traffic lights flick from yellow to red in a busy intersection, Blake bent the squirming guy's arms over his back and cuffed his wrists with a plastic band. He swaggered off like a cowboy who'd roped a calf in record time and placed his firm boot in Bobby's upper back. Without shifting his gaze from his prisoner, he addressed Janie. "You okay?"

She swallowed and squeaked out a "yes."

His chest heaved up and down in rapid succession, but his face color lessened. "Good. Mildred, call 9-1-1. Tell them we need back up."

She stood stone-still, blubbering.

Blake swerved his torso toward her. "Now, Mildred."

She snapped to as if she'd been slapped with a frozen mackerel. With a shaking hand, she reached for her flip phone and punched in the emergency code.

Blake cocked his revolver. "It's aimed at your head, boy. I'd stay put if I were you."

Bobby groaned and slammed his forehead into the floor.

Mildred knelt down to Janie and pressed a wad of tissues to her cut cheek. Tears streamed from her eyes. "I'm so very sorry."

Janie placed a hand over Mildred's and smiled. "It's going to be all right."

Mildred raised her head. Locking gazes, the two friends conveyed their sympathy for each other without another word needed.

The next half hour blurred into policemen stomping around, the medics checking Janie out from head to toe, and Ethel rocking Mildred on the couch as she shook. Bobby never cast an eye in his aunt's direction. With his jaw clenched, his Adam's apple bobbed as two officers escorted him from the premises. Through the wide open front door, Janie caught a glimpse of the crowds gathering once again. She groaned.

Blake rushed to her side. "Janie?"

"The village association will oust me for sure, now."

He rocked back on his haunches and let out a hoot. "You are a tough ol' bird, you know that?"

The emergency medical tech arched an eyebrow.

"It's okay. She's my mother-in-law. Family joke."

"Yes, sir."

Blake squeezed his mother-in-law's arm. "Anyone else would have shriveled into oblivion if they went through what you just did."

Janie jerked as attendant dabbed her cheek and applied an anti-hemorrhagic bandage to the slash. "You're lucky, ma'am. Not deep enough for stitches. Shouldn't leave much of a scar. But you may wish to make an appointment with a plastic surgeon."

"Pfft. At my age? The wrinkles will hide it."

They all chuckled.

"Blake, may I sit in on Bobby's interview?"

He brushed a silver curl from her forehead. "Sorry, not kosher. Besides, you need to go home and rest or my wife will tan my hide."

Her lower lip protruded like a two-year-old's.

He kissed her on the temple. "I'll report to you as soon as possible." He rocked to a standing position and sauntered away. A few paces later, he turned back to her with a waggled finger and a wink. "I mean it, Janie. Go take a load off."

She rolled her eyes. "Okay, I'll obey you. This time."

His laugh echoed off the door jamb as he exited.

CHAPTER FORTY-FIVE

Within the hour, all eleven of the Bunco Biddies crowded Janie's living room as salads, brownies, casseroles, and appetizers cluttered her dining room table. Clucks of sympathy mixed with curiosity hovered over her and Mildred, who didn't want to stay "one more minute" in her house while the police wrapped up the crime scene and the local press, along with a few stragglers from the neighborhood, milled around outside.

Through all the chatter, Janie heard the front door bell. Before she asked someone to answer, the thing flew open and Melody rushed in, followed by Jamie and Emily.

"Mom, your cheek." Melody hugged her to her bosom, leaned back to examine the bandage, and then drew her into another embrace. The kids sat on either side, rubbing her shoulders and back.

Janie struggled to be released. "Enough. I'm fine. Just a scratch. All in the line of duty."

"I will strangle my husband when he gets home." Melody spun her finger to everyone in the room. "You are my witnesses." Her attention shifted to Janie as she sniffled. "Oh, Mom. Whatever possessed you to get involved in all of this?"

Janie pressed her hands onto her daughter's shoulders. "Mel, they involved me when they dumped a neighbor of mine in my community's dumpster. I did what any ordinary citizen would do."

Melody lifted her mother's fingers. "Who decided her son-in-law seemed too swamped to handle it. Mother, really. Didn't a lifetime with dad teach you detective work can be dangerous?"

Janie giggled. "Yes, and also very exciting." She patted her chest. "Keeps the ol' ticker ticking."

Mildred, Ethel, Betsy Ann, and Janie sat at her kitchen table, picking at the King Ranch chicken casserole Anne brought. A tossed salad began to wilt, untouched, even though Janie's favorite yogurt dressing drizzled over the top. All four of their appetites had vanished even though the time edged way past their normal lunch hour.

Over the previous half hour, the other ladies filtered away. The battery-operated wall clock resembling Felix the Cat ticked in the background.

Janie glanced up. "Almost two in the afternoon already."

Mildred's eyes swam. "I can't stand not knowing what's happening to Bobby. Excuse me. I need another tissue." She rose from the table but turned with the other three to see Blake tap on the backdoor glass.

He entered, nodded to the ladies, and took a cold soda from the fridge. After three large gulps, he set the can down and brought in one of the dining room chairs. Straddling it backwards, he draped his chin on the carved, high-back wood and sighed.

"Well?" Janie's left eyebrow imitated the St. Louis arch.

Mildred slid back into her chair to his left, hands clasped in front of her.

"Bobby, as they say in the films noir, sang like a canary." He glanced at Mildred. "He's in custody, but I will put in a good word for him. He has agreed to testify against the killers—yes, Janie, there were two as you suspected. In exchange, we are placing him in witness protection. So, I am going to take you over in a minute to say good-bye, Mildred."

She gulped in a half-lung of air, hankie to her mouth, and bobbed her head.

Blake reached over and squeezed her hand. "Could be the best thing for him. He will be under the FBI's watchful eye so he will have to fly right. Might be the start of a new life for him. They will set him up in housing, find him a decent job. No one will be allowed to discover his past...good or bad."

Betsy Ann took her other hand. "God can purpose good from evil. Saint Paul said so."

Mildred smiled through her tears.

Janie tapped the table with her nails. "So...?"

"Ah." Blake eased back and stretched like a cat in a sunbeam. "It seems when Edwin's niece brought forth proof he was who he'd claimed all along, he endangered the real Edward Norman. Alarms went off and the Feds began to comb the bushes lickety-split."

Ethel clicked her fingers. "So that's why the Federal Bureau of Investigations became involved."

"Right. Bank robberies are a federal issue if the branches are Federal Deposit Insurance Corporation protected. And nowadays, a vast majority are."

"But they learned Edwards died, right?"

Blake shifted in his chair. "True. Which led to them investigating Edwin's story. That and the evidence of his baptismal certificate, clearing up the Houston records snafu."

"Why kill Edwin once he got out, then, if everyone knew he wasn't Edwards and Edwards was dead?"

Blake's lips curled up on one side. "Because Edwin slipped up. Instead of returning to Oklahoma as he should, he settled here, near the scenes of the robberies, under the guise of choosing a community where he could blend in and live a controlled, normal retired life."

Janie shook her head. "So? Maybe they don't have communities like this in Oklahoma."

Her son in law gave her an I-know-and-you-don't grin. "He chose to live here because ten years ago, Sunset Acres didn't exist."

The four ladies gasped in unison.

"The stash is hidden here?" Ethel jutted forward.

"According to Bobby, Eduardo Lopez believes so. That's how he got Bobby involved. Smithers and Lopez used to go dove hunting in a dilapidated cabin out in this area. The land belonged to a rancher who made his millions by rather shady means, though no one proved how. For a price, he'd let thugs hang out in the boonies until things cooled down."

Ethel nodded. "A modern day Hole-In-The-Wall, where Butch Cassidy and other notorious stagecoach and train robbers hid in the Wild West. Where we get the term, 'holed up,' I believe."

"Correct. Excellent analogy."

"Ahem."

All eyes turned to Janie. She huffed. "Back to the case at hand. So they figured Edwin moved here to locate the loot?"

"They must have. Which attracted way too much attention."

Betsy Ann's face lit up.

"Uh, oh." Janie chided. "The light bulb just came on."

"Poo on you." She stuck out her tongue but then winked. "So y'all think the bank robbers hid the money here while they were…um, what's the term? Laying low?"

"Well, it makes sense. They weren't caught until almost two weeks later."

Janie wiped the idea away with her hand. "Wait. Surely Smithers and Lopez knew he wasn't Edward Norman."

"They did, according to Eduardo Lopez—who by the way, is in the federal clink. Agents transferred him yesterday. Anyway, Eduardo states they had some of their underlings hire Edwin to take the fall because he resembled Edward Norman. That, supposedly, would give Edwards time to secure passage for them to South America with the dough where they would live happily ever after. Unfortunately for them, Lopez and Smithers were spotted and arrested."

"So, I was right about that." Janie puffed out her chest.

"Yes, and about a few other things as well." He winked at her.

Blake scratched his temple. "But, Janie. What made you figure Edwin had agreed to impersonate Edwards?"

Janie fiddled with the corner of her napkin and titled her head. "Last night, I had a nightmare and fell out of the bed." She shoved her index finger at her son-in-law. "Do not tell Melody."

Blake smiled.

"As I used my metal peg leg thingy to right myself, the concept occurred to me. Maybe Edwin needed a financial boost. He never had a steady job. Was known to hang out with thugs. If they offered him a piece of the pie and guaranteed him a light sentence in exchange for his pretending to be Norman, it might stand to reason he'd take the deal. Even ten percent could set him up for life."

Blake concurred. "Uh, huh. Seems our dear friend loved the Oklahoma casinos a tad too much. He squandered all of his savings, his earnings and, in the end, lost his wife and his worldly possessions. So he engaged in petty thievery. In other words, he made a few enemies in Oklahoma, so spending a few years under tight surveillance in Texas didn't sound half bad."

"Ah, and he assumed all would be well." Ethel grinned.

"Seven years commuted sentence for keeping his nose clean, then out on parole on good behavior. He'd find the cash with the help of Emilio, Eduardo Lopez's nephew, whose term also came due about the same time his did. They planned it all while doing the laundry in the clink." Blake stretched in the chair before continuing.

"Except Edwin gets wind of this attorney who's helping a few inmates in Wallace Pack and elsewhere sue the state for the unlivable conditions in summer. Edwin becomes vocal about it to get the lawyer's attention, then gives him his sob story when they meet. The attorney takes his case, promising him mega bucks in compensation for being wrongly convicted."

Janie broke into the conversation. "So now Edwin can kill two birds with one stone. Take the quarter million settlement and help locate the real dough."

Mildred pressed her lips into a thin line, her gaze darting to whoever spoke.

Blake took a sip of his soda. "Bobby says Emilio and Edwin were going to split the cash and leave the country."

Betsy Ann's mouth dropped. "Emilio planned to steal from his uncle? That's gutsy."

"Yep. But he'd be long gone, basking on some island, by the time Lopez and Smither's sources discovered his treachery. Emilio and Edwin offered Bobby twenty-five thousand to help out."

Mildred slammed her hand on the table. Everyone jolted.

"When? Edwin Newman lived next door for only a few days."

Blake gave her a soft smile. "When Bobby went over to confront him for whacking your dog, the two began to talk. Edwin recognized Bobby as a fellow ex-con. Like a secret brotherhood, they can sniff each other out. Don't ask me how." He rocked back in his seat. "My guess is Edwin figured Bobby could help him scope things out."

Janie snapped her fingers. "But Bobby had second thoughts, figuring Edwin might split with the dough and cheat Emilio?"

Blake tapped his temple. "Good reasoning, Janie. You're correct. And he tells Emilio that. So Emilio coerces Bobby into helping him kill Edwin. Emilio gets a buddy of his to steal and drive the van, which we found burned and ditched south of Llano, by the way. Bobby lets them into the butcher's section of the grocery store after hours so they can dice and chop."

All four women shuddered.

"Then they leave Bobby to clean up the mess while they bring Edwin back to the dumpster."

"Because Bobby gave them the codes and knew the trash pick-up schedule." Mildred dropped her eyes to the table.

Blake lowered his voice. "I'm afraid so."

Janie flashed an I-told-you-so gander at Blake. He nodded back. "So, Emilio Lopez and his accomplice do away with Edwin. We have enough evidence to charge them both with murder one."

"Do you know who this accomplice is, Blake?"

"Yeah. Bobby told us. An old pal of Lenny Weber's named George Mc-something, I forget. It's a weird name. Older dude with a white beard. We just tracked him down in downtown Austin outside the newspaper building and booked him."

Betsy Ann gasped and swooned.

CHAPTER FORTY-SIX

Ethel fanned Betsy Ann as Mildred got her a glass of water.

Blake helped her to the living room couch as Janie hobbled at the rear of the parade.

He whispered into his mother-in-law's ear. "What's wrong?"

Janie sighed. "That's Betsy Ann's George. The one who befriended her in the archives." She turned to side-hug her friend. "Oh, I am so very sorry, dear."

Her voice warbled. "I honestly thought him to be charming. Even someone who I might..." Her hand trembled as she wiped away a tear with her finger. "How could I be so stupid?"

Blake patted her arm. "It's okay. He is a grifter from way back. I am sure he's fooled many a lady in his day."

"Piece of slime, that George McGuffy." Ethel crossed her arms over her chest. "I thought he lathered on the charm a bit too thick."

"Wait. No. That's not right." Blake straightened up. "The George I meant had the last name of..." He dug his notes out of his jacket pocket and dabbed his finger to his tongue. As he took his sweet time flipping through the pages, Betsy Ann held her breath until Janie figured she'd keel over from lack of oxygen.

"Ah. Here we go. McBerger." He laughed. "Reminded me of a fast food joint."

Betsy Ann let out a whimper of relief and gripped Ethel's hand.

Janie squeezed her other one. "Oh, Betsy Ann, I am so glad." She smiled at her sweet, ditzy, but lovable friend whose countenance once again glowed.

"Me, too." She took a gulp of water.

For a moment, a quiet peace hovered in the room.

Then Janie did a double take. "Wait. Did L.W. stand for Lenny Weber?"

Blake perched in the arm of the couch. "No. For the Lazy West."

Janie slapped her forehead. "Of course. From the court transcripts. Where Lopez and Smithers were arrested."

Blake nodded. "The ranch is now Sunset Acres, along with the upscale subdivision down the road called Westfield Ranch. The owner, Lawrence Westmont, sold his acreage to your developers eight years ago after he suffered a stroke. Wanted a place to live out his old age on the land he once loved. The full care unit was built first, then the assisted living and the condos. He died in the nursing unit about two years ago."

"But Lopez and Smithers didn't know the ranch had been sold?"

"That's right, Ethel." Blake grinned. "You ladies do have a flare for this sleuthing stuff. They hid out in the old cabin, which by then had become deserted, and buried the loot somewhere on the acreage. That cabin sat where the middle of Westfield subdivision is now. Little did they know their one-time benefactor resided just down the road with round-the-clock care."

"Emilio wanted to get hold of the loot, huh? So why try to free Lenny?"

Blake chuckled. "For the same reason Edwin agreed to go to prison. Money problems that would not go away or wait until he chased after the legendary bank loot. He had hoped Edwin had lots of ready cash on him, so he killed him. Edwin didn't. After he paid his lease in cash so no background check would be needed, his niece placed the rest in a trust, set up by the attorney so Edwin could live off the dividends. Not finding the cash at Edwin's place, Emilio felt the pressure breathing down on him, so he came up with a plan B to get quick cash."

Janie leaned back, hands folded. "Spring Lenny Weber and get not only money but protection in return, which would allow him time to locate the loot with Bobby's help."

"Exactly."

Betsy Ann scrunched her eyebrows. "Is all that stolen money really somewhere around here?"

Blake shrugged. "Lopez and Smithers won't talk, so the banks are hiring land investigators to find out. I know one thing. I'd not want to be Emilio right now."

Everyone laughed.

CHAPTER FORTY-SEVEN

The next Thursday at six in the evening, Janie's living room filled with her friends rattling dice and chatting, Mildred included. The Feds allowed her to spend a good hour and a half with Bobby before they whisked him away. She knew it was for the best and all would work out as God planned. Even so, she couldn't go back to her garden home so she put in a request to move into one of the vacant condos after the management painted and did minor repairs. In the meantime, she occupied Ethel's guest room.

Janie now sported a Velcro-laced boot and received permission to drive again. Her mood improved dramatically. The cut on her cheek had begun to heal, which Babs attributed to the special essential oils and herbal cream she sold on the side to supplement her widow's benefits. Janie didn't have the heart to tell her she'd thrown the little jar in the trash the second day.

"So, Janie." Roseanne glanced at her as she rolled for threes. "Have you gotten the sleuthing bug out of your system?"

Ethel giggled as she rolled the dice at the next table. "I think Melody will beat it out of her if she doesn't."

She twisted to catch Janie's eye. "Though for an amateur, you did good, my friend."

Janie thrust her hands to her hips. "I beg your pardon, Miss nose-in-a-mystery-book. I lived with the best detective this area of Texas has ever seen for—"

"—forty-two years." The three women at her table chimed together.

Every one of the Bunco biddies laughed.

Roseanne halted her roll. "Well, I thought you might like to know about the young woman found dead behind the Get 'em and Go today. And get this. The real estate agent listing the Newman residence found a newborn infant this morning in the bathtub!"

Janie and Ethel gazed at each other wide-eyed.

Betsy Ann rested her head in her hands. "Here we go again."

And even more from Julie B Cosgrove...

The Bunco Biddies Mystery Series

Three widows, who live in a Sunset Acres retirement community, host Bunco games every Thursday evening.

Betsy Ann, a retired columnist for the Alamoville, Texas community newspaper, considers herself a seasoned reporter, due to her articles in the Garden and Home section.

Ethel, a cozy mystery aficionado, can recall each episode of *Murder She Wrote* and *Columbo*. She catalogs every one of the who-dunnit paperbacks in her library by how the murders were committed.

Janie is the widow of a renowned Austin, Texas police detective. He often bounced his most difficult cases off her brain.

So when their neighbors start reporting bodies, the three hop into action, despite the fact that Janie's son-in-law happens to be Alamoville's competent chief homicide detective.

Up next is *Baby Bunco*, releasing in Early 2017...

"Did you say she found a baby?" Janie stopped mid-roll, the pink and white dice warming in her clutched fist. "Here in Sunset Acres, a retirement community?"

Babs, seated to her left at the Bunco table, nodded. "That's what Mildred told me as we were walking up to your front stoop tonight. Right, Mildred?"

"I went to collect a few more of my things since I'm staying with Ethel, and no more than three minutes later the leasing agent pounded on my door. 'Come see,' she motioned to me. Her eyes grew as wide as those mega donuts at the Crusty Baker." She thumped her pencil against her score pad and groaned. "It took every ounce of gumption to follow her into that—ugh!—place next door." She quivered her shoulders.

Janie shifted her gaze to the woman sitting across from her. "Ethel, you knew about this?"

"I did."

"And you didn't tell me?" Her voice elevated to echo-off –the-ceiling volume. She humphed and pivoted to face the storyteller. "Mildred. What happened?"

The other eight ladies halted their Bunco round. Each swiveled to listen in, their eyes fixated on the first card table.

Mildred leaned. "I paused at the steps, determined to not go inside. Only peek in from the front door. Then high-pitched, frantic cries came from the direction of the bathroom. Well, I had to rush to its aid. Every motherly fiber in my being dictated it."

Murmurs and head bobs filtered through Janie's living rom.

Mildred sniffled. "Poor little thing. Alone, scared and red as a beet from wailing so hard. That house is cursed, I tell you."

Janie patted her hand. "Now, dear. Just because someone murdered Edwin soon after he moved in there doesn't mean..."

Mildred shot from her seat and paced, her arms flaying in circles, resembling the duck windmill on top of the antiques barn down the road. "Ever since I relocated into Sunset Acres it's been one thing after another. Edwin murdered, then my nephew Bobby arrested, and now an abandoned newborn in a bathtub? This is supposed to be a quiet retirement community."

"Maybe because you live on Solar Boulevard." Annie huffed. "Nothing weird ever happens on my street, Sunrise Court, except for an occasional stray golf ball. Then again, if you kept your nose out of everyone's business..." Her voice trailed off with a smug cock of her head.

"*My* nose?"

The other ladies mumbled to each other.

Ethel blew a whistle through her teeth. "Okay, everyone calm down. We all lived through the ruckus of one of our neighbor's brutal murder last month. It's not Mildred's fault. Nor mine or Janie's that this happened..."

Betsy Ann raised her hand, as if her legs once again dangled from under her desk in Ms. Everett's kindergarten classroom.

Janie rolled her eyes. "What?"

"Well, it is sort of our fault." She pointed to Janie, Ethel and herself. "We helped solve the case and Bobby did wind up in the middle of all of the commotion. That's why he threatened you and tried to break into your house." She folded her hands and gazed down at them. "I'm just saying..."

"Duly noted." Janie felt the healing, pinkish wound on her neck where his knife grazed her skin. "I must add, my dear son-in-law, Chief Detective Blake Johnson, appreciated all of our..." her hands encircled the room..."research, sleuthing and cunningness. He told me so."A smile curled along the edges of her mouth. "Besides, it did beat back the doldrums a while, right?'

A few silvery head bounced in agreement as the condo sprinkled with giggles. Annie crossed her arms and harumphed.

Janie eased over to Mildred and led her back to her designated chair. She patted her on the shoulders and scanned the room, making certain every slightly glaucoma-pressed or cataract-corrected eye fixated on her. "Now we must figure out who placed a newborn baby in a vacant garden home bathtub and why?"

Babs cocked an eyebrow. "We do?"

"Absolutely. Let's face facts. Someone put the little thing in a home in our community so she would be discovered. Therefore it is our responsibility..."

"Well, now. I'm not sure..." Mildred frowned.

"We are all over fifty-five, correct? The child certainly doesn't belong to one of us. If so, we should be renamed Sarah after Abraham's elderly wife in Genesis."

"Or Elizabeth in the New Testament." Betsy Ann added, this time with a forefinger, not a full hand, aloft.

"Exactly. Therefore, unless one of you wants to confess..."

Cackles ensued.

Janie allowed the cacophony to settle, her eyes glimmering with escalating excitement. "I, for one, do not think this is a coincidence that this wee one ended up in Edwin's old garden home. There may be a connection we overlooked. Blake never discovered who left long, black hairs in that comb or ruby red lipstick on those empty beer cans when the police searched his place for clues."

Ethel scoffed. "Pffft. We all can guess what she was, even if we don't know who."

The women eyed each other and chuckled.

Annie shook her head. "But the officials only released him from prison a couple of days before he died, right? Last I heard it takes nine months to make a baby."

Mildred arched her eyebrow. "I thought it only took one night."

Several of the elderly ladies laughed so loud Janie's china tea service jiggled.

Janie pumped her hand toward the floor. "All right. All right. Even so, someone knew that home remained unoccupied."

Babs flipped up her palms. "His demise dominated the local news for several weeks. Which means thousands of readers learned it."

Roseanne Rodriguez spoke up. "More than that. Hundreds of thousands. It was all over the news, too."

Mildred flayed her arms. "That narrows it down a bunch."

More laughter.

Janie tapped her fist to the card table. The hum of comments faded. "True, Roseanne. However, I don't recall them specifically giving out the address, even if everyone heard Betsy Ann and I discovered him in the community dumpster here at Sunset Acres."

"So, whoever dropped the baby girl off cased the joint and determined no one lived there anymore." Ethel, the one with the massive catalogues mystery paperback collection, offered the proverbial gumshoe response.

"Which means they planned to leave her at that garden home." Janie snapped her fingers. "Yes, that has to be it. So a person or persons unknown, who wouldn't attract attention as they wandered around our senior retirement village, knew about this pregnancy and somehow persuaded the mother to give up the poor thing."

Babs clucked her teeth. "Well, it does happen."

"Yes, but what gets me is they figured someone would find the infant fairly quickly."

"A 'For Lease or Sale' sign is planted plain as day on the front lawn." Annie shoved the last bite of butterscotch brownie into her mouth.

Janie gave her a nod. "Good point. Still, there must be homes all over this area for sale or rent. Why our little corner of the world? A fifty-five plus community. Why not a neighborhood with young families? That's what we must discover. Something tells me the answer might be the key to the whole dilemma."

Ethel leaned into Betsy Ann. "Get a load of Janie. Proud as a peacock and giddy as a school girl. She's in her element. A new game's afoot."

Betsy Ann lowered her auburn, curly head into her hands. "Here we go again. Bunco Biddies to the rescue whether anyone wants us involved or not."

Coming in 2017 from Prism Book Group!

ABOUT THE AUTHOR

Julie B Cosgrove is a novelist, but she also writes devotionals and inspirational articles for several publications and websites on a regular basis. She won national awards for her creative writing skills in high school. In college she won the American Bible Society's Religion Major of the Year award and went on to study in seminary until the birth of her son, who was in and out of the hospital most of his childhood. However, she never lost the itch to write. After a hiatus of thirty years, she once again picked up the pen and became a freelance writer.

In 2015, Julie was selected as "one of the fifty writers you should be reading" by the nationally syndicated radio broadcast, The Author Show. She has four novels, two novellas and six non-fiction works published as well as a short story which won second place in a state-wide competition. *Dumpster Dicing* is the first of several Bunco Biddies Mysteries. Be sure to check out her Prism Book Group suspense romance novels, *Hush in the Storm, Legitimate Lies* and *Freed to Forgive*.

When she isn't writing, she is a part-time church secretary, active in her own church, and a spokesman for anti-trafficking missionaries. She also is a professional speaker and leads women's retreats, Bible studies and writer workshops.

A native Texan, Julie is a widow who lives in Fort Worth with two spoiled-rotten and lovable house cats whom she dubs her "beastie boys." She enjoys clean, cozy mysteries in print and on film, especially British ones. She is an avid word puzzle player and loves to spend time floating in the Guadalupe River at her maternal family's property in the Texas Hill Country.

Visit her website, www.juliebcosgrove.com and follow her devotional blog, http://wheredidyoufindgodtoday.com.

Thank you for your Prism Book Group purchase! Visit our website to enjoy free reads, great deals, and entertaining, wholesome fiction!

http://www.prismbookgroup.com

Made in the USA
Middletown, DE
10 May 2021